King of Odessa

King of Odessa

ROBERT A. ROSENSTONE

Northwestern University Press
Evanston, Illinois

Northwestern University Press
Evanston, Illinois 60208-4210

Copyright © 2003 by Robert A. Rosenstone. Published 2003.
All rights reserved.

Printed in the United States of America
10 9 8 7 6 5 4 3 2 1

ISBN 0-8101-1992-7

Library of Congress Cataloging-in-Publication Data
Rosenstone, Robert A.
King of Odessa / Robert A. Rosenstone.
p. cm.
ISBN 0-8101-1992-7 (cloth : alk. paper)
1. Babel', I. (Isaak), 1894–1941—Fiction. 2. Fiction—Authorship—
Fiction. 3. Odesa (Ukraine)—Fiction. 4. Jewish authors—Fiction.
5. Authors—Fiction. I. Title.
PS3618.0839 K56 2003
813'.54—dc21

2003000694

Book design by Vincent Chung

For a list of Babel's friends and associates, see page 237. A chronology of
Babel's life is found on page 239.

For Janima

King of Odessa

Prologue

In the summer of 1936, famed Soviet writer Isaac Babel returned to his hometown of Odessa for the last time. For over six decades the only record we have had of his three-month stay has been what was contained in seventeen letters and seven postcards that the forty-two-year-old author wrote to his mother and sister, who were living in Belgium. Composed in Russian and flavored with phrases in Yiddish and French, they were produced by a man who understood that what he wrote would be scrutinized by government officials. From Babel's careful words we have long known that during the summer and autumn he underwent medical treatment for his asthma and his sinus problems at the Lermontov Sanitarium, swam often in the Black Sea, visited aunts, uncles, and his high school mathematics teacher, attended synagogue once, hunted for a villa to exchange for his house in a writers' colony near Moscow, and in October took a boat to Yalta to help longtime friend Sergei Eisenstein polish up the script of the film *Bezhin Meadow,* then in production.

Absent from his pages is any mention of the great social and political events of the day: the beginnings of the Civil War in Spain that followed the rising of the generals against the republic; the proclamation of the new constitution of the USSR, hailed in the Soviet press the most democratic in the world; the first big show trials of Old Bolsheviks in Moscow, with the startling courtroom confessions by Lenin's old comrades Grigorii Zinoviev and Lev Kamenev that they had conspired with Trotsky against the leadership of the regime. Prominent in the letters is information about Babel's wife, Zhenya, who had left him ten years before to live in Paris, and about their seven-year-old daughter, Natasha, conceived during Babel's first sojourn abroad in 1927 and 1928; repeatedly he speaks of bringing the young girl back to live with him in Russia. Yet nowhere does Babel even hint that he has for two years been sharing his apartment with an attractive young woman, the only female among the engineers overseeing the construction of the new Moscow subway.

One theme running through the letters is the steady progress Babel claims to be making on what he describes as the most important, the most personal, the best piece of writing he has done in years—a book he calls a new departure, one meant to finish with the old Odessa. For decades scholars have speculated about this last phrase and about the contents of this work, apparently seized with all Babel's other papers when he was arrested like so many Russian artists and intellectuals— allegedly as a spy—in 1940. But now, more than sixty years after his death and over a decade after the collapse of the Soviet Union, a manuscript has been found in the archives that, internal evidence suggests, seems to be the work Babel was writing in 1936. It was not, to be sure, in the Babel archive, but located among the papers of an obscure government official named Svetlana Kripinskaya, about whom very little is known though she seems to have worked occasionally with the secret police. We are privileged to publish it here for the first time under the title Babel himself chose, *King of Odessa*. Devotees of the author will notice immediately that—even in an English translation—this work shows a startling departure in tone, voice, and style from anything Babel had previously written. Whether the change was a sign of a new artistic direction or simply a response to the crisis in which the writer found himself that summer of 1936 is something that scholars will no doubt debate for years to come. Certainly as a historical and biographical document, *King of Odessa* is full of revelations from a man who in his closest relationships and every other piece of writing was exceedingly careful to conceal all issues of personal history and identity.

*I*f this were an American story, it would begin with a dame. But that word hardly applies to the female who knocks on my door and barges into the room. A dame has long, silky hair that covers one eye. A dame is dressed in something low cut, slinky, and suggestive. The only thing suggested by the drab, olive suit of this stocky woman with a face like a potato field after a rainstorm is an institution where doors have to be locked day and night. But who am I to complain about looks? When I take off my cap on a sunny day the gleam off my head can blind people within fifty paces. I've been told that if I ever lose my spatula, this nose of mine will serve as a good substitute. Besides I'm not a private detective and I don't have an office. When she enters, I am sitting on a couch in my study, twisting a ball of string around my fingers in complicated patterns. Wondering why I can't find words for the pages of the notebook that lies open on the table.

As if I don't know.

She may not look the part but she does what a dame is supposed to do. Looks around nervously. Asks in a low voice if I am Isaac Babel, the writer. Says that she has a very important message for me from a very important somebody in the Kremlin. Somebody I know. Somebody who cannot be named.

It's about K. His troubles are about to get worse. His troubles are about to kill him.

K?

That's all I can say. You figure it out.

I do.

She continues. There are new charges against him. Very serious charges that will lead to a new trial. A public trial at which he will be found guilty and sentenced to death for plotting to kill half the members of the Politburo. But someone close to the Boss thinks that what we don't need right now is the negative publicity from a big trial of one of the original Party members. Not with the Popular Front in full swing and all the support we are getting in Western countries. Not with the Civil War that has just broken out in Spain and the possibility that Mussolini and Hitler may intervene. Not with our new alliance with France and our recent diplomatic recognition by the United States. What we need now is the world to see we Russians as good guys. Good guys don't plot to kill their leaders. Good guys don't execute their old comrades.

Very interesting. No doubt true. But what's this got to do with me?

The Somebody in the Kremlin thinks there is a way out. K could plead guilty at the trial and then be allowed to escape. That way we would not have his blood on our hands. He could vanish. Get out of the country. So he would be out of the Boss's way. Alive but impotent. If he criticizes the regime from abroad, we can say, What can you expect from a traitor who has fled his homeland? A man who is alive cannot become a martyr, a rallying point for our enemies. He can be no more than a nuisance. K will be neutralized. Getting rid of him like this will be good for all of us.

Us?

The Somebody in the Kremlin knows that I am desperate to make a trip to France. That permission for such a trip has been denied and will keep being denied until I publish some new stories, stories that show I understand the social realities of today. That the thirties are not the twenties and the Civil War is long over. That it's the duty of writers to forget about the troubles of the past and instead describe the glorious process of collectivization, the workers of the Donbass who are happy to overfulfill their production quotas, and the shining new city of Magnitogorsk. The Somebody knows that I am having great trouble writing anything that suits editors these days, let alone the bureaucrats in the passport office.

All this is not exactly secret information. In recent years I have become equally famous for not publishing any new stories and for having a wife and daughter who live in France. All this is a cause for suspicion. Things got so bad that two years ago, at the First Congress of the new Writers' Union, it was necessary to make a speech explaining myself. I chose as my topic the aesthetics of silence. Told my assembled colleagues how important it was to refrain from writing until you have something to say. A position that, though I could hardly say this in public, would wipe out most of the literature being produced in our country. And almost everywhere else.

Potato Face continues: The Somebody in the Kremlin knows lots more. That I am about to leave for Odessa to spend the summer having treatments for my asthma at the famed Lermontov Sanitarium. That I am well connected in my old hometown, know all sorts of unusual people there, including some in the underworld and some on the waterfront. Boats leave Odessa almost every day for the West. The Somebody suggests that if I could provide a way of smuggling a special passenger out on one of those boats at just the right moment later this summer, permission for a trip to France would be granted. Without my having to publish any new stories.

Questions fill my mind: How would the escape from Moscow be arranged? How would K get to Odessa? How soon would all this take place? What happens if I say no? But the only one I put into words is *Why me?* I don't expect an answer. A good thing, because I don't get one. Only a slow shake of the head that leaves us staring at each other like two mutes. Potato Face is the one to break the silence.

You will be contacted in Odessa.

By whom?

It doesn't matter. Someone.

She turns away and walks to the door just in time. Staring at her face was beginning to make me feel as if I were in a small rowboat in the Black Sea on a stormy winter day.

The view of her from the rear is not much better than from the front.

I wait a minute after the door slams, then go downstairs. My housemate, Herr Bruno Shtainer, is in the kitchen, drinking coffee and eating what seems to be a mountain of whipped cream. Typical. He's an Austrian, an engineer, a representative of a machine tool company who manages to find the most astonishing pastry in Moscow. An Austrian? Yes, I know it as well as you: to share a house with a foreigner is dangerous these days. But there are real rewards. More than half the year Shtainer is at home in Vienna, which leaves me with that rare luxury for Moscow—a place to myself.

She's not exactly your type, he suggests.

I decide to head off any leading questions:

She came here direct from the Kremlin. The Boss wants to hire me as an undercover agent. Spy on foreign capitalists like you. Find out your secret plans for drowning the Revolution in whipped cream.

Things must be getting desperate if they're turning to you.

Truth is always less believable than fiction. Half-truths even more so. We laugh together. Shtainer has seen a few females come and go over the years. You can't conceal much from a housemate. But he's a good guy. Discreet. Self-protective too. While his wife stays at home with the kids in Austria, he indulges a taste for local women. Large women, the larger the better.

Large women are passionate, he says. *And Russian women are very passionate to begin with. So a large Russian woman? These aren't casual affairs, my friend. They're part of my job description. Scouting out new secret weapons! Women are what I mention in my monthly reports to my government. Who knows how many secrets the body of a large woman contains. I tell them to hire some Russian women and maybe we'll win the next war.*

Since Nina moved in with me a few months ago, Shtainer has refrained from mentioning any of the earlier females in her presence, so it's not necessary to say anything specific about Potato Face. Not that Nina is the jealous sort. By now she is used to women coming around, but usually they look a touch more helpless, or poetic, or in need of literary advice than Potato Face. It's just as well that she's at work. This is not the moment for answering questions or trying to make explanations. At least not until I can make them to myself. Not until I can figure out if, after avoiding it all these years since the Revolution, I am going to let myself climb into bed with the government.

2

*F*or the next two days I am busy—packing, buying train tickets, meeting with the head of production at Mosfilm, having lunch with two of my too many editors. Who can tell them apart? They shrug the same way, toss back the same number of shots of vodka during the meal, ask the same question: When will the manuscript on collective farms be done? I avoid the vodka, do my best to look troubled, plead unspecified personal problems, hint at writer's block, and assure them both: *Soon, soon.* Each is too polite to mention what is on both of their minds. The large advances on the manuscript. The fact that if I don't deliver soon, their asses are on the line.

If I do deliver, my ass is on the line. I have promised the same manuscript to each of them.

These arrangements occupy only a fraction of my mind. What I am really chewing over is the visit by Potato Face. What she proposed. Trying to separate fact from fiction. Not an easy thing to do in this surreal country at this particularly surrealistic time. K is simple enough. Lev Kamenev. An Old Bolshevik, left over from the time when that term seemed a badge of honor. Today it's closer to being a death sentence. Kamenev was one of the ten members of the Central Committee of the Party during the October Days. One of two who, in the crucial meeting on October 20, voted against Lenin and against the Bolsheviks taking power. Grigorii Zinoviev was the other. Both changed their minds at the last minute and for a long time this blot on their records was forgotten. Kamenev went on to chair the Council of People's Commissars, Zinoviev to head the Communist International. In the early twenties the two of them took sides with the Boss in order to head off Trotsky. A smart move that eventually turns out to be foolish. Winning in this country can be more dangerous than losing.

Both Kamenev and Zinoviev have been in jail for a year. After the murder of Sergei Kirov, Party secretary in Leningrad, they were tried and found guilty as distant accessories—connected to the killer but not fully implicated in a widespread plot. The truth is the Boss was behind the murder, but truth is a scarce commodity these days. Now I have to wonder: Has some new evidence turned up? Will they be tried again for the same crime? Or for something else? Anything is possible these days. This Revolution is not devouring its children. It's swallowing its parents.

Lev Kamenev. Not much surprise that he voted against seizing power in 1917. A gentle sort, more a schoolteacher than a revolutionary, a theoretician than an activist. He used to come by some of our evenings at the Writers' Union in the late twenties. A few glasses of vodka and he would begin to quote the most sentimental passages from Pushkin or Blok. Is the literary connection the reason they want me for the job? They? Let's not kid ourselves. He! This has to be one man's idea. Not the Boss, but somebody who wants to please him. The best candidate is my old buddy Genrikh Yagoda, head of State Security. But it's strange. Why wouldn't he ask me directly, as he has so many times when we are playing cards at his house.

Babel, he says. *Listen to me. You may not know it, but there's more to life than cards and women. You get around. You are trusted. You could give us a hand. You could help us find out all sorts of valuable things. And don't think we wouldn't be grateful. We would. You might be surprised how our gratitude would show itself.*

This is one of those situations where my reputation for silence is well earned. I trump him, raise my eyebrows, puff on a cigar. He demands to see my winning hand and I lay it down with a secret smile. Everyone knows Yagoda is not suited to head the secret police. He's too tactful. He wants people to like him too much to press a point, so he picks up the cards, shuffles, deals a new hand. Yagoda would be far better off far from the Kremlin, back where he started out, in Nizhni Novgorod, mixing up prescriptions for headaches in his pharmacy rather than messing around in secret labs trying to develop odorless poisons and truth serums. Assuming that rumor is true.

A less pleasant possibility is Nikolai Yezhov. Nobody ever dares call him by his first name. Just as everyone pretends not to notice the limp when he drags his foot across a room. Yezhov will be Yagoda's successor. That's already clear. He very well might want to get me into a compromising situation. He's always been cranky with me, but recently he's become openly nasty. At that last party hosted by Yevgenia Yezhova in their apartment, he confronted me in a loud tone meant to be heard by everyone:

Babel. When will we see this masterpiece on collectivization you've been writing for—how long? Since the end of the Revolution, isn't it? The French Revolution.

No doubt about it: Yezhov has long known that Yevgenia and I once were lovers. Maybe he's lame enough to think we still see each other. But we haven't, not alone, not in nine years. Nine years! If he knew anything he'd know that's far too long to keep an affair going. Even an affair turbulent as that one. She doesn't look well. This marriage is bad for her. No wonder. He's a brute.

We met in Berlin in 1927. Except for the few days during the Civil War when our regiment rode across the Polish border, this is my first trip abroad. All my life I have longed for the scent of Western Europe. The first breaths of it are intoxicating. Yevgenia has just arrived to work here as a secretary in the office of the Commissar of Foreign Affairs. She feels much the same as I do about Europe. Yevgenia loves literature and loves my Odessa tales and *Red Cavalry* and, soon enough, me. Or so she says. For two weeks we are inseparable. At night we drink French champagne and go to the theater, the opera, music halls, and cabarets where black jazz musicians play into the wee hours or men dressed as women do stripteases for shouting crowds. We ride in a horse-drawn carriage down Unter den Linden at dawn. We pick up a hooker on Kurfurstendamm and take her back to my cramped hotel room, but the three-way turns out to be less erotic than humorous.

Somehow I never get around to mentioning that I have a wife in Paris and a lover in Moscow who is the mother of my first child. A year later when we are both back home we meet at her tiny apartment on the outskirts of town until someone gets the word to Kashirina and she delivers an ultimatum: *I haven't said a thing about your wife, but I won't stand for another lover. It's her or me!* The choice is not difficult to make.

I never returned to Yevgenia's apartment. Never gave her an explanation and to this day she's never asked for one. Maybe she knows. Five years later when she becomes the editor of the monthly review *USSR in Construction,* she phones and asks me to write some stories. The timing is perfect. I am in desperate need of work that will pay well. It's expensive to have a family abroad, to have them writing letters all the time asking for money. Not that they can use the word. You're not allowed to send assets abroad. To avoid the censors we decided to use *bagels* as a code word for money.

Maybe Potato Face's story is on the up-and-up. Someone in the Kremlin wants to keep the regime from embarrassment. Lots of people might want to do that. Including the Boss himself. Why me? Benya Krik, of course. Write about gangsters and people are sure to think you have all sorts of special contacts in the underworld. How many times over the years I have been approached by con men, or thieves, doctors, members of the Party hierarchy, all of them with elaborate schemes for making a million if only they could meet the kind of people who could break into a villa or crack a safe or get something smuggled across a border. All willing to cut me in for a good percentage if I can introduce them to one of the kings of the Odessa syndicates. When I say no, they stare, stutter, press their case, refuse to believe I can't help. Some even get angry when I repeat, no, sorry, can't do it, it's impossible.

What I never admit is that I don't have any more contacts with the underworld than anyone else. Never really did, save for a single, three-day stay in the house of a well-known Moldavanka con man more than ten years ago. I paid for the stay up front, in hard cash. My aim was to get the old juices going. To gather local color for more stories. But somebody in the neighborhood must have gotten the wrong idea. Someone must have thought that I was an undercover cop. On the third day the still-warm body of my host, his throat slit from ear to ear, was dumped on the doorstep. His wife was clawing my face when the police hustled me away. They suggested that I not show my face again in Moldavanka—at least not for a long time and not after dark. It took more than a month for the scratches to heal. I have followed their advice ever since.

*V*areniki with cherries are the treat I make for special occasions. That's what I served Nina the first time she came over for lunch. It was February. Straight out of Siberia, she couldn't believe you could get cherries in winter.

Simple, I said, *if you know the right people.*

Now I serve up the same dish every time I leave for a while. She loves the combination of salty cheese wrapped in thin dough and covered with the sweet fruit. Her eyes mist up slightly when I sit her at the table and set the plate before her, but she's not really a sentimental type and she knows that I'm long past the age where tears and threats excite me. Besides, in a few weeks we are going to meet in Yalta for a real vacation.

Nina is the only female engineer working on the Moscow subway project. To be absolutely accurate, for the Metropolitan Construction and Design Institute. It's a big job. An important job. The Boss has decided that our subway is to be the chief symbol of modern civilization. His current favorite, Lazar Kaganovich, has taken personal charge of the project and is pushing it forward. Don't ask with what methods. Soon it will be complete. Which means soon we Soviet Russians will be civilized. But don't hold your breath.

Nina is superb at what she does. Any woman in such a job would have to be. She is stable, hardworking, serious, with little interest in things political or artistic. One of those people who believe the Party is actually working for the good of everyone. Nina knows little and cares less about things not reported in the pages of *Pravda*. All the emotions she has to suppress on the job come out when we are together, alone, in the bedroom. The first time I visited her office, the wall newspaper had a huge feature article on Nina as a model worker. The headline was an imperative: *Keep Up with Pirozhkova.* That line has become our theme song, one we play with endless variations. Today it goes like this:

Even on the beaches of the Black Sea and in the steam room at the Lermontov Sanitarium I will do my best to keep up with Pirozhkova.

Saying goodbye is not really difficult. It's a pleasure to leave Moscow. But the train ride is another story. Twenty-six hours to Odessa. The Ministry of Transportation can brag to the skies that this is half the time the journey took ten years ago—it still feels endless. And believe me, the Ukraine isn't Tuscany or Provence. Rarely do I glance out the window at the spectacle—brown wheat fields, sagging towns, slow rivers where naked peasants gather on grassy banks to sunbathe and get drunk. My eyes focus on the copy of Maupassant's stories I bought nine years ago on my first trip to Paris. At a stall on the Left Bank, just across from Notre Dame. The elderly bookseller seems disappointed that I pay fifteen francs without bargaining. He pushes back his beret and says, *You are not French, monsieur?*

This question is the product of a long tradition of French philosophy? My summer suit may be the height of fashion in Moscow, but in Paris the square, baggy cut makes me look like a visitor from another planet, or century.

No, I am not French, malheureusement.

But you read our language, you speak our language. A shame, monsieur, but of course not everybody can be French. We need other people in the world so we can know we are French.

Gallic wit? Insult? Both? I touch my fingers to the brim of my straw hat and stroll away. The same hat that hangs on a hook in the corner of the compartment. The train is new, but the style is strictly prerevolutionary: thick upholstery and pillows, velvet curtains, a polished wooden table with a fake Tiffany lamp. One wall features a much retouched photo of the Boss. He looks almost handsome—strong chin, stern, kindly eyes, cheeks free of the pockmarks that fascinate and frighten all of us who get to see him up close. Opposite hangs a mirror where a patriotic traveler might see the glory of our leader reflected once again. My suit jacket hangs over the mirror.

Natasha is on my mind. She's my second child, but it's different this time. I ran away from the idea of Misha even before Kashirina gave birth and never even saw him after the age of two. Who's to blame? I was young, foolish, married to another woman. Now he has the name of the father who adopted him. But Natasha is mine. With my genes, my name, and as many of my wayward impulses as can show in an eight-year-old. And I'm not raising her either. Fifteen hundred kilometers separate us. We may as well live in different universes. Different galaxies. Every hour or two I pull out the picture taken last summer. It's only our second long period of time together, the second time I have made it to France since her birth. We are sitting on the outside steps of a summer cottage in Normandy side by side and looking intently at each other. Is that me? Have I ever been capable of such a sweet smile? Natasha's expression is quizzical, guarded. It says: If you are really my daddy, why don't you stay and live with Mommy and me?

Last year's visit almost did not happen. My name was conspicuously absent from the official list, so the Soviet delegation to the Congress of Writers for the Defense of Peace and Culture went off to Paris without me. Without Boris Pasternak, too, though it's difficult to know what his literary or personal sins might be. But we were lucky. Our foreign friends and colleagues found the situation impossible. On the first day of the congress, telegrams came to Moscow from the delegates of twenty-five countries: No Babel, no Pasternak, no Soviet speakers will be allowed to take the floor. The next day we are in an Aeroflot plane together. For hours I have to listen to Boris: *I'm an old man. I don't like to travel. I hate congresses. Writers aren't politicians. I have nothing to say that's not in my poetry. Why don't they leave me alone?*

When we enter the huge hall at Mutualité, the speaker on the podium shouts *Here they are!* A thousand people roar approval while we are hustled to the platform. Boris waves, sinks into a folding chair. Not me. I never miss an opportunity to speak in French: *Sorry to be late, comrades. We had to change the oil on our tractor before we could get away.* Laughter and cheers. I bow, continue for twenty minutes. Carefully, for someone will report every word back to Moscow. On the flight I practiced phrases that, stripped of the irony in my voice, would sound the way a Soviet writer's speech should sound to anyone reading a transcript in the Kremlin: *We are reaching a new stage in social development. The collective farmer has bread, he has a house, he even has decorations. Now he wants poetry written about him.*

The collective farmer! Poetry? Not from this speaker, who is not meant to write about the collective anything. If I didn't know it already—and I did—that was the lesson of that sugar beet farm in the Ukraine. Living in a hut with a leaky roof and a floor so muddy that putting on my pants in the morning is an acrobatic feat of hopping from one leg to the other. Undertaking days of the miserable work in the fields to get the feeling of collective life. Attending the long meetings to debate such fascinating topics as the shapes and depths of toilet pits. Around me all day long, the thoughts of the peasants scream aloud: Be careful around this Jew. He must be reporting to the NKVD. What else but a job with the secret police would bring him to our godforsaken farm? What else would make him sit through these dreary meetings?

In ten weeks the only time I feel like picking up my pen is the morning they find the body of a young peasant at the edge of a field. One of those types who gets up at every meeting to make a speech urging everyone to work harder and harder to fulfill the production quotas. One of those who then goes out and overfulfills his own. Thirty, forty of us stand quietly in the mist, remove our hats, look down at the bloody scythe, the head, the limbs severed from the torso. All placed neatly next to each other. By late afternoon, everyone refuses to answer questions about him, his family, or possible suspects. The next day nobody mentions his name. Other than the old man who pulls me aside and whispers: *Beware.*

It's an apt metaphor for our generation? Fame if we are lucky. Notoriety if we are not. Silence either way. That's the story. Six years past his suicide, Mayakovsky is honored as the great poet of the Revolution, but who dares to quote his flaming calls for social change? And who speaks of Mandelstam two years after he has been disappeared for a single poem about the Boss, a poem never committed to paper and spoken but once to an audience in a private apartment in Leningrad? Akhmatova has descended into silence since the arrest of her son. Blok was lucky to die in 1921. Would anyone today dare to write a poem in which Red Guards are led by a vision of Christ? Would anyone read it? Or take its sentiments seriously?

Now Gorky is silent too. The great Maxim Gorky, buried with state honors. The Boss himself, serving as one of the pallbearers. We'll never know if his death was natural. It doesn't really matter. He has been heartsick and dying, dead in terms of creativity or force, ever since his return from Italy two years ago. Surrounded by doctors, journalists, young writers, all posing as friends, all reporting back to the Kremlin. Not a healthy climate, but for an old Russian at least it smelled of home. Gorky was Russian to the core. Even after all those years of living abroad. Especially after all those years. When I visited him in Sorrento four years ago, all he wanted to talk about was the solemn beauty of twilight over the grain fields of the Ukraine. We strolled together in his garden overlooking the spectacular cliffs and the sea of the Amalfi coast. He took me by the arm and said: *This view breaks my heart. But not as much as being away from my native soil. Each hour I long for the language, the music, the passions, the sadness, the insanity of our motherland.*

My mentor. That story has protected me for almost two decades. Say Maxim Gorky loves you and government officials tremble. Everyone knows he is the Boss's favorite author. The soul of the new Russia. During the dreadful spring days of 1918 he published lots of my stuff in his journal, the *New Dawn*. My clever, unfair, brash reports on the inefficiency, corruption, and stupidity of the new Soviet institutions—homes for the blind, the pregnant, the delinquents. Reports that supported his own criticisms of the regime for the way it squelched democracy and debate. But soon enough he made his peace with the regime. That helped me too. In the midtwenties he stood beside me against the attack of General Budyenny, when the old hero of the Civil War accused me of slandering his beloved Cossacks in *Red Cavalry*. Why, he demanded in the press, does Babel highlight their atrocities? Why does he fail to show their revolutionary élan? Because, Budyenny answered his own question, Babel was never at the front. He was a coward, a soldier at the rear. Two years later the general returned to the attack. This time he called me womanish. This time it was not only Gorky who came to my rescue. Wonder of wonders, the Boss himself settled the issue by telling someone who would get the word out: Red Cavalry *is not all that bad—in fact it's a very good book.*

Another benefactor.

All that was less than a decade ago. It seems like a century. Now Gorky is gone. The single dissenter ever tolerated both by Lenin and by the Boss. A sign, like so many other signs these days, that things are changing and not for the better. Getting tighter. So tight there is a real possibility that I won't get to see Natasha again. And now this offer by Potato Face. It could be a godsend. Or a trap. Why me? Because I'm proof that the Soviet state is generous enough to honor writers who no longer write. But a boat from Odessa seems too much like a story. Hard to believe they would really let him escape. If it proves possible for him, why not someone else. Why not me? Do people really believe my claim to have the same problem as Gorky. But it can't be quite the same. No Jew is as Russian as a Russian like Gorky. I love the taste of the West. The freedom, the erotics of the grand boulevards. But when I am there it is not me that is there. It's as if someone else is pasted onto me, someone whose perceptions and language are not quite familiar. Anyway, this time it's not a question of Paris, but Natasha. My child. It's worth a try. Nothing to lose by checking things out and you never know: something might well turn up. Characters for a story. Settings or situations. Inspiration. There's always something to be learned from literary shadows. About continuities with the past. Richer than any future we can now imagine.

4

*T*he guy who dreamed up the train schedule deserves a stint in Siberia. Six A.M. is a ridiculous time to arrive in a southern seaside town like Odessa, where everyone goes to bed late and wakes up even later. It's far too early for passengers to enjoy the nineteenth-century showpiece station, its broad platform, frescoed walls, and bright tile floors all washed in light from the glass ceiling. In front of the neoclassical facade with its heroic arches, I look around. Not a single taxi in sight. What else is new? Okay. After twenty-six hours in a compartment, I can use a little exercise. Shake out the kinks in my legs. See what's new in the only place in the world where my breath can sometimes get the better of my asthma.

A few minutes' stroll confirms what I noticed last year: the old town is shabbier than ever. Someone in the Kremlin must have it in for us. Jealous of our climate or resentful of a city where half the population are Jews. Moscow has been getting more modern and elegant the last couple of years. New apartments and office buildings, worker's co-ops, paint jobs on old palaces, iron lights to brighten boulevards like the Tverskaya and the Arbat. But Odessa grows more and more dingy. Along the main street, Catherine the Great, renamed Karl Marx and still called Catherine by everyone except Party officials in public speeches, lots of store windows are blacked out. At the corner of DeRibas, the striped umbrellas over the tables of Café Fanconi are in shreds. Robinat, its old rival across the street, squats behind wooden boards. In Cathedral Square, the iron benches are gone and the genitals, noses, and fingers of all the classical statues have been chipped away. From their heads and shoulders you can tell it has been years since anybody has dealt with the creative efforts of the local pigeons.

Every trip home begins with the same ritual: a visit to the Second Jewish Cemetery. A walk along a stony road, past shanties and weed-choked fields, brings me to an imposing stone gate with an iron fence. A cemetery doesn't change much. This one has been the same jumble as long as I can remember. Plots with tilted stones, mostly overgrown with weeds, a few with fresh flowers, line the walls. In the center, screened by rows of acacia and chestnut trees, you find pink marble monuments, the resting places of the merchants and brokers, misers and philanthropists who tried to turn this town into a Russian Marseilles. Tombstones with inscriptions in Hebrew. In Russian. In both. None is simpler than Father's: EMMANUEL BABEL, 1868–1925. Can it really be eleven years since we buried him? The last time the family was together all in one place. Always I have a feeling here of too much left unsaid. No surprise. Neither of us was good at listening. He didn't hear and I didn't care. Or thought I didn't. Now I would. Now I could use some good advice. Did he ever feel the need for advice and find that he didn't trust anybody enough to give it? No doubt.

He stopped listening when I began to talk back. In my teens, he became afraid to hear what I was saying. Before that it was always, yes Papa, I will study hard after school and at night and on Saturdays, and take special lessons in Russian and Hebrew and math, anything to make you proud of me. But once I began to speak of writing. Once I began to write. Once I published my first story, he closed his ears. Writing might be something to admire, but in others, not in your only son. Words were no way to make a living. He wanted something different for his son. A future. Wealth. A businessman with a future. But give him this: he had his own quirky taste. He wanted a son to be a special kind of businessman. A businessman who could play the violin.

Poor Stolyarsky. My teacher. Did he ever have a pupil with less talent? He who started off greats like Oistrakh and Heifetz. I can see him now. He flings his hands about in wild despair. His voice cracks into shrieks: *Don't hold the bow that way, hold it this way, I've told you a million times, don't you ever listen, can't you remember anything, don't you practice?* Yes and no. I prop up a book—Dumas, Scott, Twain, Tolstoy —on the stand next to the music and saw away like a mechanical toy. Father is tone deaf. He never complains at any sound that issues from my room. Silence is what he fears. One day the bow stops moving. I stand there, absorbed in a story by Maupassant. Two seconds later, Father yells from the living room. *Isaac, what's wrong. Why did you stop?*

You think I'm paying for lessons for you to stop? Next morning I hide the violin in the back of my armoire, put a bathing suit and towel into the case, and march past Stolyarsky's street and down to the harbor. I hang out at a waterfront café full of sailors. Buy a hand-carved pipe from one of them, light up, get sick to my stomach. In the afternoon I make for the beach. Put on my bathing suit. Tiptoe into the sea. Tiny waves knock me over. I swallow water and choke. Nikitich and his band of athletes take pity and come over to teach me. A week later I can swim out beyond the buoys. For months I fear Stolyarsky will appear at our house to denounce me. Father will have a stroke. The store will be sold to pay for funeral expenses. Mother and I will have to go to live with relatives. But Stolyarsky must have been happier than I was. I never did learn how he got the message to Father that he need no longer pay for lessons.

After the cemetery, I devote the rest of the day to practical matters. Find a temporary room in a small hotel on Gogol Street, just behind the Opera House. Stop by the Lermontov Sanitarium to make an appointment with the director. Visit the Writers' Union to arrange for the occasional use of an automobile. Wait in a line at the main post office to send three telegrams. To Nina: *Your babushka is safe.* To Mother in Belgium: *The prodigal son has come home once again.* To Zhenya: *Tell Natasha Daddy will come soon to teach her how to swim.*

Another ritual ends the day: a visit to the Duc. There he stands, rooted in place at the head of the wide Primorskii Promenade, near the London Hotel and the once grand Stock Exchange, now a dilapidated nursing home. The Duc, a bronze figure in a toga, looks out over the steps, arm raised, staring out to sea, waiting for someone to come and take him home to France. Poor Armand du Plessis, Duc de Richelieu, grandson of Louis XIII's great cardinal, forced to stand here eternally because Czar Alexander picked him as the first governor of Odessa. The ruler's goal was simple: Get a European to civilize my barbaric subjects. Fat chance! But Richelieu gave it a good shot. He told the emperor: *You want a port? You want business? You want trade with Europe? You want civilized? You have to let in the Jews.* Alexander signed the decree without blinking. In less than a century, Odessa is the richest port in the empire. The liveliest. The one with the best bagels.

Say Odessa and what do people think? What do they see? A long flight of stone steps down to the harbor. The boots and rifles of soldiers in formation descending those steps. Crowds of people, young and old, bourgeois and worker, scattering every which way, fleeing for their lives. A middle-aged woman with shattered glasses carrying a child. A baby carriage bumping downward. Cossacks on horseback riding at the bottom of the steps. Pandemonium and mayhem. You know what I'm talking about. Eisenstein's steps. As if he invented them. As if they didn't exist before *Battleship Potemkin*.

Don't get me wrong. Sergei Mikhailovich is a good friend of mine. A great director. A great artist. And that sequence on the steps, that brilliant montage, is to film what Brunelleschi's dome is to churches or Beethoven's *Eroica* to symphonies. People will be exclaiming over it centuries from now. But you have to remember: Eisenstein is from Latvia. A gloomy northern country darkened by perpetual clouds and storms that get into the souls of its native sons. So he can look at our Odessa steps and see blood, anguish, horror, destruction. But not me. Nor anyone else from Odessa. To us, these steps speak of opportunity, success, romance, happiness, love. They are the place where you take a girl's hand for the first time. Where you nuzzle her cheek. Where you taste the sweet pleasure of her soft lips. Where you sit and plan the wonderful future you will have together.

Here's a little-known historical fact: I'm the one who first turned Sergei onto the steps. It is early 1927 and he has just arrived in Odessa, ready to shoot two films at the same time. He's always been ambitious. One is the homage to the Revolution of 1905, which ends up as *Potemkin*. The other is to be *Benya Krik*, from my screenplay based on the first of my gangster stories. Five minutes after the company moves into the London Hotel, I march Sergei out the door and across the road to see the Duc and the harbor view and the steps below. I'm not thinking of his film but of mine. Won't this be a splendid site for one of Krik's adventures.

Tell the truth, I already used it as a setting the year before. The film was *Jewish Luck*. An oxymoron? Perhaps. But I didn't write the story, only adapted it from a tale by Sholem Aleichem, one that features his favorite character, the schlemiel and perpetual schemer, Menachem Mendel. On the lam from creditors, Mendel falls asleep on a train and dreams a grandiose dream. A dream in which he sees himself wearing a formal suit and riding into Odessa in a gilded carriage attended by footmen in livery. Mendel descends from the carriage right in front of the Duc and, there on the steps below, spies an elegant and attractive woman. Down he goes to meet her, but no, they don't do the expected. They don't fall in love. They do something far smarter: they go into business together. The matchmaking business. Next scene they sit in a café with a view of the harbor and listen to a rich American lament that in New York City real Jewish brides cannot be found.

Mendel lights up like a menorah and immediately gets off a telegram to a shtetl town and, before you can say *gut yontif,* trains of boxcars are arriving in Odessa loaded with girls clad in wedding dresses. Hundreds of young women in white flounce along the docks where Eisenstein will later have sailors wave their fists and shout revolutionary slogans. Cranes lift the girls like cargo onto the deck of a big liner until, overflowing with females, it steams out of the harbor. Dockside crowds cheer. Mendel, puffed up as the savior of America, climbs to the top of the lighthouse to wave goodbye. But at the moment of his great triumph, he loses his footing, plunges into the sea, and wakes to find himself back on the train, a schlemiel still on the lam.

That's the Odessa where I grew up. A place where big things happen. Where the unexpected is reality and reality is unexpected. Where dreams can begin and dreams can end.

5

*S*ome days everything happens as if in a movie.

In the morning I make my way to the Lermontov Sanitarium. One of the showplaces of Odessa. A big white building with Greek columns and a grand portico set on a bluff, with terraces leading down to the sea. Set in the midst of expansive gardens. The kind of place you don't want to inspect too closely. Paint peels from the walls. Floors sag. So do the faces of the nurses and helpers. But the head of it, Professor—*Don't call me Doctor*—Kalina knows his gestures. His lines. He pokes and prods my belly, places a cold stethoscope against my back, looks down my throat and up my nose with a small flashlight. Then we face at each other across a desk. Neither point of view is very inspiring. He pats his ample belly. Begins to speak in the voice of a character actor who isn't getting as many roles as he used to.

Overwork, my boy. Nothing but overwork. Well, it's not easy to build a new world. You're run down.

He pats his belly again.

Me too. I'm run down. We're all run down these days. We work too hard. Another pat. *My prescription for you is no smoking, no alcohol, no greasy food.* He pauses and winks. *And no wild women! In a few weeks you'll be good as new. Better than new.*

My asthma?

Asthma? Oh yes. Asthma. All a matter of general health, my boy. Get you in shape and you'll be breathing like a long-distance runner.

Before or after the race? I refrain from asking.

The treatments begin. Suddenly I seem to be part of a badly edited silent comedy. I'm Buster Keaton or Charlie Chaplin. Doctors, nurses, attendants, guards: everyone seems to be wearing smocks either far too tiny or way too large. Everyone moves in quick jerks. Nobody smiles. Everybody shouts and points as I am pushed into a locker room and forced into striped pajamas so huge there's room enough for a couple of other guys inside them. An attendant hustles me into a mud bath so deep I must breathe through a straw. I dry out under a sunlamp until the tiny hairs in my nostrils begin to smolder. The word *Fire!* appears on the screen. Someone rushes over carrying a huge extinguisher and sprays me with foam. A gigantic masseuse drags me away like a sack of potatoes, hurls me onto a table, and proceeds to pummel and twist me into a pretzel. When she departs, three attendants stand around the table, scratching their heads over how to straighten me out. The final sequence takes place at lunch. A close-up of tears running down my cheeks. Cut to a long shot of a bare room full of mostly toothless folks, sitting on hard chairs, staring with hollow eyes at tables full of plates heaped with nothing more than leafy greens.

Afternoon brings a different genre: the social problem film. A story of the good citizen battling faceless bureaucracy. The opening image: a ponderous government building, a wide flight of steps. Flags, posters, armed guards at the door. A life-size stone image of the Boss sitting in a chair on a pedestal. The hallways are crowded. Young people and old people, peasants and city folk, the ragged and the well-dressed, lean against walls, squat on bundles, read books, deal cards, throw dice, munch on cold *pirojki*. In the long green hallways, acronyms impossible to pronounce are stenciled in black letters on doors just above the equally worrisome names of departments. MACENTSUPMATMAT—Main Central Supply of Matchmaking Materials.

Inside a door labeled TEPHOOSU, Temporary and Permanent Housing Office for Odessa and the South Ukraine, a male secretary is shocked by my request. A villa? I want a villa? Out on the Fountains? Out beyond the Sixth Station? Impossible. Absolutely impossible. Don't I know there's a housing shortage. Don't I know there are too many people who have no roofs over their heads? And were such a thing possible, this would not be the right office. I need to go to the Department of Russian Housing Resources and Family Matters.

The clerks at DRHRaFM are stunned to learn that I have been sent to them, since everyone knows, or everyone should know, that housing is handled by the Inter-Soviet Resource and Transfer Administration

Program. Not at all, comrade, not at all, says a jovial secretary at ISR-TAP. He shakes his head and sends me on to his distinctly less jovial counterpart at the Soviet Transfer Administration, who insists that his office handles national housing, that local housing is not at all in their jurisdiction. This is clearly a matter, he says, for the local branch of the Party. They have taken over anything to do with housing. But not, I learn at local headquarters from a Party secretary who looks at me suspiciously, if you do not have a Party card. Besides, decisions like this are always made by the Russian Party. At whose office a bunch of workers find the idea of a villa on the Fountains so amusing that they shout the news around the office, laugh together, and tell me, *Tovarisch,* we are far too busy running a country to worry about housing. Housing is under the jurisdiction of TEPHOOSU. Why don't you take your problem there?

This time the door is locked. I pound vigorously and, after five minutes, it opens to reveal a round man in a suit so shiny and a necktie so bright that you need sunglasses to look directly at him. *Sorry,* he says, *sorry, we're closed.* I speak quickly. Start with my name.

The Isaac Babel? He takes my hand, shakes it furiously.

A pleasure. Isaac Babel! In my office. Bagritsky. Vladimir Bagritsky. What a pleasure. My wife will be so happy. She reads your stories over and over. She loves Benya Krik. Soviet literature begins and ends with Isaac Babel—that's what she says.

The door opens wide. We sit and drink tea. Discuss housing problems. *Of course, comrade, there is a shortage. There is always a shortage. We don't have enough space for our own people, but I know how it is with a writer. My wife is a writer too. A writer needs a quiet place to work. A writer needs space. I'm sure my boss will understand.*

His boss, Anatol Zirinovsky, in a dark brown belted leather jacket and with a face made of much the same material, looks like he has never read a book. Never wanted to read one. Would like to shoot anyone who suggests that he read one. He sits behind a large desk. Shakes my hand without rising.

Comrade. We recognize you and your great contributions to Soviet literature. But it is not easy to arrange for accommodations in these days of struggle.

Comrade Yagoda thought it might be possible.

He stiffens. Bagritsky stiffens. I relax.

Comrade Yagoda?

He and I had a good talk about housing just before I left Moscow. Talk to the boys at TEPHOOSU, he said. At TEPHOOSU they know how important writers are in the struggle against capitalism. They'll fix you up with something nice. Give the boys at TEPHOOSU my best regards. Tell them to keep up the good work.

Zirinovsky doesn't miss a beat.

The truth is, comrade, we of the Odessa Soviet, we servants of the Russian people never use the word impossible. *Certainly not for such a well-known local citizen. Of course we must remember: Leningrad wasn't built in a day. Give us a little time, comrade.*

No rush.

I smile. They smile. We all shake hands. Bagritsky leads me out into the hallway. Takes me by the arm.

My wife would love to meet you. Love to hear you read. Could you do her writers' club the honor of appearing one evening. Nothing too formal, you understand. Just a few words from a great writer to his loyal fans. Or perhaps something new about Odessa. We'd all like to hear something about Odessa.

There is no question mark in his tone.

It will be a pleasure, I say.

Knowing very well it will not.

6

*F*ive days later I am all set up. The boys in the housing office have moved quickly. Somewhere my credit must still be good.

I'm in a villa out on the Fountains. Not the Middle Fountain, but the fancier area, the Big Fountain. Just past the Twelfth Station on the trolley line. The place has seen better days. Haven't we all? Crumbling pink stucco. Pipes that shake and rumble when you turn on the water. Sagging furniture—what few pieces have not been stolen or burned as firewood by previous tenants. A flagstone terrace with jagged edges onto a hillside overgrown with dead bushes. Fragments of tile and pieces of broken concrete lie on the rocky beach below.

Sitting at the table in the dining room I see nothing but sea and sky. If only I felt like writing.

Along this coast the rich once built their mansions. The year my parents were living in Kherson and I had to stay with Uncle Wolf and Aunt Bobka, she often brought me out here on the horse-drawn trolley. Bobka wanted to teach a lesson to this nephew who spent all his time in his room, reading, writing, playing alone. She was worried: What kind of future can a kid have if his nose is always stuck in a book?

Friends are important, she says. *And always remember this: It's as easy to be friends with someone from the Fountains as with someone from the Moldavanka.*

Eventually I do have a good friend who lives in the Fountains. In the ritziest area, beyond the Sixteenth. Mark Borgman. His father is a businessman who is in importing and exporting and stocks and bonds and just about everything else in which there's money to be made. His mother heads a dozen charity committees. Mark is a good boy, a sweet boy who has absolutely no imagination. He is fascinated by the stories I tell. Like the one about how Uncle Wolf fought against the Turks and visited Cairo and slept all night inside the Great Pyramid and was haunted by the ghosts of the Pharaohs. Or how Grandpa Yitzhak, once a famous rabbi, was run out of Lvov for forging checks against the account of his own synagogue.

Mark wants to be an aeronautical engineer. In his room in the huge villa he shows me how to build model airplanes. We swim on his private beach. Soon I am spending so much time out there that Aunt Bobka says, *I never get to see you anymore.* At night, through the bedroom door, I hear her complain to Uncle Wolf. The Borgmans are not exactly what she had in mind. The mother is the kind of woman who perfumes her underwear, spends too much time playing cards, and wears a pound of makeup and a ton of diamonds to services at the Brody Synagogue, even on Yom Kippur. As for Mr. Borgman, his behavior is scandalous. He makes no attempt to hide the fact he is having an affair with a pudgy Italian soprano from the opera. Bobka sounds angry when she says: *That woman is not even as attractive as his wife!*

What's an affair? I ask at dinner the next day.

Aunt Bobka gets up to clear the dishes. Uncle Wolf answers: *It has to do with business. You'll understand when you grow up.*

He's right.

Those trolley rides must have had an effect. Over the years, whenever I imagine the ideal place to write, the Fountains is it. Odd. In three decades this is only the second time I've stayed out here. How different the world is now from that first time. The year was 1921. I am twenty-eight. The first of my Odessa stories, *The King,* has just been published. The first about the Moldavanka district, with its working-class Jews, famed whorehouses, and thousands of bandits and thieves. *The King* tells how the handsome, feared gang leader Benya Krik plays host to a huge wedding banquet for his homely sister and, on the same afternoon, has his boys burn down the local police station. It's a ploy to divert the cops who, he has learned through an informant, plan to raid the wedding to capture the underworld elite who are in attendance. The publication gives me what I longed for without admitting it: fame. First in Odessa, then across the country. Immediately I begin to learn some of its costs. At cafés and in libraries, strangers begin to pester me. Everyone seems to be a writer who needs advice. Everyone comes up to ask how to get their stuff published. Journalists, librarians, schoolteachers, waiters, busboys, hang on my every word. Thrust manuscripts into my hand. Become cranky and abusive when I refuse to read them.

I escape to the Fountains. Hide out. Avoid town. It's the start of a lifelong pattern of avoiding other writers, their salons, organizations, colonies, meetings. People who do things are always more interesting. Jockeys, pilots, con men, hunters, thieves, cabbies, members of the secret police. I prefer people who don't spend all their time living in their heads.

That glorious summer of 1921. Zhenya is radiant. Her red hair glistens as she awakens to the sea, the sun, the air. We have been married three months. Her father refused to attend the ceremony at the Public Registry Office in Kiev. What's wrong with a synagogue, he wanted to know. What he really meant is, What's wrong with my daughter? What did I do to have her pick this young man? A kid who abandoned a good commercial college degree to become a writer. My daughter is an only child. A Gronfein. An heiress to a fortune built on a machine factory. And she's marrying a man without a job, without a future.

We told him that synagogues belonged to the past. That we were children of the future. He denounced me and disowned Zhenya. And cursed my family for ten generations.

Zhenya and I are in love like neither of us will ever be in love again.

Maybe it's time to reconsider the power of curses.

It's the first good summer in many years. The Civil War is over. The Bolsheviks are finally in control of the whole country. All the invading troops and foreign legions have left Odessa—the French, the Germans, the British, the Ukrainians, the Whites. The city is a ruin. Pavements have been torn up for fortifications, trees in the parks cut down and burned for firewood, stores looted of everything that could be carried away. But the war is over. Everyone smiles. So does the weather. One sunny afternoon follows another. Each morning I write like a madman. Each afternoon we walk on the beach. We swim. We eat melons. We make love. We are immortal.

It's too good to last.

The first hint of change comes the afternoon when we learn that Alexander Blok has died in Moscow. Age forty-one. Three years younger than I am now. He was one of our great literary heroes, even if the years have made it difficult to remember exactly why. During the war I visited him one afternoon in Petrograd. A disappointing experience. I ached to hear Blok say the secret words that would make me become a great writer, but all he wanted to speak about was the war, the horrendous numbers of deaths, the wave of destruction that he feared would carry us all away. This was a year before the October Days. How odd it seemed when this great poet grasped at the Revolution like someone who was drowning, clung on to the Bolsheviks like a life jacket. At least the Revolution let him begin to write again, write in a new language full of hope, one that, for a brief time, made us believe in the possibility of a new age. A better world.

Some local writers appear at the door of the villa with the news. It's depressing enough to make me welcome their company. Together a bunch of us grieve through the night, drinking wine on the beach, reciting Blok's famed revolutionary works, *The Twelve* and *Scythians,* into the light of dawn. After breakfast, my new friends don't leave. For days, weeks, they hang around and talk about the future. Sharing their dreams. Konstantin Paustovsky. Valentin Kataev. Others whose names are now forgotten. Not one of them has published a word, but they overflow with ambition, with big plans for the future, for the revolutionary literature they will help to create.

Literature! The word makes me cringe. Reading these guys today, I know what I should have done: given lectures on the perils of writing when you have neither talent nor guts. But I was young and they treated me as someone famous. So I played the role. Preened, pontificated, expanded my chest. Told them in great detail of my trips to Paris. Described the sounds of lovers in the next room of my hotel on Place Contrescarpe. The smell of the flowers in the Bois du Boulogne. The beauties of the women on the boulevard des Italiens. The solemnity of my visit to the Maupassant museum, in the writer's former home, where I sat in his chair and felt his spirit enter me, heard it whisper that I was destined to be his literary heir.

They swallow it all. Years later they put the things I said into so many essays about me that the stories become part of my official biography. Never do they suspect that I have not been to Paris, that I was inventing Paris. Inventing experiences I would not have for many years.

Midsummer brings more changes. The Soviets take full control of Odessa. Half of my parents' apartment is requisitioned for the family of a Party member. Seven strangers suddenly move into what used to be my bedroom, the dining room, and my father's study. The kitchen and two bathrooms are now communal. Father is away in Nikolayev, vainly trying to sell a piece of property before it is confiscated. My mother and sister last four days before they pack suitcases and arrive at our villa in tears. We newlyweds now have our own communal house. One that grows a few weeks later when the state expropriates Gronfein's factory. Suddenly the son-in-law proves to be not such a bad sort after all. Zhenya's mother arrives with a belated wedding present: a thousand-ruble note. It turns out to be worthless when the old currency is abolished.

A household full of people disrupts my schedule. It's far more difficult to get anything done. Each morning I must get up very early to write. It doesn't work. Zhenya's mother makes it her business to get up even earlier to cook eggs for me. I hate eggs. I hate seeing anyone first thing in the morning. She is not good at taking hints. She says: *I made them specially for you.* She gets coy: *Don't you like your mother-in-law?*

I hurry to my workroom, but each day it is less and less a refuge, more and more a site of struggle. I am trying to write the stories about the Civil War that will become *Red Cavalry*. The stories that will later make me famous. That will bring me an international reputation. But all that is in the future. Right now it's painful coming to grips with the shattering experiences of last summer. Trying to understand the horror and the odd exhilaration of those months riding with the Cossacks. I am desperate to turn my notebooks into something publishable and suffering from a problem that will over the years plague me: the original words, scribbled during the advances and retreats and horrendous confusion of the war with Poland, notes jotted hastily on horseback or in leaky barns or in the bedrooms of filthy hovels in one devastated shtetl town or another, are more powerful than any finished stories. Fresher. More concise. Truer to what I witnessed and felt. The notes say what needs to be said about our cavalry in the summer of 1920 as we rode from Kiev toward Warsaw. That this was less a revolutionary army than a Cossack rebellion. That we—I was working at headquarters—were less an army of liberation than a barbarian horde. That our men could kill prisoners in cold blood for the sheer joy of killing. That there is no difference between a Cossack pogrom and a Polish pogrom. The hatred is just the same, the cruelty just the same, the results the same.

If I don't know it before, I learn this in Komarow. Despite my assumed Russian name, Lyutov, and despite my best attempt to pass as Russian and not be labeled a Jew, the family of David Zys suspects otherwise. Indoors they whisper to me of atrocities they have seen. Wandering the streets I smell the stench of blood that pervades the town and see the evidence for what they say: the child with fingers chopped off, the mother sitting over her sabered son, the old woman cut into many pieces, the rape victim lying twisted like a pretzel in the muddy street, the family of four sunk in pools of their own blood, the seventy-year-old Hasid and the shammes, his wife, and his fifteen-year-old daughter lying in a heap.

I learn the same lesson again that gray afternoon we ride into Zhitomir and find a grisly present left by the retreating Polish army: forty-five dismembered bodies, heads, tongues, limbs, fingers, and ears scattered like bloody pieces of meat in the yard of the local slaughterhouse. Our captain finds the scene amusing. *Who needs all these Yids?* he says. *They're not Russian. They don't belong to us. Let's do the world a favor. Let's take care of them the kosher way.* He grabs a frail, elderly man. A skullcap slips off as the captain roughly places the gray head beneath his left armpit, brandishes a bayonet in his right hand, and then, like a kosher killer, slowly draws the blade across the scrawny neck and holds the old man tight while blood spurts and splatters onto weapons, clothing, boots, the ground. The captain tosses away the bayonet and raises a bottle of vodka aloft. Shouts *l'chaim,* laughs, drinks deeply, passes it to the surrounding troops.

This is what people need to know about the Civil War. What I must let them know. But nobody will publish notes and nobody will dare publish such a view of the Cossacks, our new heroes. Some of the incidents can be used. But the overall narrative must have some hint of redemption, something more in keeping with the ideals of the Revolution. Something that says all this horror was only a prelude to a better world. For me to say this is difficult. So I tone down some of the worst atrocities. Swallow hard and have my narrator speak of Lenin, quote documents from the Second Congress of the Communist International, praise the new trains on which we will ride to future stars. Even so, I am compelled to make changes before the book can be published. A book I now dislike for the way it shades the truth. For the way the narrator can sometimes seem to enjoy the intensities of horror and war.

Cossacks in my study. Women everywhere else in the house. Mother, sister, Zhenya, and her mother. They cook, argue, bewail our fate, criticize, shout, demand, complain, worry the future. The villa overflows with too much emotion. It's no longer a refuge, no longer a place to write.

I am twenty-seven. A time of life when no line separates the practical from the romantic. In September we flee across the Black Sea to Batumi, on the Turkish border. It's a different world. Palm trees against startling sunsets. Muslim women, their heads covered with scarves. Five times a day the wail of the muezzin from the local mosques. Four kilometers from town we rent a shepherd's hut on a hill overlooking the sea. The perfect place to write. The perfect place for Zhenya to paint and sketch—lone trees on the rocky hillsides, the faces of women carrying baskets of olives to market. Nothing here to disturb us but the barking of dogs. For six months we live with the smell of sheep. We begin to smell like sheep ourselves. A smell I will always associate with the beginning of the end. Of our marriage.

Zhenya was raised with maids, cooks, a chauffeur, tickets to the symphony, cafés where you drink hot chocolate and giggle over handsome young officers in their cavalry uniforms. Seven years of war and revolution have taken care of the chocolate, the officers, and everything else except the desire for them. Her hands weren't meant to haul buckets of water from a well. But she is not the only one dismayed by country life. Soon I grow tired of sheep, olive trees, perfect sunsets. I go into town. Hang around with local journalists, members of the Soviet, schoolteachers and clerks who are trying to learn how to govern a city. I attend trials of counterrevolutionaries. Lounge in cafés. Listen to Socialist revolutionaries criticize the Party for shutting down their newspaper. Chat with disgruntled soldiers who deserted and are being denied pensions. Sailors of the Black Sea merchant fleet who made the mistake of supporting the wrong side in the Civil War. The local Soviet has pulled them off their ships, stripped away their citizenship. Penniless, stateless, they cadge drinks and smokes, try to get hired on Turkish or Greek freighters, talk vaguely of making a fresh start in Constantinople, Piraeus, or Marseilles.

Zhenya thinks it's a crime: *They are Russians. They were born here. They can't throw them out of their homeland.*

It's a revolution, I tell Zhenya. *They're alive. Worse things happen.*

It's not our first quarrel on the topic. Nor our last. But it is the one that makes me leave her in Batumi to spend a few months in Tbilisi. In this mountain town that reeks of almonds and roses, I rent a garret that hangs over the seething rapids of the Kura River. Take a job as a typesetter and reporter for the *Dawn of the East.* Begin to investigate the changes brought on by the Revolution: the creation of secular schools to rival the *madrasas* run by mullahs. The refurbishing of run-down dachas for workers' vacations. But it's the life of the region that grips me. This is my first time in the Caucasus. I love the masculine sense of freedom here, the soft winds off Mount Kazbek, the turquoise twilights, the stands smelling of lamb kebabs, the bazaars with their mixture of types and languages: Tartars in blue tunics and soft boots, Persians jabbering in Farsi, shopkeepers in alpaca jackets, Georgians with fur hats and tight leggings, and those grim harbingers of change: solid Russians wearing military boots and peaked caps with red stars.

When I return to Batumi, Zhenya and I pretend that Tbilisi was not a separation but a career opportunity. Soon we take the boat back to Odessa. The stories from *Red Cavalry* have begun to appear in journals. Critics are calling me the first writer to capture the spirit of the Revolution. Moscow beckons. Zhenya is not sure she wants to brave the climate there.

Meteorological or political? I ask.

She doesn't find my question funny.

Twelve years later, neither do I.

7

*M*orning sun. Curtains. Breeze. The smell of sea. Remnants of dream images: distorted faces, a palace, a gymnasium? Lines of people in overcoats, high cliffs, storm clouds, snatches of conversation in French? Yiddish? Thighs of women. Dreams elude me. Always fragments. Not since childhood have I remembered a dream intact. Could Freud explain? He knows how to tell a good story, I'll give him that. But a science of the self makes less sense to me than a science of society. You can see exactly where that idea has gotten us. Maybe it's just as well that Freud's works are banned here. Somebody in Moscow would no doubt find a way to use psychoanalysis to mobilize our inner selves for greater productivity. For the good of the state.

Put away the shadows of night and the shadows of day. Get back to basics: a burner, a kettle, a teapot. Persian tea I am able to get through connections in Moscow. No woman has ever been able to drink my morning brew undiluted. Nina, Zhenya, Tamara Kashirina, Yevgenia Yezhova—none of them. None of the others either. Maybe a good test. A smile across a morning cup of tea.

More sensible than whatever criteria lurk in my subconscious. Sex and the Jewish question. Sex and the pogrom. Grandpa Shoyl, stretched out on the stones of the courtyard. He who was so alive telling tall tales that fired my imagination. Who was so loud yelling his wares in the fish market. Now he lies still, one live fish in his mouth and another flopping out of the fly of his pants. In the house of the Christian neighbors who have taken us in, Galina, the officer's wife, leads me by the hand into her kitchen. For how many weeks I have stared from the bushes at her blond hair, green eyes, high cheekbones. A boy's dream. A Jewish boy. She washes the blood of dead pigeons from my hands, arms, face. She holds me close. Calls me her little rabbi. Bends down to kiss me. I grow faint with her perfume. With the powerful smell of the female. Ever since then I have fainted with startling regularity at this same smell.

Zhenya liked the fainting as little as she liked the Soviets.

Less.

Concentrate on what is at hand. This battered table. My notebook. My pen. The slightly cracked cup filled with tea. Fringes of dying bougainvillea on the terrace wall. A freighter far out at sea. To mind comes an encounter I had with Yagoda shortly after Gorky's funeral. At a very solemn party. Everybody there with a long face, even the Boss. This time he really does have something to be sad about; he's lost one of his chief excuses to the world. With Gorky alive, he always had an answer to those foreign critics who worry about the lack of freedom in the Soviet Union:

Don't be ridiculous. Writers are free here. We are all free. Look at Maxim Gorky, how he criticizes the government. Gorky writes what he wants. Goes and comes as he wants. He lives in Italy. He returns home. It doesn't matter to us. We honor him as we honor all free men.

Yagoda pulls me aside. Tries to soften me up by quoting a few lines from one of my Benya Krik stories. Then asks if I prefer Russian vodka or French wine. *Now you take Lev Kamenev and me,* he says, *this is something we have in common. We both think the Revolution will be finished and complete and triumphant the day we Russians can make a really good burgundy. What a pity. Some of us will never get to see that day.*

Maybe I was wrong. Maybe Yagoda is the one who sent Potato Face.

K has not been far from my thoughts. Every day I pick up *Pravda* to find nothing about him or Zinoviev. Instead the pages are full of news of the Civil War that broke out in Spain last month. The resistance of the workers of Barcelona and Madrid to the Fascist uprising. The expressions of solidarity from Soviet factory workers, who have already donated millions for their Spanish brothers. What is never explained is, Exactly which workers have enough money to make donations?

The other topic that fills the newspapers is the new constitution. Reporters, analysts, professors, experts, and Party cadres agree: it's the most democratic constitution that has ever been written. Already hailed by hundreds of thousands, millions of people in meetings held in factories, offices, shops, and on collective farms. Endorsed in tens of thousands of letters to the editors. Blessed in numerous public forums.

Who knows? Maybe all this is even true. I managed to skip the meeting at the Writers' Union devoted to the new freedoms promised by this constitution. On what grounds? That for us, for me in particular, constitutions are a mixed blessing. The last one we got was in October 1905. A constitution by order of his gracious majesty, Czar Nicholas Romanov. What followed was a brief period of press freedom, a long-winded duma, and the worst pogrom in our history. Eight hundred dead in Odessa alone. One of them is Grandpa Shoyl.

Forget politics. Concentrate on my daily routine. Simple enough. Morning hours I stare out the window. Wait for inspiration. There is one more Benya Krik story in me. I know it. The final story. Benya in the Revolution. Benya and the Revolution. What he does to it. What it does to him. But Benya stories never come easy. So I write these pages instead. Odd pages to be sure. A mixture of chronicle, autobiography, fiction. A new genre perhaps. Certainly new for me. More like something Bulgakov would write, much like his first book, *Off the Cuff*. The only one they've let him publish. People who know my work will say this can't be Babel. It's not his style. Too stripped of imagery, too simple and direct. What they don't realize is that style can be a trap. A burden. Twenty-five years of elaborate imagery and I'm ready for something simpler. A new voice. A simpler way of looking at the world. One that does not call for rewrites. It can be so tiring to seek the perfect image, the perfect word. And what in the end is the point. Some stories I have redone more than twenty times. This one I will leave as it emerges on the page.

Midday I go into town. Stroll around, strike up conversations with street sweepers, clerks, waiters, men on park benches, take lunch in a café, then check my mail at the old post office on Sadovaya Street. I avoid the new one on Catherine Street—that huge, modern triumph of Soviet architecture, a space in which the New Soviet Man can buy stamps, send telegrams, and make a long-distance phone call. If he can afford it. A better description would be: a monument to bad taste. Ornate as everything else these days. Like the model for the Palace of the Soviets that has been on display in Moscow for a year. We should all become religious and thank God that the ground is sinking so much they'll never be able to build it. Too bad the ground isn't equally soft under the subway. Poor Mayakovsky would commit suicide all over again to see the monstrosity they've named after him. Mosaic tiles, fake Greek statues, frescoes, putti, glass chandeliers—all to honor our leading Futurist, the man who wished to strip the world to a few spare lines of type.

At least Nina has taste enough to be embarrassed. More than once she says: *I do the mechanics, not the decoration.*

She was nervous at preview day last year. We all were. Members of the Politburo, heads of government agencies, regional Party chiefs, diplomats, journalists, scientists, artists, academicians, ballet dancers, packed together like cattle as we ride back and forth between the first four stations. Noisily trying to outdo each other. Talking in loud voices about how much more magnificent this is than the Paris Métro, the London Tube, the Berlin U-Bahn. A splendid buffet awaits but the long speeches make my appetite vanish:

We are surpassing the world, comrades. Surpassing even ourselves. Life is getting better and better.

The Boss is not there. You won't catch him underground. In crowds. Some say he has claustrophobia. The proper word is *paranoia.* A condition that feeds on itself and everything else. Like cancer.

After the post office comes the Lermontov. The massages are getting less painful, the heat lamp and baths more soothing. By late afternoon I am ready to check out an old rumor about one of my classmates that has never much interested me before.

I begin with a visit to Alexander Kirilovsky, my high school mathematics teacher. Twenty-five years since I've sat in his class. So stooped over, so fragile is the figure standing at the door of his apartment in Peresyp that it's hard to believe this is the same man who terrified us by thundering equations. Kirilovsky leads me into a shabby room crowded with dark furniture from the last century or the century before that. His white-haired wife hovers over us, refills cups from a copper samovar, insists I take slice after slice of home-baked kugel from a silver tray.

Well, well, well, well. Young Izzie, my prize pupil, and he ends up as a writer. A famous writer. You've put us on the map. And I picked him for the next Lobachevsky. To be Odessa's great gift to mathematics.

His classes, I explain, did not go to waste. Thanks to him I can keep track of what publishers owe me. And do a better job than their book-keepers.

You remember Schloime. Schloime Rotenstein. With a big nose and hair down to his eyebrows. Lots smarter than me. There's a rumor that he got himself smuggled out on a Turkish ship, that he's living in New York, that he's become a rich man.

No reaction. I put the question again. Kirilovsky shakes his head slowly. Shakes it again.

My old high school friend Fyodor remembers Schloime. Fyodor has done well. He lives in Arkadia, not far from the beach. Throws his arm around me. Pats his tummy and says, *We aren't kids anymore.* I pat mine and try to smile. We sit on a couch made of light wood at a light wood table laden with black bread, caviar, olives, bottles of vodka and wine.

The furniture is from Finland.

Fyodor sounds proud. His wife, a fleshy bleached blond, laughs at everything you say and lots of things you don't. Fyodor works at some vague job for some vaguer government agency. I don't press the point. These days we all grow vague about whom we work for and what we do.

A few glasses of vodka put us back in high school. Sneaking into the bars on Greek Street, watching belly dancers and sipping ouzo, lusting after a redheaded Uzbek with long fingernails. Too many *Remember whens* send his wife out of the room. Fyodor relaxes, stretches out.

Who would have expected Schloime to be the one. That kid was all brain, no balls. I understand it was a ship to Greece, then Italy, then America. I hear he does some kind of research for a big corporation. Not that I told you. So don't quote me. You've been away a long time. Odessa has changed.

Nikitich I save for last. His single room is sparse. Neat military bed in the corner, tiny kitchen area against the wall, small window looking out on a tree. He is well into his seventies now, but his back is straight, his hair thick. He looks like he could still swim ten kilometers. We sit on chairs at a small wooden table. Drinking beer, eating nuts.

Nikitich taught me the two most important lessons of my life. That water would hold up Hebrews (his word) as well as Russians (also his). That writing well was more than a matter of words.

You have a spark of genius, but something is missing. Something I can't put my finger on.

We were sitting on a bench in the botanical gardens. In his left hand he held the pages of my first stories. With his right he tapped the ground with a cane—his sole affectation. A proofreader by trade and inclination, Nikitich had read everything and forgotten nothing. But all that reading did not spoil his beliefs. He feared God and loved nature. When I confessed I did not believe in the first and knew nothing about the second, he was stunned enough to clap his hand to his forehead. Then he pointed: *What's the name of that tree?* I shrugged. He pointed again: *What's that one? What's the name of that bird that's singing?* I pleaded ignorance. He shook his head and muttered to himself: *Your parents, what can they be thinking?*

After reading my stories he said: *No matter. Believer or nonbeliever, the Divine is in you, like it or not. The day you can touch it and get it onto the page is the day you'll be a great writer.*

Nikitich was the first to put into words the most secret desire of my heart. To name the only thing I ever wanted to be. Ten years ago it was possible to believe I was on my way. Everyone agreed: *Red Cavalry* was a masterpiece. The Benya Krik stories were gems. But something happened. To me, to the world, to the fit between us. The words stopped flowing. The kind of words you can remember. There were enough words for screenplays. My own. The rewrites of others. Enough for articles in *Pravda* and *Russia Constructs* and a bunch of other publications best forgotten. But something happened. History. Love affairs. Ambition. A mixture of them all. Or maybe it's simpler. Maybe it's not historical. Maybe I could never fully accept the Divine. Maybe faith in storytelling was the closest I ever got. Maybe that's close enough. Maybe it really doesn't matter.

Nikitich sips a beer and says I don't look too bad for someone who lives in Moscow. Flabby, but nothing a few weeks of exercise wouldn't fix. He asks about my writing. I confess that I have no new stories. That I seem to have lost the desire to write. That I feel like time is running out.

No wonder. It's impossible to write without love, and there's no more love in this country. Love is like nature: God created both to feed the soul. Without love there is no soul.

I tell him that sometimes I think of moving back to Odessa. That sometimes I think of leaving the country.

Good idea. Get away! Everyone should. You're young.

I put a finger to my mouth.

He raises his voice. *Let them hear, if they want to. Let them do something about it. At my age you're not afraid of anything.*

Does he remember Schloime? Does he still have connections on the waterfront? Can he put me in touch with stevedores, warehousemen, pursers, captains? With anyone else who might help one get away.

Nikitich ponders. Shakes his head. Everyone he knew is dead or gone, but there is someone in my family who might be able to help.

My family?

That relative. The one married to the dentist.

Lyosha? That petty crook!

Nikitich looks pleased. He believes in the importance of family because he doesn't have one.

What I don't say is that I am not asking for myself. Not exactly.

8

They say there's no such thing as coincidence. Not in Odessa. Just as I have begun to wonder how to approach Lyosha without having Aunt Katya get me involved with half the people in the city, we meet. I am sitting in a café with my nose in a book when I hear the unmistakable sound of her voice.

No phone call. No telegram. No letter. A fine how do you do. This is the man I call my favorite nephew?

I look up. She leans over, kisses me on the cheek, and they sit down. Lyosha is with her. She is round as a bagel, he lean as a bread stick.

You weren't going to call?

Not right away. I've got things to think over. I need to be alone for a while.

This is news? As fresh as the news that the pope is Catholic? When didn't you need to be alone?

I like Katya. I love her. She is direct, honest, with no inclination toward nonsense. A dentist with the steadiness of the profession and the heart of a mother for the children she never had. Lyosha on the other hand is nothing but trouble. Pettiness clings to him like body odor. For thirty years he has been edgy and sarcastic with me, and things have grown worse since I had to make a few visits to friends in the right places and grease a few palms to get the charges about stolen goods against him dropped.

We talk about the family. The weather. My treatments at the Lermontov. I complain about the vegetarian luncheons. She makes an offer I can't refuse.

You want a real meal? I'll cook you a real meal. Come Sunday. You will eat a meal like a Babel should eat.

Okay, but do me a favor. Don't invite half the people in Odessa.

Fat chance. When I enter their apartment that afternoon, ten people shout hello. Elderly people who knew my parents in the old days. Who knew me when I was in knee pants. A quick glance at Katya's table takes away my annoyance. This is Sunday dinner in Odessa. It's been far too long. Chopped eggplant, steamed bluefish, roast brisket, fresh poppy seed bagels, two kinds of melon, wines from Bessarabia, apple strudel, honey cake.

We begin with toasts to our dearly departeds. Then we stuff our faces and raise our glasses and toast again and again. Voices grow loud. People have to yell to make themselves heard. Not me. I chew, nod, smile, chew, listen.

Hymie Rabinowitz, once a rich grain broker who had outlets in Brazil and Southeast Asia, says: *This brisket is delicious, but Izzie, your mother's was better, the best, the very best. What an elegant woman. And her heart, oy, did that woman have a heart. Today we could use such a heart in our community.* Mrs. Knadelman of the sharp tongue and the nervous twitch in her right eye is not to be outdone. *You forget, Hymie, that Fenya is still alive. But Manny, your father, Izzie, may he rest in peace, he was a prince of a man, so handsome, so smart, honest as the day is long, always willing to lend a hand. A real prince, I tell you, a Prince of Odessa.* Abie Dubinsky, the one-time kosher meat killer who now manages a state slaughterhouse, was always sweet on Mera: *Your sister. A rare combination: both a good girl and a beauty. And such a beauty. Well behaved too, not a troublemaker like her brother who broke his parents' hearts running off to Kiev, to St. Petersburg, to Moscow, and God knows where else.*

They don't expect answers. They are talking not to me but to themselves, their own younger selves, and the me at the table is only the excuse. But I am respectful. I put in a few words about Mama, and Mera, talk about their apartment in Brussels, their vacation in Ostend. Nobody has mentioned Zhenya. Of course. She's not from Odessa. She's a stranger, so she doesn't get mentioned. Our daughter is also not from Odessa, but about her they are curious. I pull out the photo of Natasha, pass it around the table to exclamations:

What a doll! Such a cutie! Such a sweet nose. Tell us, be honest, who's the real father?

Three empty bottles of wine are on the table when we get to the kind of questions that come up every time I am here.

So, Isaac, tell me, how is it writing for the movies? You get paid well? You meet lots of pretty girls?

You're in Odessa to make a movie?

*No, I'm here to take treatments at the Lermontov. And to do some writ-*ing. I pause. They deserve more. *Truth is, in a few weeks I will be off to Yalta to finish work on a film. With Eisenstein. I've been rewriting a script for him.*

Everyone stops chewing. Then they all start to speak at once. Saying more or less the same thing. *They're letting him make films again?*

I'd rather stay in Odessa. But Sergei's an old friend. He claims he can't do without me. I won't mind a trip to Yalta. It's been years.

At this point, their voices become almost interchangeable. Who is saying what is less important than what is said.

So what are you writing. Are you writing about Odessa again?

What's to write about Odessa? There's nothing to say about Odessa. Nothing works here anymore. The town has gone to hell.

Synagogues! You should write about synagogues. That's where things happen.

What can happen in a synagogue?

Everything happens in a synagogue.

Give me a for instance?

God! God happens in synagogues.

God? A synagogue is the last place God would happen. God would commit suicide rather than happen in a synagogue. You'd be more likely to find him in a coal mine.

Isaac, don't listen to him. Abie's always been an anarchist. Come see for yourself.

Maybe you are right. Maybe I should pay attention to synagogues. Maybe some Saturday I'll come to services.

Don't maybe me. Come. It will do you good. I guarantee. You'll be a better man.

That's when Lyosha starts.

My nephew the Cossack lover getting religion? Tell me another.

In Odessa these are fighting words. But Lyosha doesn't want a fight. With him it's what passes for affection. Never letting me forget that my reputation is based on writing about Cossacks and what they did, or refused to do, for my father in 1905.

Going to synagogue doesn't mean you're religious. Writing about Cossacks doesn't mean you're in favor of pogroms. That was a long time ago. Recently I've been writing about collective farms.

Another red flag. Lyosha raises his voice. Starts to shout about the madmen who are ruining the country. Running it for their own profit.

Collectivization? *A nice word that really means millions of people are having their land stolen. So now everybody owns everything? You mean nobody owns nothing. Not even you, Mr. Famous Writer. Your dacha. Your car. Your chauffeur. Your money. How long will that all last when you're no longer writing what they want?*

I never write what they want.

Before Lyosha answers, somebody interrupts:

Izzie, do me a favor. Do us all a favor and don't write any more about Odessa. Oy, what stories you told. You made us all sound so crazy.

We are crazy. Who else but crazies could live in such a country?

You think we're crazy. What about the people in Moscow? They have to be crazy as loons to live in a city with such a climate.

It's poetic license. Izzie is a writer.

License? It was exaggeration. It was lies. You really think gangsters are like Benya Krik. You really think gangsters are Robin Hoods? Let me tell you: think again.

Sometimes I feel the need to defend myself.

I make up things. It's what they pay a writer to do. You think it's so easy to make up stories. You think stories have to be about the world as it is? Who wants to read about the world as it is? Who wants reality? People come up to me and ask, Was your grandfather the rabbi really run out of Lvov for forgery?

Nu, nu. *Was he?*

I don't know. I turn to Katya. *Tell me. Was Grandpa a forger?*

She shrugs, holds her hands out palms up.

If I knew I wouldn't say. Not to a writer. You never can trust one. You never can know what he will say.

Lyosha looks surprised when I ask him to walk with me after dinner.

On the street he mumbles an apology. Something about the difficult times. Lousy business. Katya and menopause.

I wave away his words. Ask about his connections. The possibilities of smuggling someone out on a freighter. He becomes suspicious. *Why me? Who told you to ask me?*

Nobody told me. I just assumed. He relaxes. Smiles but not with much conviction. Asks if I am in danger. When I say it's not for me, that it's for someone else, his expression says: Yeah, sure, tell me another. I insist: *It's for someone else.* His expression says: Have it your way. His voice says: *I'm only a small fish. I change a bit of money. Help move around things that have been liberated from their owners. Occasionally enter a building after hours. I don't do anything big. I don't do overseas. I don't do people. Only Odessa stuff. Overseas is out of my league.*

You must know people. People who know people.

He hesitates.

Listen, Lyosha. It's true. You and I, we've never exactly seen eye to eye. We've never been close. But we're related. We're family. We stick together. I help you when you need it, remember. Now I'm the one who needs help.

His smile says: So it *is* for you.

Okay. Let me see what I can do.

9

Dear Izzie:

Lately I have been thinking a lot about Grandma. Funny the way you don't think much about someone for years and then suddenly they are in your mind all the time. Haunting you like the past haunts you. The might-have-beens. The way we might have been a normal family, all living in the same town or at least the same country, and getting together every Passover for a seder, and at Hanukkah to light candles, and breaking the Yom Kippur fast at a big family party. You, me, our spouses, children, parents, grandparents, all of us overeating and complaining about our swollen bellies. I know. I can hear your response. What's the use of might-have-beens? Right? For a creative person you can be terribly literal-minded when it suits you. Or is it just that the Revolution suited you a lot better than the rest of us. It certainly gave you something to write about. It made you famous. It's the reason you're still there while all the rest of us have gotten out. Almost all of us. It killed Father, that worry over what would become of us. Have you visited his grave yet? Does it look cared for? Did you remember to bring flowers?

I think about Grandma in that stuffy room she had at the back of Aunt Bobka's flat, with the small stove roaring away summer and winter and the old copper samovar always boiling. She smelled of old fish and stale horseradish, and I never really understood what she was talking about. Thank the folks for that. They wanted us to be Russians, to speak Russian and write Russian, but not to think Russian. Oh no. We had to think Jewish. But not Yiddish. Yiddish was a special language they used when they didn't want us to understand what they were saying. With Grandma the Yiddish was all mixed up with something she thought was Russian but was really some odd mixture of Polish, Ukrainian, Russian, even a few words of German. Did you ever wonder where she learned all that?

I hated that room. You couldn't breathe. Grandma scared me. And now, twenty-five years after she's gone, keinahora, I find myself thinking of her and wondering about her life in the shtetl before she and Grandpa came to Odessa and wondering how they were brave enough to make the decision to come. I wonder if it really ever did make any difference to her where she lived? She never went out. So what did it matter being in Odessa except for the freedoms for her children and her grandchildren. For us. Or for one specific grandchild, you. Not me. Oh no. The future was you. Her boychik. Her sheyner mensch. How she stuffed you with gefilte fish and bought fresh bagels, but for me it was a crust of whatever bread was around, a piece of cheese, it didn't matter because I shouldn't get fat, a girl should wait to get fat until after she was married. She made that clear without language. Girls didn't matter. You were the one who had to know everything—the Talmud, the violin, mathematics, music. You were the one who had to know everything so that the world would fall at your feet. Me. It didn't matter. I'd get married. I'd go away. But not you. You didn't just write King of Odessa by chance. You were raised like a King. Or at least a Prince and heir apparent. Not only in her eyes. In the eyes of our parents too.

That, my dear brother, is what I always resented. I resent it still. Izzie gets to go to Russian High School. Izzie gets violin lessons, even if he hasn't the slightest shred of musical talent. Izzie gets new uniforms for school, and a fountain pen, and all the new notebooks his heart desires, and when Izzie is sick, when he has a stuffed nose, the whole household goes into mourning. You can't speak aloud, you can't play, you can't run down the hall because the Prince of Odessa might lose a moment's sleep or, God forbid, he'll get a nosebleed. You know what? I was the one with musical talent. I used to sneak into your room and get out your violin and pluck the strings. I vibrated to them as if I was plucking the strings of my own heart or soul. How much I wanted to play. But when I went to Mother to ask whether maybe I could have lessons, she said, One violinist in a family is enough. And when you stopped lessons and I asked her again, she said, I'll teach you how to bake strudel, it's more important, and then I went to Father and he threw up his hands and gave me that look he had, you know the look, and said, What, you think I'm crazy, you think I'll go through with you what I went through with your brother?

It wasn't just the violin. It was everything. College, trips, new clothes, special food—nothing was too good for the Prince of Odessa. The world revolved around him. And if you wonder why I'm writing all this now, it's be-

cause as far as I can tell you take it for granted that the world still revolves around you. Even now, Mother wanders around the house worrying, Is Izzie okay? Is he eating right? Keeping warm? It's summer, I tell her. He's back in Odessa. He's probably too warm. But this doesn't stop her. I wonder if they're treating him all right at the sanitarium. He's a delicate boy. They have to be careful. Not to overtire him. He works too hard. He worries too much. He's just like his father.

She's the one who's tired. Life here is no picnic. Not for her. Not for any of us. At least Grigorii and I have learned to speak French, but for Fenya it's hopeless and Russian and Yiddish don't take you very far here. You know that. You've been here. You see how we live, crammed into this tiny apartment, all three of us, while Grigorii works his heart out for almost nothing. Yes, yes, yes, we appreciate the bagels you send. We could not live without them. But we could do with a little less advice. Get a car, you say. Go to the seashore for a month. Enjoy yourselves. Life is too short. You are deserving. Fine. But who is supposed to be paying for the car, the seashore, all the other things we deserve. You think we have piles of money stashed away somewhere. What little we have saved is not for trifles. It's for a rainy day. So please stop going on about such luxuries. It only makes us feel worse. Certainly one thing we never want to do is ask you to do more for us.

Izzie it's not just the advice. It's the way you act too. You don't come here often enough and when you do you lie around like a spoiled child and let Mother cook for you day and night. And you order me around as if I were still a kid and not a married woman with responsibilities and not all of them to you. Sure you send lots of bagels. How I wish we could eat them fresh once again. Real bagels. Hot bagels with poppy seeds still warm from the oven of that bakery behind the Opera House. Remember how Father would take us there every Saturday to buy a bag full, ten or twenty, and by the time we got home the bag was half empty. Don't stuff on bagels, Father would say, but even he couldn't keep from eating one after another. May his soul rest in peace.

How come you have never written about Odessa bagels? The bagels of our childhood. It's too realistic a subject? You couldn't make up things about them the way you made up everything else? Except me. How come in all your stories of childhood you never have a little sister? I didn't count for anything? Or is it a play for sympathy, this poor orphan boy with the thick glasses, forced to live half the time with his aunt and crazy uncle, and his grandmother, though you know perfectly well that was only for one year so you could attend a good school while Father wound up his affairs in Kherson. And the father in your stories: what a tyrant, forcing you to take violin lessons and Hebrew lessons, bargaining with you over grades, demanding you work before play, refusing you a dovecote until you got into the best high school. Whose father was that? Not ours, that man who gave you everything, including a second dovecote after you burned down the first one and roasted half your birds and all because of doing what we were told never to do, play with matches. And then you blame it all on pogromniks. Well why not, they're to blame for so much else. But Father. That man who thought of nothing all day long but his family and asked nothing other than that we behave decently and bring honor on our name. What would he think of us now, scattered all over the world?

I suppose you know what's coming. You must know that when I write like this it usually means we need another order of bagels. Lord I hate to ask right now, for things must be uncertain for you too. The news we get from there isn't reassuring. You have probably heard what's going on here, the local Fascist Party, and believe me they look very much like Nazis only in silver shirts, has been beating up workers, rioting, demanding representation in Parliament. Izzie, if you really cared for us as much as you claim to you would come to us. Take care of us in person. I know what you are thinking but the answer is No. We won't return there. For all the problems, we like it here. Grigorii's work is here and this is not the time for a move toward anywhere, let alone the east. Why won't you come west, where your books are loved and you are loved and we can all take care of each other?

Mother asks me to send her love. She prays for you every day and especially every Friday night when she lights the candles. Yes, we have a white linen cloth on the table and a twisted challah, so it feels homey. She covers her eyes and sways back and forth and mumbles in Hebrew and I wonder when did she learn prayers in Hebrew? Do you remember either of our parents using Hebrew? I never heard a word of it from her until we got to Belgium. Maybe she has a secret plan to immigrate to Palestine?

Take care of yourself, my brother. I love you. We all love you and are proud of you and are very disappointed you were unable to come here this summer. Soon, soon, we all hope. Our thoughts go out to you and our prayers, even if you don't believe in such things. I can see you in Odessa, lucky you, getting to visit all our old haunts. Stop by the Duc and talk everything over with him—maybe he'll give you good advice on how you can get to see your family soon.

Mother joins me in sending much love,

Mera

10

I should know better. But we all need a little diversion. So what if they're doing that chestnut, Chekhov's *Cherry Orchard,* at the Sibiriyalovsky. I've always been a sucker for the magic of theater. Ever since I was fourteen. A lad who became soundless as a young deer in front of more than three people, I snuck into the Municipal Theater to see the tiny Sicilian actor, De Grasso, transform himself into a giant figure, swooping across the stage like an avenging angel. Kashirina completed my education in the pleasures of make-believe. She gave me the nerve to turn to theater.

What a mistake. It's the one genre where the critics have always killed me. They tolerated *Sunset* in spite of the oedipal theme because it was about the well-loved Benya Krik. But they had such a field day with *Mariya* that the production was canceled before a single performance. The problem is not with the title character, Mariya, the only fulfilled person in the work, the only one who looks to the future, the only one committed to Bolshevism and social change. The problem is we only know her through the letters she writes, for Mariya never appears on stage. The characters who do appear there are all what our critics like to call degenerates, neurotics, sickly folk who cling to the outmoded values of the vanishing bourgeois world. Such folk don't make them happy. You have made a big ideological error, comrade. Such sadness, such gloom. Remember: This is the new Russia. This is the Soviet Union. Today we have a right to the future, a duty to it. Depression is out. Joy is in. Both in our daily life and on the stage. And certainly if you expect to have your plays produced and well reviewed.

It will be dark in the theater. Who will see me? I sit in the orchestra staring intently at the pages of Maupassant. Try to ignore the figure of the manager when he sidles up, bows, starts to speak: *We are honored. You must.*

People turn their heads, stare, whisper to each other.

Must I? Evidently.

A few minutes later I stand in front of the curtain, look up at crystal chandeliers, frescoes on the ceiling, worn velvet walls. The manager rubs his hands, hovers nearby, apologizes that there is no microphone. I take a few deep breaths through my newly cleared nasal passages, project my voice. The speech is short. Full of the kind of sentiments that would make any other city put me on the payroll. I finish like this:

It is good to breathe the air of Odessa once again. Air full of poetry, literature, and happiness. I have always placed great hopes in the air of Odessa. For myself, for you, for the Soviet state, for the world.

Coming down the stairs into the audience I see her. Look away. Look back. This one is a dame. You could tell that from a mile away, let alone the twenty meters that separate us. Her face shows a touch of the Tartar. High cheekbones, green eyes, blond hair to her shoulders. If my childhood were a play, I would cast her as Galina. She stands straight, holds her hands up high, claps in front of her face. Our gazes meet. That's enough. Maybe too much. I have reached that age when you know what you know and you know it far too well. My head nods ever so slightly. Call it instinct. Habit. It amounts to the same thing.

At intermission she is on the other side of the lobby, standing with a bunch of smooth-looking, theatrical types, men with soft faces who wear flowing ties and specialize in extravagant hand gestures. Our eyes meet again, over the shoulders of the mob of fans, young writers, old friends who have me surrounded. Questions come at me from every side. How to get a publisher in Moscow, a job with a studio, an essay into a thick journal? A long-haired youth whose breath suggests he must live on nothing but garlic presses close. I turn away but he moves with me, his words exploding like bombs that have been outlawed by the Geneva Convention. My knees start to buckle. He pushes a huge manuscript at me. *It's about the war, the Revolution, brother against brother on the shores of the Black Sea. It's just like* War and Peace, *War and Peace in Odessa in our time.* I shake my head. He pleads. *Read a chapter, a page, a paragraph. It could change my life.*

She is suddenly next to me. Speaking in an official voice. A gentle but commanding voice. A voice that makes you think of a bedroom with a view of lingering sunsets over the sea.

Enough, comrades. Comrade Babel is on vacation. The Party has sent him to Odessa to rest. It is our duty to leave him alone.

She takes me by the elbow, pushes through the crowd, and leads me into the auditorium and back to my seat. So startled and pleased does this leave me that I don't thank her properly until much later, at the dinner after the show. The manager insists on dragging a bunch of us to the nearby Red Hotel, and for once I don't refuse. Some twenty of us take over the nearly empty dining room. My savior and I are seated at opposite ends of a long table soon loaded with heaps of food—*shashlik, pirojki,* caviar, summer salads, bluefish. Seated among a motley crew of actors, stagehands, and technicians in various stages of dress, undress, some with greasepaint on their faces, some in parts of period costumes, others sporting hairpieces or false beards. It's a lively crowd, as such crowds always are. Huge amounts of vodka are downed. I stick to wine. Doctor's orders. Maybe she has the same doctor, for I watch her sipping delicately from a wineglass. She catches me gazing her way, tilts her head in my direction.

The manager jumps up to make a series of extravagant toasts. *To the members of the company for creating this fine production. To the spirit of Chekhov, a man who understood the decadence of the bourgeoisie and the necessity of social change. To our two distinguished guests. Isaac Babel, most famous of our native writers in a town as famous for writers as Lake Baikal is for sturgeon. And to Nadja Kamenskaya, the great actress from Kazakhstan, who is currently honoring the soundstages of the Odessa Studio with her talents and this banquet table with her beauty.*

It figures. Is there anyone in the world who doesn't know of my weakness for actresses? We raise our glasses and look directly at each other for the first time. A good thing we are seated so far apart. Good too that the men around her keep leaning close, touching her on the arm, the shoulder, the hand. Better they than me. She is far too stunning a woman for this summer. The kind of dame who could get things very confused. The kind you could build a story around, only it wouldn't be a story with a happy ending. Not that anyone in this country has ever believed in happy endings. Except me.

Only when the party is breaking up at some ungodly hour do we finally have a moment together. Even without all the wine in me I would have raised her hand to my lips.

My deepest and most heartfelt thanks. You saved my sanity, if not my life. I am forever in your debt.

Always happy to help a fellow distinguished visitor in distress.

You haven't been here long? You probably don't know that we Odessans are famous for our gratitude. It is at once our duty and our joy to repay favors. Lucky you. Your action has won you a native guide for a tour of this most fascinating town. A guide to show you Odessa's famed and ancient historic monuments.

She pauses just the right amount of time before delivering her line.

I thought I was looking at one of them right now.

I block out the amused sounds from those who are standing nearby. All I hear is the gush of her laughter. A surprise fountain bubbling in a tropical garden. The mating cry of some exotic bird.

Believe it or not, there are more interesting sights than this face that has sunk a thousand ships. We have beaches as golden as wheat fields. We have steppes that roll like the sea. We have hospitals that are grand as palaces. We have bagel factories that are like bagel factories.

Our film schedule doesn't leave much time for sightseeing. It's early to bed and earlier to rise and in between nothing but work, work, work.

The tone of her voice says two things at the same time: go away and come close. We kiss on both cheeks. She says, *I am staying at the National,* then hurries out the door, surrounded by the same crowd of theatrical types, all of them gesturing broadly into the Odessa night.

11

For two days I avoid thinking about Nadja. Or try to. Life is already complicated enough. *Pravda* is the same as ever. Nothing about K, but today there is a suggestive editorial about how to recognize an enemy of the state. It quotes the Boss as saying that some degenerates, even some who are members of the Party, remain intransigently opposed to the process of building a classless society. Such people are no better than counterrevolutionaries. They must be driven out of the Party, out of our midst, off the face of the earth.

At the post office I find similar notes from my two editors: each hopes the treatments are going well; each is too polite to mention the manuscript on collective farms. An envelope with a clipping that has *Good news!* in the margin in Nina's handwriting and *Pirozhkova* under-lined in a story that praises the new subway for being ahead of schedule. A bulky package from Eisenstein: his rewritten version of my rewrite of the *Bezhin Meadow* script. A brief glance shows he has put back all the religious imagery, the themes of blood sacrifice straight out of the Old Testament. The most illiterate censor wouldn't let such things pass. Let alone Shumyatsky, who is all too literate and out to get both of us.

Today the Lermontov features a new kind of inhalation therapy. The nurse pushes my head under a towel and tells me to breathe deeply. What she doesn't say is that they are boiling up what must be prehistoric eggs. I gag, choke, collapse. She leads me to a cot. Assures me that in a couple of days I will enjoy the smell. No doubt. But this first treatment leaves me so weak that after resting on the cot, I get no farther than the lobby. Lyosha finds me there, relaxing on a couch. He asks if I have come down with a new form of jaundice. That would explain my odd shade of green. There's something else, too. With Lyosha there is always some-thing else: am I still interested in what I was interested in a few days ago? Good. He has found someone for me to meet. No specifics about time and place. But it will be soon.

Midafternoon I stroll into the Moldavanka. Two decades of Soviet life have changed it less than you might expect. On the corners, hustlers in tight jackets and snap brim hats. Men wearing oversized coats that conceal whatever you might want: watches, rings, diamonds, political tracts, pornographic photos, hunting knives, small pistols. Women with too much lipstick or too little hair.

The open air market behind the railroad station may not be as crowded as it used to be, but it's not empty. Men, women, children buying, selling, bargaining what they have used, found, produced, grown, or stolen: fruit and vegetables, scarves, clocks, radios, magazines, shoes, books in leather bindings. I linger by the stalls of birds I loved in my childhood. On a whim I ask about my favorites, Kruykov pigeons. *Haven't seen one in years,* says the keeper. *They're rare as dodo birds.* Stares at me as if searching for a distant memory. *Do I know you?*

I check the time on my father's gold pocket watch. Someone in a long coat bumps against me. An old man. Maybe not so old. He looks directly into my eyes and says: *Two hundred rubles for the watch.* I shake my head. He blocks the way. *Top prices for rings.* He grabs my arm. Pulls up my sleeve. *Nice cufflinks. Gold, no? A hundred rubles.* I try to move on. He says: *Do me a favor. Do yourself a favor. The watch. Four hundred. Five hundred. My top offer!*

I shoulder him out of the way and find myself face to face with a face that doesn't belong here.

Remember me? says Nadja.

I suppress the questions that spring to mind. She answers some of them anyway. No scenes for her today, so the director said get out of here. Enjoy yourself. Go see some of Odessa. Soak up local color.

Nothing more local than this market. Nothing more colorful.

I take her arm. We move together from stall to stall. I glance at her out of the corner of my eyes. We leaf through old books. Check out porcelain vases. She picks up a small bronze bust of Czar Nicholas. *Genuine!* The merchant rubs his hands. *From the Winter Palace. Direct from the bedroom of the czar's mistress.*

We sit in a café near the market. A once-elegant place. You can tell from the dusty crystal chandeliers, parquet floors, wrought iron tables, remains of a past nobody dares to care about. Papers and refuse strew the floor. A waiter in a badly stained white jacket refuses to acknowledge my signal and turns away.

You don't look like someone from Kazakhstan.

What does someone from Kazakhstan look like?

Darker hair. Hair you couldn't see because it would be covered with a scarf.

We Russians get around.

So I notice.

Silence. A silence that grows awkward. Time for the ploy for which I'm so well known that it gets mentioned in articles about me. I reach toward her purse, hanging over the back of the chair.

Let me see what's inside?

Nadja has, apparently, not read those articles. She puts out a protective hand. While her face says: What to do when you learn that someone you know turns out to be a bit of a nut? Maybe more than a bit.

I place a ruble on the table. Explain that it's out of a research fund provided by the Writers' Union. I am composing an essay for *Pravda* on the contents of women's purses.

She forces a smile, thrusts the purse across the table, opens it with a flourish. I bow and begin to pull things out one by one—a lipstick, crumpled handkerchiefs, a powder case, coins, keys, a small notebook, ticket stubs, an announcement of a poetry reading, an address book, a volume of stories by Tolstoy, half an apple wrapped in wax paper, wads of cotton, a large notebook, a wallet, another stick of lipstick, a single earring, scraps of paper with words scribbled on them, a few pages torn from a screenplay, an envelope with photos of some elderly people. A pair of panties make me feign a look of shock. I restrain the impulse to hold them to my nose and stuff them back in the purse. When the table is covered with debris, the waiter shows up, yawns while taking our order for coffee.

Your turn.

I hesitate. Her smile is earnest. I put my hands into my pockets and heap stuff on the table. Scraps of paper, pencil stubs, dirty handkerchiefs, a case for glasses, bottles of pills, a fountain pen, a well-worn wallet, and a tiny notebook that she grabs. I snatch it away.

You're not cleared for state secrets.

Don't bet on it.

The ice is broken. Now we can settle back and talk the way people talk when they are thinking of becoming lovers. Or in my case, mostly listen. To the difficulties of an actress getting roles without sleeping with every theater manager or director. To the heavy-handed plot of this film on collectivization in the Caucasus, a tale of peasants who must overcome the schemes of wily kulaks, locate the pots of gold hidden away by these counterrevolutionary traitors, and use the money to purchase a new tractor. She is the romantic lead. The guy who gets the tractor gets her too. Not the most original of stories, but a good opportunity for her, a chance to get out of the clutches of local managers and into the larger world of film.

Nadja stops herself. Says *My, I do seem to be dominating the conversation.* And continues with a confession: she has never read my work. My expression changes enough for her to add: of course she knows all about *Red Cavalry* and *Benya Krik*. Has been meaning to read them forever. But life, you know how it gets in the way of so many things. She is always on a tightrope, balancing the demands of career and family. Her two daughters, three and five, the sunshine and the starlight of her existence. She misses them desperately but her husband is good at caring for them. Even if he's only the father of the youngest. This is her second marriage. She smiles. My family life must be less complicated than hers.

Don't bet on it.

Eventually she gets around to the inevitable. They all do. Are you married? Do you have children?

Of course, I say, surprised at my own words. Of course? As if it is illegal not to be married. Immoral not to have children. Usually I duck such questions, but now I follow up with a wife and child in France. A mother and a sister in Belgium. A father twelve years in the grave. A great uncle who died in a pogrom. I might have kept on going, back through the generations, but a hand placed on my forearm stops me.

We leave the café and I lead her deeper into the Moldavanka. Happily point out the originals of sites I once appropriated for stories: the rutted courtyard surrounded by sagging porches where Benya Krik pistol-whipped his father to keep him from leaving the family for a teenage Russian girl. The cabaret and whorehouse of the powerful woman called Lyubka the Cossack, who specialized in arm wrestling with stevedores and in punching out customers rude enough to spit on her floor. The bench where Froim Grach's huge daughter, Bassya, swooned over the tiny feet of Hyman Kaplan, of the famed grocery family, and lingered to sew her own trousseau.

After a while the expression on Nadja's face says this is far more fascinating to me than to her. So we leave Moldavanka and I take her into the old cemetery behind Kirchhof. She brightens up. We sit on a bench. Nadja gazes around intently at crosses and mausoleums.

I've always liked cemeteries. Ever since I was seventeen and a gypsy street fortune-teller looked at my palm and said I would not live to be forty. My mother was hoping for good news about my wedding prospects. She became so outraged that she dragged me away without handing over a kopek. The poor old lady ran after us yelling for her money but my mother raised her arm and clenched her fist. It's the only time I ever saw her raise a hand to anyone.

I touch her arm.

Not that I really believe it, but it's a comforting idea. Knowing how much time you have for things you want to do. Until you realize you can't do them anyway.

What exactly is it you want to do?

She shrugs. *Whatever it is, I'd do it all the way. No excuses. No limits.*

Talk like this is too portentous for a sunny afternoon. I go into my fake Yiddish accent: *You like cemeteries, we've got cemeteries. We've got big cemeteries and small cemeteries, old cemeteries and new ones. Enough cemeteries for every taste. One kind of cemetery if you are Greek Orthodox, another kind if you are Russian Orthodox. We've got a Catholic cemetery*

with enough crucifixions to please the pope and two cemeteries with no stat-
ues at all for the Jews. We've got a Protestant cemetery for the Lutherans, or
maybe it's for the Presbyterians. And we have an old Muslim cemetery, dat-
ing from the time of the Turks, set aside exclusively for old Muslims.

We devote the rest of the afternoon to cemeteries. I deliver a jumbled patter full of architectural and historical details, a mixture of fact,
fiction, memories, and old wives' tales. Once, when Nadja stumbles on a
bridge over a fishpond, I grasp her arm and hold it just a touch longer
than necessary. Once we both raise our heads from a beautifully carved
headstone and look directly into each other's eyes. Once we sit on a
grassy slope and talk of life, death, and the problems with our first mar-
riages. Hers ended more disastrously than mine. When she left her husband, he threatened suicide. A year later he fulfilled his promise by
breaking into her apartment when she was away, placing a gun at his
forehead, and pulling the trigger. She and her daughter found the body
in a pool of blood on the bedroom floor.

By the time we stand on the terrace of my villa watching the sun
sink behind the mast of a fishing boat, we both feel very conscious of the
cliché we have been living for the past few hours. Of our bodies, too. In
the kitchen, I fuss with the kettle and teapot. Nadja picks up journals
and books from the dining room table, asks if she can help, remarks on
the noisy birds singing in the bushes against the twilight. The water
boils. She sits on the couch. I place a plate of biscuits on the coffee table,
sit across from her in an armchair. We drink tea. Neither of us looks toward the door of the bedroom. We are out of words.

What happens next happens this way. I excuse myself and go to the
bathroom. When I return, Nadja is standing. We face each other in the
semidarkness. I start to say something but she raises a finger to my lips.
For a moment we are frozen into a photo, twilight silhouettes, then we
are fumbling with each other's hands, mouths, bodies, groping toward
the bed, pulling off pieces of clothing, choking out words. We lay quiet
and I become aware of the chorus of birds, screeching farewell to the
day. I slide my hand along her thigh.

I can't, she says. *Boris will know.*
Not if you don't tell him.

Yes, he'll know. I can't hide anything from him.

The birds are silent. The room is dark.

Okay, I say.

We get out of bed. Dress on opposite sides of the room. Say nothing while she pushes her head against my chest, I bury my face in her thick hair. A sliver of moon rises over the Black Sea. I take her back to town. At the door of her hotel, kiss her on the forehead.

12

When we're young we think that women are the goods. But after all they're nothing but straw that is set on fire by nothing at all.

It's a line from one of my stories. Spoken by Benya Krik at dawn as he leaves the beautiful Katyusha, a hooker who all night long has been moaning and opening her Russian paradise for him. He's young as I was when I wrote it. Late twenties. Best dressed of all the gang leaders in the Moldavanka. Like all of them, a premature cynic. At least until the night his gang invades the estate of Zender Eichbaum, a wealthy dairy farmer who has pointedly ignored Benya's letters demanding protection money or else. The *or else* is Benya's men carrying torches. Firing pistols in the air. Dragging five prize cows from the barn and one by one slitting their throats. A sixth animal is mooing a death song when across the blood-soaked yard comes a slender vision in a white shift. Eichbaum's daughter, Tzilya, seeking her father's arms. Benya stands in the posture of a man who has seen the end of the world. Hides the pistol behind his back. Sends his thugs home and returns the next afternoon wearing an orange suit and a diamond bracelet to ask for Tzilya's hand. Eichbaum suffers a slight stroke but recovers in time for the wedding. The couple take a long honeymoon in Bessarabia, three months of rich food, sweet grapes, and the many tastes of love.

Don't ask me if they live happily every after. I'd answer your question with one of my own. Remember: I write short stories, not novels. Continuity is never an issue. Nobody seems to care that in later tales Benya is again a single man.

He's not the only one.

I sit here at the table drinking tea, thinking about Benya and wondering where I wrote that story: in Odessa or in Moscow? It's one way of not having to think about last night. The implications. The reasons we ran into each other in Moldavanka. The reasons we got out of bed.

A knock on the door. Strange. Nobody ever comes out here. I open it to find Lyosha, looking flustered. Beyond him, parked in the road, a black Packard sedan with two men in the front seat. They wear light-colored suits and straw hats. Lyosha points, gargles something incomprehensible, and hurries off to the nearby trolley stop. Five minutes later, clad in my linen jacket and summer hat, I sit in the back of the Packard as it races along the Fountains.

Headed in the wrong direction.

Not east toward Odessa but west toward the steppe. Past crumbling cliffs, villas with orange tile roofs, fisherman's huts, scraggly vineyards, cornfields full of withered stalks coated with the yellow dust that billows behind the car. Not a word passes between us. No communication after the slightest nod from the hat next to the driver when I climb into the back seat. Both chew toothpicks. Stare straight ahead.

We roar past the final tram stop at the Sixteenth Station and head directly at the dark finger of Kovalevsky's Tower. The Packard screeches to a halt. The hat next to the driver gestures toward the tall sandstone structure the size and shape of a lighthouse. I get out. The car races away.

I stare up at the tower. Intense sun on my neck. Many decades ago a very rich merchant named Kovalevsky—nobody remembers his first name—built a villa out here, then commissioned the tower. For six years workmen hauled huge chunks of sandstone to the site and set them in place. Once it was completed, Kovalevsky would climb the tower every day to drink tea and gaze at the stunning sunsets. One afternoon he placed his cup next to his armchair and leaped to his death.

You can imagine the stories told about why he did it. An unhappy love. A business failure. The diagnosis of a fatal illness. Despair at the meaninglessness of wealth. Or existence. Equally imaginable is the legacy: Kovalevsky's ghost haunts the tower. Especially during the dark of the moon. For Odessa boys in their teens a moonless night alone at the tower was once considered the height of bravery. Maybe it still is. Many of my friends managed it. I could never bring myself to try.

The crumbling rooms are filled with stones, the charred remains of open fires, torn papers, rusty cans, sticks of wood. Lizards disappear into cracks. Rickety stairs lead me up to the first level, the second, the top. A figure sits in a chair. An old man with a long gray beard in the black coat and hat of a rabbi gazes out to sea through a huge hole that once held a pane of glass. It's crazy. Some sort of joke. He looks exactly like Arye Leib. One of my characters. The one who sits on a cemetery wall and tells the stories about Benya Krik.

Well, well. Mr. Babel, I presume. Sit down. Take a load off your feet. You look surprised. You were not expecting me? You were expecting someone else?

Just the accent I would pick for Arye Leib. I sit in a chair opposite him.

I was expecting someone.

Nu, nu. *I'm someone, Mr. Babel. So what can this someone do for you?*

What should I call you?

A name. What's in a name, Mr. Babel? Gefilte fish by any other name would not smell sweet.

Okay. Have it his way. I tell the story. Make the request. A boat out of Odessa for an important person without papers. A person who has to remain nameless. No exact date yet. But sometime soon. Is such a thing possible?

Now Isaac. May I call you Isaac? Before I answer, I must ask a question. Why are you, a famous writer, trying to act like a smuggler? You have a reputation. An audience. So tell me this: Why should you get mixed up in something like this? Why should we? And by we, you know who I mean. Not just you and me. Our community. One must always consider the question: Is this good for our people?

The person in question is Jewish.

The person is you, no?

No. The person is not me.

This is the truth?

I say nothing. Stare directly at him. There's something more than a little fishy here.

Okay. So it's the truth. But does this person call himself a Jew? Or has he, like so many others in these dreadful days, turned his back on the religion of his fathers. You, for example, Isaac. Do you say your prayers every morning? Do you go to synagogue every Friday? Do you eat treyf? *Are you, in short, really a Jew or no more than a goy with the neuroses of a Jew?*

To me the real question is: Can we get him out of the country?

Hold on a minute. Tell me first: Your wife is Jewish? Your girlfriend? Your mistress? All your mistresses?

Before I can reply, there is laughter. Hearty laughter. But not from the rabbi. A guy in shirt sleeves strolls into the room. The sort you would not want to meet in a dark alley. Or anywhere else. He is powerful, with sandy hair, strong forearms, the shoulders of a stevedore, a black patch over one eye, a wide face cracked into a wide smile. He sticks out his hand for me to shake. Breaks into laughter once again.

Sorry. I like a joke. A good joke. Admit it: We had you puzzled, Isaac. My name is Jacob. Don't worry about the last name. These days one name is more than enough. Business goes better if we keep people puzzled.

The rabbi rises. Up close I can see the makeup. He pulls off a false beard. Puts out his hand. *Boris Aronovitch.* A pleasure to play one of my characters.

There aren't too many roles for a specialist in Yiddish theater these days. So when Jacob asked, Could I play Arye Leib? and when he asked, Could I play him to his creator's face? how could I say no? I'm a great fan of yours.

We're all great fans of Isaac, says Jacob.

Aronovitch exits down the stairs.

I know, Isaac. I don't look like your idea of Benya Krik. But even the original didn't look like him. Efraim Sharpolinski. He's your model, no? Before my time, to be sure. But long before your stories, he was already a legend. Every profession has its legends. Sharpolinski was known as a snazzy dresser but not exactly a looker, and certainly not a Robin Hood. A killer when he had to be, and he had to be more often than not.

Jacob sighs.

Those were the days, my friend. A time when a gangster could hold up his head. A time when there were things worth stealing. Now? Tell you the truth, I sometimes wonder if it's worth the effort. In the old days you had a chance to handle masterpieces. Now all we get is garbage. All the good stuff has been stolen by Party members. In the old days, new treasures would come into the country all the time. Now who would be crazy enough to smuggle things into Russia? It's depressing. We keep recycling the same old schlock. Believe me, it's no challenge.

Another sigh. We both stare out to sea.

Maybe I can provide a challenge.

He shakes his head from side to side.

You're hardly the first to come to us with such a request. Getting out is not such a bad idea. I consider it myself from time to time. But where to go? There's the rub. Marseilles, Naples, New York, Buenos Aires. The Italians have a lock on all of them. Besides, there's my mother. She's getting on in years. Jacob, she tells me when I talk about going somewhere else, listen to your mother. Be smart. Odessa is the best. I was born here, she tells me, before anyone thought of making a revolution and, as sure as God is in heaven, my grandchildren will die in Odessa after everyone has forgotten what the Rev- olution was about.

Maybe she's right. My voice is noncommittal.

He looks directly into my eyes.

And your mother in Brussels. She is well?

She's doing fine.

Your sister?

The same.

Isaac, in this business you have to be frank and you have to be careful. So tell me: How do we know this request is on the up-and-up? How do we know you are not trying to nail us as a way of helping the government. Buy- ing yourself a trip to France to see your wife and daughter.

My face must betray something. Jacob makes sympathetic noises. It's nothing personal. But in his line of work, he has to know things. He has to be careful. He reads newspapers. He talks to people. He sympa- thizes with a man whose family is so far away. He understands that writ- ers have problems. Understands it must be hell trying to fit my talent for the ethnic, the grotesque, and the symbolic into the straitjacket of the Party line.

Socialist Realism! He spits out the phrase. *An oxymoron, my friend. Socialism is the farthest thing from realism and vice versa. It's the death of literature. Besides everyone knows Russia has always been the land of Dada. Long before the term was coined.*

He stops himself.

Okay. We have to know who we're doing business with. Why we're do-ing business. Tell me, who is this mysterious person who must get away.

Sorry. That's impossible.

Nothing's impossible when you're trying to make a deal.

It's the one thing I can't tell you. Ask me anything else.

Okay. Who do you know in Moscow? Who would vouch for you?

Lots of people.

Who do you know that we might know?

What kind of people do you know?

Heads of things. People in the Kremlin. Hustlers on the Arbat.

We must have some friends in common.

I give him names of writers, actors, directors, editors, police high and low. When I say Yagoda, he smiles.

Not that we couldn't get to him. But perhaps someone a touch, shall we say, less official.

I mention hustlers in Moscow cafés. Buy them a drink and they will provide a fascinating story or invent one. Tell you which government of-ficial has been buying jewels for whose wife. Or who has sold off what masterpieces from which museum. Or who has a taste for cocaine or for girls under fifteen. I go on to jockeys. Horse trainers. Touts. The fruits of my passion for horses that has gotten the better of my lifelong desire to sleep late in mornings. A good tip and I am out at the track before dawn, watching the workouts. Enjoying the sunrise. The sounds and sweat of man and beast.

Jacob stands up. It's been a pleasure. He'll be in touch. Soon. He gestures me down the stairs. The Packard is waiting. The two guys have taken off their hats and jackets. They smile and introduce themselves. Josif and Moishe. They offer me a good cigar, then hold out a flask of brandy. We pass it back and forth all the way back to the villa, while they talk about the world of Benya Krik and I pretend to drink.

Didn't we get it right? The hats? The gestures? Did we scare you? Make you think something might happen? Hey, how about putting us in a story? Two handsome guys in a black Packard with holsters in their arm-pits. Guns that don't bulge. They hold open their coats. Pull out pistols and wave them around. *Not that we use them often. But it's part of the outfit. Part of the job.*

We halt in front of the villa. They hand me the flask one last time. I pretend to drink one last time. We toast. To the story I will write about the new Odessa gangsters. The children and grandchildren of the King.

13

*F*act. Fiction. Art. Life. People always like to make such fine distinctions. Especially critics! Ever since I have been putting down stories about gangsters and tales of childhood, the same responses, the same complaints repeated over and over. Babel writes autobiography. Babel writes fiction. Babel writes nothing but fact. Babel writes lies. Babel gives us Odessa exactly as it is. Babel invents an Odessa that never was.

All are true.

Except that I don't invent anything. I don't have any imagination. All I do is describe what I see. But you have to understand: my eyesight has never been all that good.

Take Benya Krik. Jacob is right. But not a hundred percent right. Sharpolinski is only the most famous of the models for that character. Plenty of other names of underworld figures were mentioned in the Greek coffee houses and Romanian billiard parlors that we snuck into after school. Chaim Drong, Yitzhak Rabinovitch, Lazar Rotenstein—in their day, all of them were known, revered, honored in the Moldavanka. One for his pinstripe suits and Italian shoes, another for his way with the ladies, another for his skill in slitting throats with a tiny stiletto. All I did was put them together. Knowing from experience that every good Jew who has shaved off his curly sideburns yearns to dress in bright suits and sharp hats. To play tough and carry a gun. So anyone who dresses and acts like that will be admired rather than feared. All the better if that someone has the panache of a Benya. If he speeds around in a red roadster with a gramophone in the back seat blaring Puccini arias. Sends huge bouquets to the funerals of those he has had to eliminate. Arranges generous pensions for their mothers and widows. Such a person has to be a good candidate for King, and believe me: Jews need a King as much as they need a promised land. Even more.

The encounter with Jacob and the guys in the Packard has left me restless and the steam room at the Lermontov doesn't do much to calm me. I wander through town. Soon find myself on the bluffs west of the harbor, not far from the Odessa Studio. Okay. So there is an unconscious. I never denied it. But you don't have to follow its dictates. I know too many people here who know too many people everywhere else. So I turn around, return to Primorskii, treat myself to tea and cakes in the elegant sidewalk café at the London Hotel, the only place in town you see scrubbed, shiny foreign faces, so unlike our own, no matter how much soap we use. At the London you hear French, English, German, Italian, Greek, see francs, pounds, marks, dollars, change hands. It's the one place where you can pretend that this is Odessa before the Revolution, or a resort in a Western country.

Twilight. I am sitting in the lobby of her hotel when Nadja enters. She's a good actress. Does an exaggerated double take. Spreads a smile across her face like a slow sunrise on the summer steppe. Thrusts her handbag toward me and says: *I can always use the ruble. But it's a hell of a time to be doing research.*

The Armenians say there are two kinds of fools. Men who have never looked into a woman's purse and men who have looked into a woman's purse more than once.

Our embrace is more polite than passionate. She hesitates at my dinner invitation. Gives the usual reasons: dirty hair to be washed, nails to be polished, lines to memorize, fatigue, the need for a good night's sleep. Along with a list of various other female tasks before she agrees that yes, a glass of wine and some food might be nice. As long as she gets her rest.

We go to one of my old favorites, a cabaret run by a Romanian in a basement near the docks, just off Greek Street. A tiny place of crowds, noise, smoke, shouts. On the bandstand, a jazz clarinet and saxophone engage in a friendly duel. Nice to be back in a place where you can avoid some of Moscow's bizarre fads. Recently some historian in the Academy of Music convinced the Boss that it was time to honor the great traditional instrument of Russia: the balalaika. Now every musical group in Moscow—jazz, dance, symphony orchestras—features rows upon rows of balalaikas twanging away. Making a sound that can drive you crazy.

The dance floor is jammed. Young people contort themselves, hurl each other back and forth in some distant imitation of Americans or Africans. The middle-aged stay sedate, upright, move around as if the slow waltz was still the rage. Most of the men are in light colors, summer suits, embroidered shirts. The women wear white shoes. If we had not done away with social classes, you might just get the idea that this is a bourgeois crowd.

At a tiny table in a corner, we drink red wine and eat kebabs and roast corn. It's too noisy for much conversation, but after yesterday it's not clear exactly what we would say. Nadja motions toward the dance floor. I wave her off. The band takes a break. A vision from some distant past, a flower girl in a long peasant dress, pushes against the table and looks closely at Nadja.

You're so beautiful. Aren't you in films? You should be in films.

I buy a rose. Lean across the table to pin it on her.

She is in films. Soon she will be a great star of Soviet cinema. Her name will be on everyone's lips. Nadja Kamenskaya. Remember that.

Nadja makes tiny, embarrassed motions with her hands. The girl bows and leaves. The music starts again. A few more glasses of wine and she gets me to dance a slow number, then another. We are neither quite steady nor exactly unsteady on our feet, but feeling a bit wobbly and good when we walk though quiet streets, stop at Primorskii Park, and look to sea. A misty night. The first hint of fall, the harbor clad in fog. A stone basin for kids' sailing boats that has been dry ever since the Revolution brims over with water. *It's something special,* I tell her. *A sign of luck.* Our hands clasp.

You are a good listener. All that stuff about my work, my daughters. Boris. Vladimir's suicide, for God's sake. I never talk about that. Most men would not come back.

I squeeze her hand. On a nearby bench, a shapeless lump stirs, moans—a drunk sleeping one off. Nadja turns toward me. Our faces share an intimate space. Her lips part and our mouths touch, our bodies press together, softly, then more strongly until we know what is coming. No need to rush. No need to speak. When we approach her hotel, she shakes her head. Not here. Not tonight. Tomorrow. Pick me up at seven.

At the Writers' Union the next day I arrange for the car. Pay off the chauffeur so I can drive it myself. I am at the hotel fifteen minutes early. She is ready. We drive along the Fountains with the windows open. Stand side by side on the terrace of the villa and drink a glass of wine before entering the bedroom. I light candles, place the open bottle on the nightstand. Nadja refuses to fully undress. In bed, she proves to be shy with her body. Her movements awkward, girlish, endearing. At the height of passion she says, *No, Boris will know,* but her hands clutch my shoulders, pull me down. I rise above her to proclaim: *This is written. This has been done before.*

The wine bottle is half full when I get up to boil water in the morning. Writing at this table I hear the movement of bare feet, feel a hand on my shoulder. Lips on my bald spot.

We drink tea on the terrace. A pale fog. The smell of salt water and fish. A dangerous sign: she likes the tea I brew. More dangerous: after a second cup we return to the bedroom.

In the afternoon we walk on the beach. Barefoot. Wearing old robes. Carrying towels. A freighter with the red flag and yellow crescent of Turkey steams away from port. Nadja's head angles toward it. Her body leans toward open sea.

Why do you always come back to Odessa?

It's my hometown.

That's not what I mean. You go abroad, right? You have a wife in Paris? A daughter. You could stay there. It's Paris.

Something in me wants to share parts of my past with her. Serious parts. Another dangerous sign.

A writer can only write where they speak his language, I tell her. *How could we exist without our language? But there's more to it. You can't imagine the life of an émigré. Five minutes at the Café Odessa in Paris and you would understand. The bickering. The scheming. The plots and counterplots. The arguments that have gone on for fifteen years and will continue for fifty more. The complaints about the French, the Soviets, each other, about the past, the future, the present.*

But it's Paris.

Her voice heavily laden with an emotion I can well remember,

Nadja begins to twirl, swinging her arms, a clumsy kid in ballet class. *Paris,* she says, on every turn. *Paris, Paris, Paris, Paris.* Each turn is faster. Each time the name of the city tears her apart with more and more feeling until she sobs, laughs, cries in my arms, then pulls away and says: *How does it feel to be in Paris? What do you do in Paris? How do you spend the days?*

I give her the expurgated version. The one about the cafés in Montparnasse where you open your tiny notebook, get out a pen, and try to look like a famous writer. The view of the towers of Notre Dame from the push-up window of the top floor of a hotel on the rue Jacob. The moans of lovers in the next room that start every day promptly at five-thirty and end an hour later. The transcendental taste of the *sandwich jambon* and *pain au chocolat* you buy from the local *boulangerie,* where the patron never fails to greet you as *Monsieur le Russe.* The feeling when you stroll along boulevards and keep saying to yourself, I am walking the streets of Paris. This is me.

Is it? Really? Or another me. Someone I don't recognize.

She is asking the right questions. The ones I cannot answer even for myself. Other than to say: *In Paris you eat and drink like royalty, you read what you want, you don't worry that somebody may overhear what you say, even when you speak on the telephone. French life is a piece of pastry, something made with egg whites and cream and powdered sugar. A scrumptious dish but one that can never fully satisfy a Jewish soul or a Russian heart. You know that when, once too often, a shopkeeper or clerk pretends he cannot understand something perfectly simple that you say. Or when he makes you repeat a word three or four times, then narrows his eyes and corrects your pronunciation with such a slight correction that you cannot hear the difference*—Ce n'est pas la rue Champollion, monsieur; c'est la rue Champollion. *A petty moment like this can become a symbol of rules in a country that has too many rules. A country where you have to pay to sit on a chair in one of their geometric parks or worry that a cop might arrest you if you dare to pick one of their precious flowers. One morning it's all too much. You find yourself wanting to break rules. Yearning for things you used to hate—the chaos, the confusion, the lawlessness, the shabby buildings, the dirt, the lim-*

itless mud and endless despair of our villages. That's the moment when you know you are Russian. That's when you know it's time to go home.

Enough lyricism. Maybe it's something simpler. Maybe it's because their Revolution was so long ago and we are still struggling with ours, and revolutions must destroy an old world before they can create a new one.

Can you really believe that? asks Nadja. *Does Isaac Babel really believe in a new world coming? For my money, long live old revolutions. The older the better. Certainly better that the violence, corruption, ugliness, and loss of ideals are safely buried in the past rather than rubbed in your face every day.*

This is unexpected. Dangerous too. We live in a time when a man talks about such serious things only to his wife, beneath the covers, at three o'clock in the morning. Now is not exactly the right moment for political questions. Not the time and place to discuss the regime. Not on a beach. Not with Nadja. It's time to drop my robe and towel, jump into the water, and take a long swim toward the freighter just disappearing over the horizon.

14

*F*irst times make you remember other first times. The good and the bad. The disasters. The times you knew everything, past, present, and future. The times you knew nothing at all. The times you thought you were in love. Like the first such time. With Zhenya. We were too young. Too anxious. Too know-it-all to admit all the things we did not know. Those icy days in Kiev when we walk along the streets and press against each other. She wears fur. I go without a hat, part of some artistic pose whose origins and aims I have forgotten. Maybe I was toughening myself for the tough days that had to be ahead.

We hang around cafés where men and women with long hair read poems full of phrases in French and Italian. The walls are covered with angular abstractions painted in primary colors. Zhenya is enrolled in a life-drawing class at art school. I volunteer to become a model. Her parents are on vacation in the Crimea. The servants are away. Until then love for me has been no more than a hurried encounter, the smell of sweat mixed with cheap perfume, the worn bedclothes of a Michelle or a Tina—they always took European names—in a tiny Moldavanka crib. I am nineteen. Zhenya's room is a girl's room. A room of pastel colors. Curtains and coverlets. Porcelain figurines and stuffed dolls. The smell of talcum powder and dried flowers. Silky sheets that stain. Sheets I carry away beneath my overcoat and abandon on a garbage heap.

Gronfein understood his daughter. Knew that all her teenage talk about a life devoted to Art was no more than part of some perverse phase of development directed, largely, against him. A phase that would end, like all such phases, with a rich son-in-law, a dining room full of sterling silver and bone china, a box at the opera, and a bunch of little ones for Grandpa to spoil. My arrival in Kiev puts a serious dent in that idea. The Revolution smashes it to bits. A decade later I am the one who must hurry to Kiev to grab his silver and china and hide it away before the authorities learn he is dead. I sell his priceless objects on the black market to raise money for Zhenya. She is already living in Paris. My affair with Yevgenia was the excuse for her departure, but the Soviets were the real reason. Redistributing wealth? Communal apartments? Disgusting. She was her father's daughter. For me, that was part of the attraction. The mansion, the chauffeur, the clothes imported from Paris, the careless attitudes about money. Her beauty too. I have never forgotten what it feels like to be a poor student in a school that you detest, full of desires to avoid the fate someone else has written on your wall.

Fate! The word always reminds me of Karima. The first of love's many ironies. Think of it. All I dream of from the time I begin reading Maupassant as a teenager is France. Paris. The gargoyles of Notre Dame, the Eiffel Tower, the green countryside, the poplar-lined roads, the walled towns of the south. Danton shouting *L'audace, l'audace, l'audace* to cheering mobs. The Sun King at Versailles. The Three Musketeers.

Women are very much part of the dream. French women! Elegant women with shapely legs, perfumed feet in high heels.

I arrive in Paris for the first time in the fall of 1927. On the boulevards, in the cafés, sitting on park benches, climbing into buses and taxis, the French women are just as I imagined: sleek, combed, aloof, maddening, beautiful. A lot of good it does me. Within two weeks I am involved with a dancer from Morocco who does an act with a live python.

I am living one of my own stories.

Shall I blame Lev Nikulin? A friend since we were kids. Another one who thinks he can write. I don't know what it is with Odessa. Everyone scribbles. Everyone thinks he has a message for the world. Lev and I were once students together at the Nicholas I Commercial College. I envied the fluency that got him the lead role in the French Club's production of *Tartuffe*. We meet again in the midtwenties at a party in Moscow given by the editor of the magazine *Thirty Days* and after that see each other from time to time, until he goes off to Paris. By the time I arrive, he has been living there long enough to know the city. He drops in at Zhenya's cramped apartment, notices how much she and I are out of sorts with each other, and proposes to help out by showing me a bit of the town.

We hit a bunch of spots in Montparnasse and the Latin Quarter, then end up at a club in a nondescript section of the Right Bank somewhere near boulevard Rochechouart. The Black Ball is a working-class joint where men shout aloud as girls on a small stage slowly remove their skimpy costumes. We are on our second Pernod and third dancer when a woman sits down at the table. Dark hair, dark skin, dark dress. Both of us put our hands on our wallets. But she's not working for the house. Just a friend of one of the dancers who needs a place to sit until the show is over. She sits here because she trusts us. We look so refined. Like real gentlemen.

So says Karima. Her voice husky, her accent musical, her beauty blinding as the desert sun. Soon we hear all about the home she misses. Ourzazate, the brown sand and rocks, the snow on the distant Atlas mountains, the casbahs and palm oases along the Draa River before it sinks into the Sahara. Her journey over those mountains to Marrakesh, city of camels, holy resting places of sultans and marabouts, and teeming squares like Djemma el Fna, where she bought the pythons. Three of them because they can be temperamental creatures. Some nights one will refuse to perform. Go on strike. Remain locked in a circle or stretched out like an eight-foot stick.

Three days later I wrestle with one of the creatures backstage at the Casino de Paris while she does her final number. Soon I have had enough of snakes to last several lifetimes. Karima's huge heart overflows with compassion. It's cruel to keep anything in a cage. We pull back the covers in her hotel room to find pythons snoozing on the sheets. She puts them on the floor, cooing softly in Berber. In the heat of love, I feel one slither across my back or along my leg.

How can I not ask: Has she ever known a Jew before? No. But she has seen one. More than one. Itinerant rug dealers in the markets at Zagora. Everyone says they are clever. Not to be trusted. They like to take advantage of Muslims. But they are better than Arabs. Everyone knows that. At least Jews work. Arabs are lazy. All they do is steal things from Berbers. Maybe it's a sin to make love with a Jew. But it can't be. It feels too good. It must be kismet. Her destiny and mine. Written on our foreheads. She closes her eyes in prayer. Above her bed, a tiny teardrop in blue glass keeps us safe from the evil eye. Each time we part, I say *A bientôt*, and she answers *Elhamdu lillah*. Praise be to God.

Our passion proves to be larger than either of us anticipates or fully understands. Some strange compound of the unknown, the mysterious, the forbidden. What gets released when you remove a veil after a thousand years or let a people out of a ghetto after five hundred.

Not for a moment do I hide the fact that I am married. A foreigner who soon must return to his native land. Not for a moment does Karima talk about the obvious: that a girl from Ourzazate who makes it to a nightclub in Paris has had more than a little male support. Must still have male protection not too far away.

I remain a gentleman. Do not ask questions or expect answers. Accept, you might say, the will of Allah. Karima, on the other hand, never stops asking and expecting. Never stops making judgments. Your wife! What kind of a woman is she? What kind of a marriage does she call it? Leaving you to go off and live in another country. She doesn't know what love is. She doesn't deserve you. Watch out. Be careful. Maybe you shouldn't go home. A woman like that might take it into her head to kill you. She might come and kill me. She must be crazy. I have a solution. You should kill her first. I will kill her for you. Karima picks up a knife and begins waving it. The snakes slither into the far corners of the room. Maybe they know something I need to learn.

How can I tell her Jews don't kill anybody. How can I explain that the worst moment of my life is a quiet afternoon somewhere outside of Czernowitz. The front has broken. We are retreating. The Poles are right behind us and sometimes even in front of us. We have been chased down. Ambushed. Shot up. My buddy, Dolgushov, sprawls against a tree, blood leaking from a dozen wounds, his face distorted with pain. Our horses graze nearby. I bend close. He whispers: *Kill me, for Christ's sake. Do it now, sweet Jesus.*

I take the revolver from his holster, place it against his temple. But I can't pull the trigger. *Do it,* he says, then begins to whimper. Tears wet his cheeks. I can't do it. He sobs, shakes his head slowly, moves his mouth but no words come out. I press the muzzle to his head. Close my eyes. Make a vow. Count to three. Nothing happens. I just can't do it.

Start to count again. A roar of gunfire stops me. Dolgushov goes limp. Laughter shatters the sudden silence. I open my eyes. Three of our troop put away their carbines. As they spur their horses away, I hear a single word: *Jews!*

One day Karima is gone from the hotel. Vanished. Snakes and all. No forwarding address. No message.

Two years later in Moscow a clipping falls out of an envelope sent to me by Lev Nikulin. It's from *France-Soir*. A photo of Karima, more stunning than ever. Maybe it's the diamonds around her neck, the tiara, the splendid gown, the limousine in the background. Maybe it's the story about how in a villa near Nice she has been stabbed to death by a jealous lover.

No snakes are mentioned in the story.

Elhamdu lillah.

15

A loud knock interrupts my morning. Lyosha, again? Wearing pajamas, I open the door.

Surprise.

Potato Face. Lumps and all. The same gray suit, the same solid shoes. Her lips turned up so slightly at the corners you'd need a micrometer to measure the curve. She seems to be attempting to do something unfamiliar: smile.

I step aside and she marches directly through the living room and onto the terrace. Glares at the half-full wineglass resting on the stucco wall as proof of a terrible corruption that she long suspected. I find my voice. Can I get her something to drink?

Water, she says in a faint voice.

I pour a glass. Another cup of tea for myself.

What a pleasure to see you in Odessa. My voice is very loud. *Take my advice. Be careful. You're not dressed for the climate. Heat stroke is common here. Northerners are never prepared. Try getting some sandals. A cotton dress. A straw hat.*

She puts a finger to her mouth. Shushes. Nods toward the living room.

They can put listening devices in phones.

I don't have one. There isn't a phone within a kilometer.

We stand side by side. Her posture is military. She gazes out at the sea, the first person in two centuries to stand on this spot and not mention the view. I refrain from asking the obvious question: How did she get my address?

On vacation?

She faces me with an expression that says, What's a vacation? I fight the antic impulse to put my hand on her tightly covered breast. To take her in my arms and kiss her passionately on the mouth. To declare an urgent desire for her flesh.

One week, she whispers. *Ten days maximum. Is everything arranged?*

I'm working on it.

Working isn't good enough.

It's not entirely in my control. I'm doing my best.

It's a matter of life and death, comrade. You must do better than your best. There is no room for error. Everything must be ready on time.

That about does it for conversation. We stare at each other. Civility dies hard.

Your first time in Odessa?

A slight nod. What to say now? Recommendations for the best beaches would be wasted, and she hardly looks like the sort who wants to spend time in old churches or palaces, or to hang around Greek taverns.

The steps from Potemkin. *The Richelieu steps. You must visit them. They're our most famous revolutionary landmark.*

The lumps seem to swell, grow slightly darker. Her tone of voice includes equal measures of pity and contempt:

Eisenstein made it all up. Nobody was killed by Cossacks on those steps. It's only a fiction. So what's the point.

History lesson finished, she turns toward the door. We shake hands. This gesture of growing friendship makes me inquisitive.

I didn't realize you were going to be my contact here.

Neither did I.

Will I see you again?

You never know. Life is strange.

A silent *Amen* from my lips as she leaves. Then I dress in a rush, catch a trolley into town, hurry directly to Katya's apartment, bang on the door. Lyosha is the one who can put me in touch with Jacob. No answer. I scribble a note saying I will return soon and go to get my mail.

Headlines assault me on the way into the post office. Zinoviev and Kamenev in big type. Traitors. Betrayers of the Revolution and the motherland. Trotskyists responsible for the assassination of Leningrad Party chief Kirov last year. Plotting to do away with the Party leaders in Moscow and seize power for themselves. And these are no mere allegations. They are confessions. Freely given words. Written and signed in their own hands. Such horrendous crimes have called forth enormous public outrage. All across the country, Soviets, unions, young people's leagues, ethnic groups, associations of retired soldiers, demand immediate action. Forget about a trial. Save the time and money. Execute the traitors now.

State prosecutor Vyshinsky disagrees. We are civilized people. We live under the rule of law. Zinoviev, Kamenev, and their colleagues shall have a fair trial. In an open court. With the press of the world in attendance. So that everyone can see the crimes of our Trotskyist enemies and the workings of Soviet justice.

An open trial? That's the real shocker. It can only mean the Boss is getting ready to make a deal with somebody in the West. Potato Face was right about K. Right about the timetable too. The opening of the trial is at hand. With confessions, the proceedings won't take long. They wouldn't take long even without confessions. The courts are one of the few institutions in the country to get their jobs done ahead of schedule. To overfulfill their production quota.

In lines at the post office, people are subdued. Nobody talks about the news. Trotsky is familiar enough. Too familiar. During the long Civil War following the Revolution, when he built and led the Red Army to victory, people in Odessa liked to brag about him as their own. Didn't he go to school here? Get his start here? Lots of old-timers claimed to remember him from the end of last century as a brilliant public speaker, denouncing the czar, urging workers to take over the factories and shipyards. Today his name makes people clear their throats and look down at their shoes.

Not that Trotsky is a real Odessan. For one thing, he was born and raised in Kherson. For another, he never, in seven years of living here, learns how to swim. Never once takes a dip in the sea. He's always too busy reading, writing, promoting the Revolution and himself. Drawing up plans for a new world. One that for all his Marxist theories of collective action he hopes to lead on a white horse. Trotsky's a dreamer, all right, but one with his own dangerous dreams. Awake he is cold, aloof, sardonic. Definitely not a man to throw your arms around in a bar. His passion emerges only in front of a large crowd. Or on the page, when he savages an opponent or a friend. Occasionally he would drop by our writers' evenings. Listen to everything, poetry, fiction, reportage, with a supercilious smile on his lips. Never does he say a word, but everyone worries over what he's thinking. Fearful that a few days later there may appear an unsigned essay in *Pravda* or the *Literary Gazette* denouncing the evening's featured author for ideological and literary errors.

Only once do Trotsky and I have a conversation. The usual kind: he talks, I listen. At the time *Red Cavalry* was all the rage. Critics were calling it the first great work of Soviet literature. A promise of the cultural heights to which the proletarian state aspires. Trotsky seeks me out after a reading. Shakes my hand. Offers congratulations. My images, he says, are brilliant. My judgments of the Cossacks right on target. They are barbarians. Just the kind of barbarians you need when you are fighting a vicious enemy like the Poles.

I wait for the but.

Babel. Your problem is that you're like everyone else from Odessa. You've got Jews on the brain. Forget Jews. You'll never be a great Soviet writer if you write about Jews. Your sentimentality about the shtetl is by far the weakest part of the book. Who cares about the shtetl anymore? It's gone like private enterprise is gone, like the czar is gone, never to return. So do me a favor and do yourself a favor: promise me no more stories about Jewish gangsters. No more about your Jewish childhood. Judaism is a throwback. A fossil religion. The Jews are a fossil people. The Revolution has done away with fossils. We'll all be better off without them.

Forty minutes in line to reach the window. It's worth the wait. A long letter from Zhenya, who hasn't written in six months. A note from Sharpelov, my landlord in Molodenovo, the retreat near Moscow where I have spent the last two summers: *We miss you. It's sad with you away and Gorky gone for good. The folks who gather on the riverbank miss your bald head bobbing in the water. The horses miss your soft touch. The mare you helped to birth two years ago runs like the wind. It's not a real summer without you. Your room is ready and waiting.*

A postcard from Bagritsky, setting a date for my reading at his wife's club. They plan to take me to dinner afterward. His conclusion will win no prizes for subtlety: *Is it quiet enough in the villa we got for you? Have we helped you to work well? We do hope and expect you'll have something new to read to us. Something about Odessa?*

A scribbled note from Sergei. Have I read the screenplay? Do I like the changes? Don't bother doing any rewrites. We'll fix any problems together in Yalta while we lounge by the sea and visit the local wine cellars. He'll be here in a week. He'll send a telegram first. How goes my own writing? Am I resurrecting Benya Krik?

No. Just beginning to imitate him.

This time Katya opens the door. The mother in her burbles, *What's wrong?* The aunt doesn't listen to my response but hustles me to the table for a piece of the honey cake that just came out of the oven. I pack away a second piece, then a third.

That's the Izzie I remember. Once you started on desserts you could never stop yourself. Remember the time you ate all the blintzes I made for a party of eight people. Eight people!

It's your fault for turning baking into a high art. Only the thought of my doctor's mug keeps me from eating the rest of the cake.

I ask for Lyosha. Katya shrugs. She rarely knows where he goes. But she's pleased to see me. I should not be such a stranger. Family has things to talk about. Have I heard from my mother? Rabinowitz and Dubinsky keep pestering her. When is your nephew coming to services? He promised. Talk to him. Get a date. It will be good for him. Good for the congregation. People want to see the son of Emmanuel Babel. They want to know what's going on in Moscow.

She lowers her voice. *What is going on? Don't you know Zinoviev and Kamenev? How can they confess? What's going to happen to them?*

I shrug and open my hands in that gesture that can mean so many things at the same time. That says: Who knows? We all know. The same only worse. If I knew details I would give you details. But I'm in the dark too.

She gets the idea.

Lyosha says you have been seen in town with a woman. A stunning woman. Nu, nu? Who is she? Bring her to dinner.

What a small town. I've seen her only a couple of times. I hardly know her. Why should you meet her? I have a wife, remember?

You have two wives, but who's counting?

Tell Rabinowitz and Dubinsky I'll come to synagogue. Soon. But one of them will have to remind me how to pray. My Hebrew is in the dustbin of history.

16

Dear Izzie:

    This letter will be a surprise, I know. You don't expect me to write to you directly in Odessa. I think it's the first time I've ever written to you there. I bet you hardly expect me to write you at all. I think you understand even if you don't like it. You know how I hate putting words on paper. Maybe that's one reason we married. I so admired the way the words came out of you and kept coming. I used to think that when I got older I would begin to like writing but I was wrong. I am older and I still want to draw pictures when I pick up a pen. Please explain this to your mother and sister. Every note I get from them is full of complaints. They keep saying I am stingy with words. Tell us more about your life. What they really mean of course is, Tell us more about your daughter. They never did care much for me, did they?

    One reason I write is to tell you how much your daughter is enjoying herself here in La Croix. It's a tiny fishing town near St. Raphael, not far from where we spent our holiday four years ago. Four years ago! Can it really be that long. Natasha is the proof. She is so excited with the postcards you have been sending. Does Odessa really look like that these days? Are the beaches really so clean and empty? Or are they crowded with lots of very fat people eating kishke and brisket sandwiches all day long like they used to? Probably it is all some sort of advertising for the city and the government to say, Look how modern we are. Right?

    Natasha keeps saying Daddy is by the sea just like us. When will he come visit. I want swimming lessons. He promised. Write and tell Daddy to come soon. Natasha is more darling than ever. She has taken over the whole hotel and charms everyone, running up to people in the lobby, asking for candy or saying those kinds of things that kids say. Yesterday she poked a very fat man in the belly and asked him why he was so very fat. For a moment I feared the worst. With the economy going down the way it is for-

eigners aren't very popular here these days so who knows what he could do or say or ask the hotel to do? But he laughed and picked her up and said I'm fat because I eat so many little girls like you. I know you would fear the worst in such a remark but it was all in good fun. Natasha giggled hysterically and he gave her some candy and this morning over breakfast he had a big smile for both of us.

You can see from the letterhead we are at the Kensington Hotel. Not a great place but pas mal. Anyway it's about the best we can afford. Half the guests are British and they are so good with kids. Not like the French, who are always scolding their children. I am glad none of the French vacationers find Natasha too annoying. You know how testy they can be with anyone who intrudes on their precious privacy. But she's your daughter. She has them all in the palm of her hand just like her daddy. I never did know how you did it.

You won't like this but I am going to tell you anyway. I have stopped the Russian lessons. It was harder and harder to get her to study and it seemed like all we ever did was fight about learning Russian. I want my daddy to teach me, she kept saying. The money was a factor too. Things are so bad in the States that my brother can't send me as much these days and I don't get much work. In a climate like this there just aren't many people who want to restore paintings. I know I could get free lessons from some of the Russians here but I am keeping away from Russians. I am sick of Russians. This is France. I want to be French. I want my daughter to be French.

Right now I know what you are going to say. I know you better than you know yourself. You will say, What will Natasha do when she comes to live in Russia. Izzie wake up. Natasha is not coming to live in Russia. I am not coming to live in Russia. We are not coming to live in Russia. I have been trying to make that clear ever since she was born. She is French by birth. She is going to speak French and go to French schools. I don't know why you can't get that through your skull. I want to say thick skull but this is the only issue on which I have ever known you to be thick.

You always loved France. You taught me to love France before I came here. I know there are some things I cannot put into this letter but I would think you would be proud to have a daughter who is French. She doesn't need to know Russian. She can become a writer and write in the language of your precious hero, Maupassant. Won't that be a treat?

I write to you in Odessa because maybe in your hometown you can come to understand the way things are between us. I have fond memories of Odessa. That year we spent there we were so happy. The war was over and you were safe and were writing every day and teaching me to swim. You'll never know how terrified I was all those months you were away, riding around with the Cossacks. My poor Izzie. I was so afraid you were too frail to live through the violence and bloodshed of those Cossacks and Polacks and worried if you ever got enough to eat. My mother came down to Odessa—it was so nice to have her help around the house. It was the biggest house we ever had. We could see the ocean and talk about the future. The books you would publish and all the exhibitions I would have and how they would help to make our country great. God! Did we really believe such stuff? Mother even got up to cook you breakfast every morning and I could sleep in late. I love sleeping in late. I wish I could do it here but with our seven-year-old there isn't much chance of that. One of the best reasons to have you around or for me to live with someone else or get married again is to have someone take care of Natasha in the morning. Not that you would do it. Oh I know you think you would do it but your writing desk would call to you and what has ever been more important than your writing?

I never did understand why you dragged me away from Odessa to that horrible Batumi. What were you thinking about? Not me. You were very convincing about why we needed to get away. You were always very convincing about whatever you wanted to do. You made me think I wanted to do it too. That goatherd's hut we lived in. What a hole. What stupid romanticism. There were perfectly good apartments in the town. Cheap apartments, everything was so cheap then. But you had to live in the country. Only a city boy like you would want to live on the side of a hill. The flowers you would say, the fresh breezes, smell the fresh air. But it was an hour walk to town and a lot longer when you were coming back uphill with an arm full of groceries and who carried the groceries? Who carried chunks of ice for the icebox? Not you. Your romanticism did not stretch that far.

Batumi was like everything else in your life. It was an idea, a matter of poetry, a way of making our life into a play or a story. So you would go into town to hang out with the guys around the waterfront leaving me to do all the schlepping. Believe me, there is nothing romantic about schlepping. But

I was young and so in love with you that I would make the excuses for you.
He needs to find out things for his writing. His career is under way. Me, I
haven't gotten started yet. I'm his wife. The husband comes first. Yes I was
that old-fashioned. But schlepping is also a way of ending romance. Espe-
cially when you began to spread the romance around to other women.

Tell me truthfully. I will now ask something I could not last summer.
Something I have never been able to. Would you really want me to come to
live with you in Moscow? I don't for a minute believe you if you say yes.
You keep urging only because you know I will say no. You would have a
heart attack if Natasha and I suddenly showed up on your doorstep. And
what would you tell Pirozhkova?

You think I don't know about her? You think it's a secret? You think
Ehrenburg and Nikulin and all your other buddies who stop by with news
don't open their big mouths? You think the Russian colony here is not the
same hotbed of rumors it always has been. And many of the rumors are true,
as they always have been. Izzie I know you. If her name weren't Nina it
would be Galina or Fatima or Michele or something else. You think I don't
know about all the others? Including that dark-skinned floozy with the
snakes you spent so much time with in '27? The summer that we conceived
Natasha. Snakes? Sometimes I think you ought to have your head exam-
ined.

I'm used to it now. I'm used to you and your stories. Kashirina was the
worst. The real shocker. I suppose the first one always is. Only recently did
someone tell me about Yezhova. Can you be honest and tell me was she the
first or did you have someone hidden away in the backroom of a taverna in
Batumi. Someone with dark skin who barely spoke Russian but was happy
to teach you a few words of Turkish or Farsi while you romped together. Or
was there someone in Tbilisi. Is that why you went off and left me alone
with the sheep for so many months. The only story you ever wrote about
Tbilisi is about a young man going to a whore. And you wrote it twice. No
doubt you can justify all that as another way of learning about the world.
With you there is no end to learning. With you there is no end to deceptions.
With you there is no end to words.

I was a young girl like any other young girl. I believed in love ever after.
I believed in the vows I took. It was such a shock to realize that the same

words do not mean the same things to your husband. When I learned about Kashirina I cried every day for a year. I hid it from you and your sister and your mother. You thought I was going to classes at the art institute but what I was really doing was walking the streets of Moscow and thinking what a horrible city why am I here what am I doing here what will I do now and the tears would stream down my face. Then I'd go home and cook dinner for you until I got tired of cooking dinner and going to parties where you were not exactly subtle in the way you talked to other women and I was always wondering if this whoever-it-was was a girlfriend or about to become one. And Kashirina, preening like a queen, dressed in low-cut gowns and with those fake diamonds and a tiara for God's sake always ignoring me and lighting up for you like a neon light.

I still cry about Kashirina sometimes. About the life I thought we were going to have.

And you know what's even worse. What you tell everybody about me. That my leaving had nothing to do with women and everything to do with my being so bourgeois. Sure Father was rich, and he was ruined by the Bolsheviks, and I hated them for that. It broke him, broke his spirit. But who says bourgeois can't have clear perceptions. And who actually was more bourgeois, au fond, than you, my dear Izzie. What could be more bourgeois than that dream of becoming a famous writer and helping to save the world at the same time. That desire to create a new literature full of the sun and salt air of the Black Sea. What's all that but bourgeois romanticism. Bourgeois grandiosity. You have always been grandiose. It's grandiose to stay on in Russia when your wife and your flesh and blood daughter are alone in a foreign country and need you. And you know what's really bourgeois. Your fears of becoming a nobody. Isn't that really why you stay. Oh I know all the excuses about needing your language, your soil, your city. But the truth is that in Russia no matter how bad things are you are always a Somebody. Even if you can't write exactly what you want or can't write anything at all, you're a Somebody. You are Isaac Babel, the writer who refuses to bend and refuses to cater to the demands of the apparatchiks. And for your refusal you get even more famous and honored for not writing. But it can't go on forever, can it?

You're bourgeois in another way too. You are rich and you like being rich. In France you would be poor. Scrambling for existence like the rest of us. A nobody. Part of a pack of émigrés who are all nobodies, arguing over the old country and what went wrong, fighting over scraps dropped from the table of foreign publishers. I'm not saying you're not a decent man. I will give you that. I will always appreciate the way you took care of my father in his failing days and took care of all the paperwork and the estate after his death, going to Kiev and wrapping things up and making sure the government didn't make off with all our personal possessions, and sending me the pictures and storing all the furniture. Not that I will ever come back to claim it.

Your streak of decency is the one counterweight to your passion and romanticism. But it's impossible to live with you. It would always be impossible to live with you because you will never compromise your precious creativity or your carnal desires, all of which seem pretty closely linked with each other. To live with you, Izzie, is to be a servant to your creativity. It's a job anyone can only hold for a limited time. Or is that just me? Anyway you never seem to have trouble finding others to fill the role.

I know this is the longest letter you have ever had from me. It's the longest letter I have ever written. I've been wanting to say these things for years but when we are together I am always too afraid you will walk out the door once more. You were always walking out the door and leaving me in tears. I don't want to cry anymore.

Natasha has just woken up from her nap and says, Are you still writing to Daddy? You've been writing for days. What do you have to tell him that takes so long. Tell him I want him to come here soon. Tell him I want a daddy to be around. Tell him I love him.

Izzie believe me when I say I love you too.

Zhenya

17

*D*riving in the country. Nadja and I. Sunday afternoon and we are off on a picnic. It's her idea. Women love picnics. They have all read Omar Khayyam but even the most romantic will put the loaf of bread ahead of the book of verses. They all love the whole process. Packing food into small containers, putting the containers into baskets, filling thermos bottles, traveling to a field, a stream, a meadow, a tree, a bush, a forest, and then unpacking, spreading food out on a tablecloth, opening cold drinks, a bottle of wine, and settling back with their lover. Karima loved a fresh baguette, brie, and a good bottle of burgundy while we sat on the edge of the Vert Galant, looking at the Paris skyline, the Seine flowing by us on both sides, our feet dangling into the brown water. Kashirina had more dramatic tastes. A picnic in February snowdrifts in a birch forest. She in a sable coat, me wearing a mink she has borrowed or stolen for the day. The cork won't pop on the frozen champagne bottle. She pulls out a flask filled with vodka. It goes well with the caviar, sour cream, onions, soggy points of toast.

Today we could use some of that snow. That cool water. The steppe bakes in the heat of late summer. A yellow world except where the occasional stream creates a startling green line of brush and trees. Dust and grit blow in through the windows, along with the perfume of tall wheat. A smell I have grown to love in Molodenovo at harvesttime. Five years now since I learned the knack of swinging a sickle, began to enjoy the delightful gymnastics of body and soul. For me it is recreation. That's the major difference from my neighbors. They aren't volunteers who can walk away. They don't spend mornings at a writing desk. They can't run off for a swim in the Moskva River in midafternoon.

I am breaking one of Papa's rules.

Stay clear of nature. He said it a million times. *The countryside is for peasants. We belong in the city. Only in the city are we safe.*

The spirit of what must be even more ancient ancestors rose up in me a decade ago when I fled the madness of Moscow and settled on a farm in Khrenovaya, not far from Rostov. Zhenya is already in France. Mama and Mera have left for Belgium. Kashirina has just realized that I am not going to marry her even if she is carrying our child. I need a place where there is no one to ask questions, no one to make demands. No family, no friends, no publishers, no editors, and definitely no directors.

The stud farm is the perfect place. My first lessons about horses began with the Cossacks during the Civil War. In Khrenovaya I work on an advanced degree. I come to love the stillness, the freshness, the quiet, the dark. The days pitchforking hay, cleaning stables. Horses have soft noses. They don't interrupt your dreams. Mine are of freedom. But just as I begin to think of forgetting the city and spending the rest of my life here, an urgent telegram arrives from the manager of the Moscow Art Theater. *Sunset* is in rehearsal. Some things are not working. I must be on the spot to do a rewrite. To take out some of the eroticism, the Freudian overtones. The censors won't accept it as is. No rewrites, no performances.

Molodenovo is almost as good. Less than a hundred kilometers from Moscow, but it seems as remote as Switzerland. I spend as much time there as I can. Friends continually threaten to visit but they never can tear themselves away from the city. My room at Sharpelov's is tiny, clean, sweet. In the spring, white apple blossoms fill the trees outside the window. In summer, the lush grass. I rise before dawn, stroll through woods, fields, and silent villages. One morning as the huge orange disk of the moon sinks toward the river, a watchman beats his gong and my heart swells with a strange joy. Papa was wrong about the country.

We stop under some trees. Along a tiny stream. Near a pasture. Nadja spreads out a cloth, unpacks food. Horses ease over to investigate. I lean on the railing, feed them carrots, stroke their noses. Turn back and her beauty strikes me like a blow somewhere between the stomach and the heart. She wears light-colored slacks, an open white shirt, a neckerchief, a straw hat. She has a face that belongs here. That belongs anywhere in the world.

You couldn't say the same for me.

We eat what you eat on these occasions. Cold chicken, hard-boiled eggs, potato salad, carrots, tomatoes, pickles, olives, bagels, chopped liver. Chopped liver? A special treat for me. Secured from some secret source. Not as good as my mother's, but what food ever is? But not bad. Not bad at all.

She raises a wineglass. Quotes from my work for the first time:

We both looked at the world as at a May meadow, through which pass women and horses.

I raise my glass.

Should we women be flattered you put us ahead of horses?

I pop an olive in my mouth. Look over at the horses.

You've been checking up on me. Reading Red Cavalry. *A dangerous book by a dangerous man. I wrote that in my twenties. What do you know in your twenties?*

I drink some wine.

What do you know in your forties? About horses or women? Except that they both seem to come and go. They both are beautiful and powerful creatures with distinct tendencies toward getting out of control.

And you. Always in control? Always the observer? Always hiding behind a disguise? Lyutov. What a pseudonym you chose for yourself in that book. Ferocious. Is that the you behind this mild facade? It's a beautiful book. It made me cry, you know. Your words made me cry. That doesn't happen often.

I stand up and wander back to the horses. Nadja follows, leans against me, puts her head on my shoulder, says she's planning to go on to my Odessa stories. Part of an effort to learn who I am.

When you find out, let me know. Right now it's something of a mystery. I'm not the same guy who wrote Red Cavalry. *That's certain.*

What's changed?

What hasn't?

Is it true Jews always answer a question with another question?

Why ask me?

We finish eating, pack up, drive on until yellow dust is so thick we can barely see through the windshield. I'm the one who knows the way, but she sees the graveyard first, the small stone church, the burned-out remains of some country houses, barns, other structures. The empty church is dark, stripped bare of paintings, benches, candelabra. Gouges in the walls where mosaics have been torn away. A small wooden crate that serves as an altar. Candles in wine bottles. Nadja lights one, bows her head, prays. Enough light to see the vestiges of wall paintings. A crude modern image of the Madonna and child.

This cemetery brings a different reaction from the ones in town. Tears. No great sobs, no heaving sighs, just drops slowly leaking from the corner of both her eyes. Nothing makes a man feel more helpless. I take her hand. We sit on a stone that covers an old grave. She says she knows me better than I think. Knows that I don't fully trust her. Don't trust anyone. Pain does that. But we all have our pains of the heart. This place opens old wounds for her. Reminds her of the moment when her world changed unalterably.

It was in 1920, this time of year, just at the end of the Civil War. We lived on the estate of my father's family, somewhere in the Little Crimea, not far from Evpatoria. Our family belonged to the minor nobility. Distant relatives of distant relatives of God knows who. Nobody could forget that many years before, my grandmother had been presented at court. By the time of the Revolution, we had fallen on hard days. By the end of the Revolution, everyone had. Most of the peasants who worked the estate were dead, or had been scattered by the war or were agitating for something. There were so few around that, at harvesttime, Father and Mother had to lead the work in the fields. Then at dinner one night we begin to hear shouts and loud hoots that grow closer and louder. Father looks out the window and sees one of our own at the head of a mob. Mitya, who grew up on the estate and went off to school in Yalta, and every time his money ran out, Father came up with the funds to keep him there. Mitya rages, Death to the exploiters! Expropriate the expropriators! Kill the czarists!

Dozens of them, reeking of alcohol, break down the door, storm into the house, and in a frenzy start tearing up the rooms. Pictures from the walls, curtains, dishes, furniture—everything torn, smashed, destroyed. Father tries to reason with them. Take what you want, he says. There's plenty for all. But they are not after anything material. What they want is vengeance. What they want is blood. Mitya does the deed himself, comes right up to Fa-

ther, looks him in the eye, shrieks and raises a shovel and smashes Father on the head. Down he goes in a pool of blood. Mother throws herself on top of him sobbing. I shriek, Daddy, Daddy, Daddy! *That stops them for a moment. Some of the peasants cross themselves, others kneel. Mitya screams:* Get up, get up. Death to all exploiters!

They drag the body away, push us into the yard, set fire to the house. They drink, they shout, they hurl themselves about in crazy dances in the light of the flames. Some begin to yell at us. I cling to Mother, weeping. Another one of our former workers, Mikhail, an older guy with a long beard and the red star of a commissar on his filthy shirt, puts his arms around the two of us, whispers, Don't worry, I'm sorry, he was a good man, *then begins to hustle us away. Mitya blocks our progress, but Mikhail knocks him to the ground with a powerful forearm. For a week we live with his family in a tiny hut. His wife takes care of us, feeds us, rocks me to sleep every night, gives me the tiny cross I still wear. My mother can't seem to stop sobbing. Somehow she manages to get us to St. Petersburg, to Grandmother's apartment, just off the Fontanka Canal. It's communal now, but we have three whole rooms. It doesn't make a difference to Mother. She never recovers from that night. Never again is her old self. Four years later she dies of no specific illness. You'd probably have to call it a broken heart.*

If this were a film, clouds would cover the sun during Nadja's story, the afternoon grow darker. Lightning would crack, thunder rumble. A few drops of rain would fall, then a torrent. The man and woman take shelter beneath a huge tree. He tries to hold her, comfort her. But she pulls away. The camera draws slowly back until we are looking at them from afar, side by side beneath the tree, the charred remains of the burned estate in the background. What we hear is rain, more and more rain, pouring, growing in volume until you feel that water may engulf the world.

But this is the southern Ukraine in August. There won't be a cloud in the sky for months. At seven o'clock the sun still blazes. Long afternoon shadows of a man and a woman embracing in the way men and women have always embraced. In life, in books, in movies. In dust, heat, cold, rain, fire, flood. In moments of desire, fear, hope, comfort, memory.

Two against a world.

18

I expect another knock on the door. The Packard. The guys in their hats. What I get is a two-ton truck almost knocking me over as I cross the street. I jump back. Maybe I am too relaxed to look both ways.

Late afternoon. A block from the Lermontov where I have been baked, stroked, steamed, and hosed. A new treatment. Good for the circulation. You step out of the steam room and into a tiled cubicle. A young woman makes you take off your robe and stand with your back to her. A stream of water from a fire hose five meters away drives you against the wall. Pounds your muscles into relaxation. She orders you to turn around. Plays the stream of water up your legs, down your arms and belly, along your thighs, closer and closer, circling your genitals, playing with your fears.

No. She wouldn't dare. Would she? She has to be teasing. It will hurt. Ruin me for days. Shall I refuse? Say, Turn it off? Walk away?

Wrapped in my robe, I exit. A glum man sitting in a chair, waiting his turn, asks: *Why is she laughing so loud? Is the treatment fun?*

The truck driver leans on the horn. I look up. Josif, with Moishe beside him. Wearing work shirts, sleeves rolled up to the elbow. Flat caps. Smiling, gesturing, yelling: *This is Odessa. Watch how you walk. Workers have the right of way.*

I climb into the cab. Cardboard and wooden boxes fill the back of the truck. Markings have been painted out. Some have the characteristic oblong shape of containers for rifles.

What's with the disguises?

Disguises? This is how the Russian working man dresses.

Relaxed again. I look forward to the ride along the seashore, the view from Kovalevsky's tower. But we turn right on Dalnitsa, go past the railroad station, through the marketplace and into the Moldavanka. The usual street scene. Babushkas in lines at stores for bread, meat, produce.

Quick-faced hustlers patrol the sidewalks, pull open jackets to reveal watches, jewelry, foreign postcards with pictures of women in lingerie or less. Drunks snooze in alleys behind garbage cans.

Moishe wants to entertain me. *Here's the latest. A woman goes into a butcher shop, looks at the empty counters, and says, Don't you have any meat? The salesgirl shakes her head. No, we're the store that doesn't have any chicken. The butcher down the block is the one that doesn't have any meat.*

Josif doesn't wish to be outdone. *A new political prisoner in Siberia is asked by an older prisoner, How long are you in for? He answers, Ten years. The older guy asks, What did you do? Nothing! The old guy says, Don't lie to me. For nothing they give you fifteen years.*

Their laughter is full of expectation. My turn. Happily I don't have to show that jokes are not one of my talents. We stop in front of a house no more, no less tumbled down than any other dwelling in this neighborhood. A courtyard surrounded by high, thick walls plastered with red hammer-and-sickle posters celebrating the new constitution. A heavy wooden gate that would be broad enough for two teams of horses to enter side by side. Down the street, beyond the factory smokestacks of Peresyp, the glowing eye of sunset drops into the sea. The sky is as red as a red-letter day on the calendar.

That's the kind of image I used to use all the time. Something about the Moldavanka calls for extravagance.

We are standing in front of the home of Froim Grach, Benya Krik's chief lieutenant. The one I chose for him when I began writing the gangster stories. It was a house I knew well. Father and I used to come here when I was a kid. Not Mother. She always makes some excuse—a headache, letters to write, time to begin spring-cleaning. On the way here Father delivers a long speech:

Izzie. I want you should always remember one thing. People are people. No matter where they live, no matter how much money they have or they don't have. They are all people. They all have a right to be treated like people. God looks at them all with the same eye. If there is a God we are his children. And if there isn't, then we have to take his viewpoint. I want you to remember that. You should always be nice to people.

This was precisely the opposite of what his mother told me on those

Saturdays in her apartment that began with me stuffing on gefilte fish and horseradish, chicken soup, roast meat with onions and potatoes, salad, compote, pie, and apples. Grandmother cleared away the dishes and the dining table became my desk for studies. Mathematics, Russian, French. Not a single page of what I had to read did she understand, but she knew that every one of them was absolutely necessary if I were to attain what I must have: wealth and fame.

Study, study, study. You must know everything. Everyone will fall down before you. Everyone will envy you. Don't have faith in human beings. Don't let yourself have friends. Harden your heart against people. Don't ever trust them. Don't lend them money. Don't give anyone your heart.

Had she given the same advice to my father? Why didn't he follow it?

Father's closest friend in secondary school was Simonovich Krapolinsky, who after graduation followed his own father into the family business: a draying company. The two young men remain friends, though they now lived in different worlds. Simon begins to drive his own team of horses, hauls heavy goods every day from the docks to warehouses, factories, and stores. He is a huge bear of a man with powerful shoulders and arms, a head taller than Father, with a mass of gray messy hair and a dirty patch over one eye. One day he is not wearing the patch. The socket is hollow, weird, frightening.

Don't stare, whispers Father. *It's not polite.*

It's difficult not to stare. The only thing more fascinating than an eye patch is an empty eye.

Manny. Let him look. He's a kid. Remember when we were kids. We would want to take a look. Come here, kid.

Simon grabs me around the waist and raises me up until our faces are a few centimeters apart. I look directly into an empty socket. A crusty slit surrounded by shriveled gray skin. Disgusting bits of dirt and gunk hang from the lid, the brow, stick to the corner of the socket, the side of the nose. I feel a touch queasy when he puts me down and roars with laughter.

Not a pretty sight, my boy. You want to know how it happened, don't you? You want to know how handsome young Simon the lady-killer became old One-Eye to everyone?

He's right. I want to know.

It happened during the pogrom of eighty-one, kid. Our first really big pogrom. Before that they liked us here. We were building up the city. Maybe we built too well. It's not that they got any poorer, but we were getting richer. Building big synagogues like the Brody and hospitals and starting newspapers. Sending pishers *like you off to school. But you know all that. You've had your own pogrom. Each generation gets its own pogrom.*

A special look passes between Simon and my father. One of those looks that each generation has, full of meanings that get lost to history.

I'm on my way back from the docks. The violence has already started and I've just gotten rid of my last load and I'm lashing the horses and racing home to safety when on Dalnitsa I see a bunch of Greek sailors waving whisky bottles over their heads, yelling, circling a young woman who is trying to protect two small kids. They are pulling at her coat, grabbing her arms, her legs when I wade into them. Seven, eight, big guys, some as big as me, but surprise helps me and I manage to occupy all of them so that she and the kids slip away. I get in some licks, smash a couple of them to the ground, but with that many it's only a matter of time until it's all arms, fists, legs, bottles over my head, boots in my face. They do a job on me all right, but she and the kids are safe, thank God. An eye for three lives. Not a bad bargain. I'd pay it again, kid. You always have to hold your head up. Remember that. No matter what the cost.

A story like that has to impress a youngster. Heroism, excitement, a clear moral. What more can you want?

Some might say the Truth.

A few weeks later I retell the story to friends. Four of us sitting near the docks, after a swim, eating ice cream. Krapolinsky drives by and waves. I start in on one of my famous stories. Elaborate it with many gory details Simon forgot to mention. Sharp punches and clean counter-punches. Sailors hurled over shoulders, against each other, tumbling in heaps. It takes six of them to hold Simon down while a seventh takes out a knife and slowly gouges away the eyeball.

Two of the guys burst into laughter: *What garbage! I bet Simon sold you that load of shit. He's been peddling it all over town for years!* They all roar together, poke me in the ribs, snap at me with towels. *Don't you know, dummy? Everyone knows Simon lost that eye on the docks tripping over his own feet and falling face down against the corner of a metal crate. He's no hero. Simon's a klutz!*

Father must know the truth but I never dare ask him. Never ask Nikitich or any other adults.

Fifteen years later I revisit Krapolinsky's yard to refresh my memory. Gathering stuff for what will be the gangster stories. Laundry hangs in the courtyard. Through the stable doors where Simon fed and combed his workhorses, a bunch of kids play on the dirt floor, a woman cooks on a brazier surrounded by odds and ends of furniture. Upstairs several families crowd against one another in partitioned living and dining rooms. Krapolinsky and his wife occupy the old master bedroom. He has suffered several strokes. Lies in bed all day, a shrunken figure staring at the ceiling. His wife brings me tea and cookies. Calls to him in a loud voice, as if he were far away:

Look, it's Manny's boy. Manny's son Isaac. Look how big he is. A real mensch. He says he's going to write about the Moldavanka. He's going to write about us. About our lives. Say hello to Izzie.

He stares at the ceiling. Blinks. Stares.

The blinks must be saying something important. They must be saying you are a good boy to come back. Now make our lives important. We all need to remember our lives as if they were important.

19

*D*ifferent yard. Different house. Different world.

Josif honks the horn, the gates swing open, we drive inside. No lines of laundry, no dust, no kids, no smells of cooking. The Packard and a Mercedes roadster parked side by side in a paved courtyard. A truck in front of open stable doors. Steel doors. Burly guys in work clothes load the vehicle with boxes.

Jacob stands on the balcony that runs the length of the second floor. Waves me toward him. We hug like old friends. He shows me around. Some rooms are outfitted like offices. Others are bedrooms or storage rooms piled high with all kinds of stuff: antique porcelain vases, statuettes, oil paintings, foreign-made refrigerators, radios, clocks, sealed cartons large and small. He explains:

Times change. Tradition remains. In Odessa we know how to honor tradition. You're part of that tradition, Isaac. You pointed the way. We needed a new headquarters and someone said, How about Froim Grach's old home. Let Babel be our guide. You described it so well that everyone around here knew which house it was. We had to move out a whole bunch of folks, three, four families, kids, dogs, cats. But we found places for all of them, better places. This was quite a dump when we took it over. Tell the truth, we would have preferred Benya Krik's home, but that was a real mystery. Nobody knew where it was. You don't give enough clues for that one. And nobody could remember Sharpolinski ever having a home. He was a kind of nomad who moved from place to place every few days.

My smile is enigmatic as I can make it.

A writer has a right to a secret now and then.

He's not satisfied.

Sure you have a right. But remember: you have an obligation too. We're not just anybody, Isaac. We're your children. Your invention. Your greatest fans. You've given us to the world. You've made us what we are.

Without Babel we're a bunch of common criminals pulling off jobs in some run-down town in a perpetually crazed and godforsaken country. With Babel we're heroes. People know about us in France, Germany, England, and America. All over the world. You've put us on the map. What does anyone anywhere know about Odessa? What do they care about Odessa? They know about Eisenstein's steps and they know about Jewish gangsters. That's us!

I decide to come clean.

Jacob, there's no mystery. A writer invents things too. It's not all from life. Benya Krik's home is an invention. It's generic Moldavanka. You can search for a thousand years. You won't find a model because there isn't one. Except in my mind.

Truth can seem stranger than fiction. His eyes narrow. He wants to know why I'm holding back. As some kind of bargaining chip? Jacob's a smart guy. Hard to believe he's that literal-minded.

We sit. He offers vodka, wine, kvass. I prefer seltzer with lemon. One of the guys brings it, along with a pitcher full of ice cubes. Something you can find at parties in the Kremlin, but rare as diamonds in this town. Rarer.

Isaac, I have to ask you one thing. Why didn't you mention that you know Yezhov?

I didn't mention lots of people.

He's too important not to mention. You visit his house. You eat his food. You sleep with his wife.

If I'd slept with him I might have mentioned it. Anyway, it's slept *not* sleep. *The past tense. We haven't been lovers for years. Just friends.*

Any other important people you forgot to mention?

Sure. It's time to confess to Jacob that I have met the Boss. More than once. Toasted the future of Soviet literature with him. At Gorky's place and at receptions for authors and artists. Twice he called me in for private meetings. You know the kind. The telephone rings at one A.M. and a muffled voice says, He wants to see you. At one A.M. in this country there's only one He. A car arrives fifteen minutes later. You sit between two men in long coats and all the way to the Kremlin wonder if maybe they're going to turn up Gorky Street and head for Lubyanka Prison. If maybe this is your last ride.

A few minutes later I am alone with him in that huge office. The Boss and me. One on one. He looms over the desk, as if his chair is very high. I sit in front, on a very low chair, looking up at him. His face is red. It must be the vodka. I try not to notice his pockmarks, glowing in the dim light. He lights a pipe. We sit in silence. The first time this happens I wonder what I'm supposed to do. Confess to something? Entertain him? Tell jokes or do a little dance? He puffs and stares. It is impossible to stare back. I look at the carpet, the walls, the chandeliers. Finally he says: *Tell me about France.*

Tell you what? I want to say, but I don't dare. So I give him the socioeconomic version. The version a leader must want to hear. I talk about the spread of the unions in the auto and steel industries, the growing strength of the Left in the Assembly, the sympathy of the intellectuals for our efforts to collectivize, the way so many workers look up to him as the one leader who can remake the world. I go on and on, saying more about economics and politics than I have in years, while he sits in stony silence, puffing, his eyes half shut. Am I boring him? Eventually I run out of things to say. He puffs. Nods. Puffs some more. Finally he gestures toward the door. Slowly I rise, back away facing him, feel vaguely like I should bow. He puffs and nods, and only when I put my hand on the door does he finally speak: *They tell me, Babel, you're quite a ladies man. A remarkable idea. You with that nose. Well, in this world, anything is possible. So tell me something I've always wanted to know: Is it true that the cunts of French women smell of champagne?*

The second visit is shorter. More ominous. He stands behind the desk and comes right to the point: *Babel, you are well known in France, England, Germany, Italy. I need an author like you, one with a world reputation. I need someone to write my biography. Not a dry academic work but an interesting, exciting one that people all over the world will want to read. You won't have to do too much research. I can tell you everything you need to know.*

Don't ask me how I got out of that. All I remember is feeling weak in the knees and sick to my stomach and blurting out the words: *I'll think about it, Josif Vissarionovich. I'll think about it.* The rest is a blank. What he said, if anything. How I answered, if I did. How I got down the hallways, the staircases, and into the car. The ride home. I don't remember a thing.

Jacob enjoys these stories. But he has other things on his mind.

Isaac. Lots of people have a high opinion of you. You're a popular guy. Especially with men. Women don't entirely trust you. They love you but they don't trust you. You're secretive. Some say sneaky. You disappear for long periods of time without telling anyone where you're going or where you've been. Lots of people think you may be working with the government. So I have to ask you as I did the first time: Are you a writer or a secret agent?

Neither.

A chuckle. A knowing nod.

Still having trouble, eh? Who can blame you? This is not an atmosphere for a creative artist. Trials, repression, everybody's nervous, on edge. So let me suggest a subject for you. Why not write about us? Gangsters in the Soviet state. Not that you could get it published here, but we have connections abroad.

Writing's not the first thing on my mind these days.

He knocks back a shot of vodka.

Business before creativity. I understand. Let's say you're not an agent and your story is true: you're going to have a big name on your hands very soon. Let's say we could fulfill your request. There's one thing we didn't talk about last time: money. Moving someone out of the country costs a lot and you can't pay in rubles. You need dollars. Say two thousand.

Neither the currency nor the amount is much of a surprise. But I had been hoping they might be sympathetic to the cause. Good luck. One thing is clear. I don't have dollars, and I can't put my hands on more than a quarter of that amount in rubles. Even if I knew where to change the rubles. Which would give me much less.

My silence says a lot.

I know, I know. You don't have that much. Who does? We're as patriotic as the next guys, which is to say not at all when it comes to things like this. We have no real homeland, we're businessmen. The money's not all for us. It's a complicated operation. You need documents, you have to take care of sailors, captains, port officials, customs inspectors. It's not cheap to make so many people look in the wrong direction.

I tell him what he already knows. That my foreign royalties have gone to support my wife and daughter and mother. My domestic royalties to travel, cars, houses. That I already have so many advances for unfinished projects that no publisher and no film studio is likely to come up with a ruble, let alone a dollar more. That my only resource is my pen. Which is not working very well or very quickly. If he really wants stories about gangsters today, I might have a go. If it would pay the bills.

Jacob waves away the offer. Far be it for him to ask an artist to compromise his vision. His creativity. Besides, there's a better way. I can work off the money. Do some jobs for them. Nothing dangerous of course. Nothing involving weapons or climbing into windows at night. Something that will draw on my special talents. My connections.

It's simple. Two of my boys were picked up a few weeks ago in Nikolayev. Somebody took a payoff and didn't come through. It's like your story about the cops, How It's Done in Odessa. *A new chief trying to follow the rules. Well, I don't appreciate a wave of honesty at our expense. Especially when they're throwing the book at them. Smuggling, carrying weapons. They'll get fifteen years, maybe more. They're good boys, but our contacts there just aren't working now. Getting them out would be worth two thousand dollars.*

What can I do?

You know people in the Kremlin. People at the top respect you. Yagoda. Yezhov. You can make a call or two. For them this is a cinch. Their arms are long enough to stretch to the Black Sea.

I wouldn't know how to begin.

Remember the old Chinese proverb: The longest journey begins with a single phone call.

Jacob stands up. I stand up. We hug. Good to have me as a guest but please, never come here to see him. It won't look good. For them. For me. They will get in touch with me soon enough. Don't mention any of this to your uncle, Lyosha. He's got a mouth too big for his brain. And think about the offer. It's the only way.

I stand outside the wooden gate. The sun is down. The sea as red as a bucket of blood. The corner of an old sign peeks out from behind posters for the new constitution. I tear them away and read the faded words, gilt on black: S. KRAPOLINSKY. HAULING, MOVING. YOU NAME IT, WE CARRY IT FOR YOU. NO JOB TOO LARGE. NO JOB TOO SMALL.

20

*T*he night of my reading at the writers' club, I get out of the bath and surprise Nadja bending over the table, looking at my pages. Not these pages. These are well hidden away. The pages I am going to read. The story I am finally writing about Benya Krik. The last story. One that should end with his death at the hands of Red Army commissars. For the good of the Revolution we must do away with such corrupt products of the old regime.

Nadja isn't flustered. She straightens up. Her eyes meet mine.

Benya Krik beginning as a child. I can see this on the screen.

I doubt it will ever make it to the printed page. Unless I get him to change professions. Maybe I should have him use his talents to manage a collective farm.

Do you know how to start a collective farm? No? The first thing you do is steal a tractor.

I didn't know they had collective farms in Romania.

Some nights Nadja stays over. Cooks us a meal. Chicken in wine, grilled fish, eggplant with tomatoes. She's not very good in the kitchen but neither am I, and a home-cooked meal is a real meal. We eat on the terrace. In the morning I send her off to the studio like a real movie star, in a car with a driver.

Benya Krik is not the only thing she's been catching up on. Now it's my life. Which leads to a familiar question.

Are the stories true?

Yes. Of course.

Did things really happen the way you describe them?

Not exactly. Some incidents are made up. But I've never thought truth is the way things happen. What really happens is that most of the hours of our lives are pretty dull. Nobody wants to read about that. Nobody wants all the details. They want the interesting parts.

Nadja comes over to kiss me on the cheek, straighten my necktie, pat my few stray hairs into place. I have put on my tan, rumpled summer suit. My only summer suit. She is a vision in white. Simple dress, cotton gloves, high-heeled sandals. Does she know I think she is spying on me? Does she understand that I don't much care?

I ask her a question about a true story. The one about her father and mother. She left out some details. Never finished it. How did she get from an apartment on the Fontanka Canal to Kazakhstan?

Grandma raised me. That woman who had met the czar worked as a seamstress, repairing old clothes, to pay the bills. She did a good enough job of hiding our background so that when I began to show some talent as a singer, there was no problem getting me enrolled in the state conservatory. Acting school came later. At sixteen I married one of the instructors. My first big mistake. Kazakhstan was the second. Never marry a man who wants to go home to Alma Ata. The place sounds far more romantic than it is.

Time to go.

The auditorium is small. Badly lit. Bare save for a huge portrait of the Boss along with Lenin, Marx, and some smaller photos of Odessa writers. There I am, side by side with Paustovsky and Kataev.

A big audience. Hard wooden chairs, all occupied. Some people sit cross-legged on the floor. Others lean against walls. From the podium I see Bagritsky of the Housing Bureau next to a heavy woman in heavier makeup. His wife. Loaded with jewels that even at this distance look fake. The smile of a shark about to devour its prey. Nearby sit Katya, Lyosha, Dubinsky, other faces of old family friends. Nikitich sits alone, erect, looking straight ahead. Josif and Moishe stand up and raise their thumbs. Others in the crowd look vaguely familiar from the streets, the markets, my past.

At the back. In a dim corner. By herself. Potato Face.

The club president, with gray hair, gray face, and gray suit, drones an introduction. If he's a writer, I'm the King of Siam. Even this local club has its watchdog. No deviations from the line, comrades. Nothing negative that cannot be redeemed. Socialist Realism today, tomorrow, always.

I try not to listen. But the last few words get through: *A name well known to we who live in Odessa. A man who has helped to put our city on the literary map of our great Union of Soviet Republics. The creator of Benya Krik, a character we would be tempted to call King of Odessa did not our Socialist principles forbid such bourgeois titles. Our own Isaac Babel.*

Applause, cheers, whistles, shouts. I gesture for silence. Bow.

Thank you, thank you. In Odessa it is always good to bring along your own audience.

Clapping, cheers. A disturbance at the door as Jacob pushes his way into the room. Steps on toes as he struggles into the row where Josif and Moishe sit. Heated words, a bit of a scuffle. Someone stands, gives him a seat, moves noisily into the aisle.

In Odessa any audience feels like my audience.

More clapping, shouts. I begin a talk given in various versions on different occasions in recent years. A talk in which intonation, emphasis, gesture help to carry the meaning. A talk jammed with ironic and playful words, phrases, and sentences that will sound serious when committed to paper in shorthand and read aloud in a police station or government office.

Thank you all for coming tonight. This has been billed as a reading, but before reading, I want to talk directly to you. Some things are too important to cloak in the artifice of fiction. We live in times that demand that things be said directly.

You all know my old stories about the Civil War and childhood and Odessa gangsters. All those were written during an earlier stage in our social development. A time before a simple but profound truth had been pointed out by our most important literary voice: that we writers are not just entertainers whose job it is to help people to relax and enjoy their leisure hours. Our task as writers is at once more difficult and more serious. We know now, as our leader put it, that those who work with the pen are like those who build our great dams, factories, and canals. We are engineers—engineers of the most important element of the social order. Engineers of the human soul.

Recently we have entered a wonderful new stage in our society's development. Some of us who began writing at an earlier stage find it difficult to change our habits, styles, and patterns of thought and creativity. That is why I have had so much trouble in recent years creating stories. But I have learned one important thing. I have learned what kind of stories we need to write.

Today we can see that the first scaffolding of the edifice of socialism is coming down. Workers today have roofs over their heads, and bread on the table, and hospitals to care for them in troubled times. Now what they need are stories to match their lives. Not stories of Cossacks during the Civil War or of Odessa in the days before the Revolution. Today we need stories full of courage, fire, strength, joy, and passion that will match the courage, fire, strength, joy, and passion of those who are building the new social order.

Today we need a new style to match our new order, new words to match our people's accomplishments. How to find such a style? Let me point to the example of a man who doesn't have any professional dealings with words yet shows the way toward this new style. Look at how Stalin hammers out his speeches, how his words are wrought of iron, how terse they are, how muscular, how much respect they show for the reader.

A few people begin to clap their hands. Others reluctantly join in. I wait until most of the audience is clapping, politely but with little enthusiasm.

When I think of an audience consisting of workers and of Party district committee secretaries, people who know ten times more than any writer about bee-keeping, farming, and how to build gigantic steel plants, people who have been all over the country, I realize that neither I nor any of us can get away with writing empty, school-kid stuff. To write you have to be serious and to the point.

As for me, I am not yet at the point where I know enough for today's reader. So I keep silent. You might say I have become a master of the art of silence. Is this bad? Think of it: in a capitalist country, I would have long since died of starvation. I am not happy about my silence, but at least it proves something very important: we have a different attitude toward writers in this country. The Party and the government have given us everything—food, medical care, housing, freedom. They deprive us only of one privilege. The privilege of writing badly. Far better for us to keep silent until we learn how to write for our society as it is now. For our society as it will be in the ever more glorious future.

Applause. Scattered, polite, bewildered. I know the reaction. Expect it by now. Acknowledge it with a slight bow. A voice shouts from the audience, then another and another. They say, *This is Odessa, this is your* home. *We don't want speeches, we want stories, we want Benya Krik, old or new. Give us Benya Krik.*

I put my palms up toward the audience. Voices subside to a loud mutter.

If you insist.

Yes. Of course. We do.

Since this is Odessa.

Bet your life.

Only here, at home, would I dare share something not yet finished. A work in progress. The beginnings of a story. No more than a fragment. One from the old Odessa. You could say it is the beginning of my attempt to finish with old Odessa once and for all. So that I—so that we, all of us, including my characters and my imagination—can move at last and fully into the Odessa of today.

21

*S*o you want to know what happened to Benya Krik? How the mighty fall. How the King was deposed. You with the glasses still on your nose and a touch of autumn in your heart. You who are at a stage of life when endings are more interesting than beginnings. And closer too.

Well, you have come to the right place. Who knew the King better than I? From the beginning to the end, I picked him out, followed every step of his career, saw him pull his first job right here, in the cemetery, as I sat on this wall dressed as I am today, in black. I, Arye Leib, looking as much like the rabbi that I am not as the shammes that I am, remember that day better than what I ate for breakfast this morning. The rich, the poor, the clerks, the bankers, the ladies of the mikvah circle, everyone standing by the open grave of Sophie Rabinowitz, may she rest in peace, president of the women's division of the Brody, patroness of the Jewish Home for the Elderly, sponsor of the bilingual kindergarten—Hebrew in the morning, Russian in the afternoon—and generous donor to every other good Jewish cause, and there are more causes than you can point to even with your nose, one that is long enough to lead us out of Egypt and all the way to the Promised Land.

Everyone is damp, and not only with tears. It was the worst time for a funeral but God is not someone who thinks about the weather when he takes us to our reward. He's got more important things on his mind. So Sophie Rabinowitz is buried on one of those midsummer days when the sky is like a bowl of hot chicken soup pouring over everyone in their dark suits and dresses and tight shiny shoes. And because she is who she was, the speeches go on and on and people get hotter and wetter and all they can think about is not poor Sophie and all she has done for our community, but how nice it would be to take off their clothes and jump in the ocean or drink an ice-cold glass of kvass.

People in such a place and time don't notice what's happening around them. And what is happening is that a little boy named Benjamin is slipping through the crowd, lifting a wallet here, a pocket watch there, a money clip *somewhere else. So that when poor Sophie is finally tucked away in the nice cool earth, and someone, trying to pay for his beer and his wife's ice cream at Fanconi, learns his wallet is no longer with him, and someone else misses a train back to Kherson because he has no watch to give him the correct time, little Benjamin is under a tree in the corner of the cemetery, dividing his loot. One third for his mother. One third to buy a bicycle for his timid friend, Reuben, whose family can barely feed themselves. One third to buy that stunning ring in the window of Kramer's jewelry. He can hardly wait until he sees the expression of gratitude and love on the beautiful face of Vera Slobodnick when he puts it on her finger.*

You could say that I knew Benya Krik before he was born and I know him still, after he has gone to his reward. Not that he believed in an afterlife. He was from Odessa, after all. This is a practical town, a place to make money, start a revolution, have a love affair. In a sense, Benya was Odessa. To know what happened to him at the end you have to know what happened in the beginning, even before he was born. You have to know where he came from and why. You have to know Odessa.

The name is interesting enough for a tale or two. It's Russian for Odysseus. Legend has it the great Greek stopped here on his wanderings home from Troy three thousand years ago. Not exactly on the direct route to Ithaca, but in those days who knew from maps? Think of them, the Greeks, the founders of our world. What do you see? Wild tribesmen in skins, slaughtering goats on the beach, cutting them open and trying to read the future by pulling out the kishkes and studying them. They eat, they drink themselves into a stupor, they fall asleep, they wake up in the morning and begin to play leapfrog and hurl spears and run races. Before you know it, they have invented sports. Soon we have Olympic games. This is what they call the golden age of Greece, the beginnings of Western civilization.

The next three thousand years people fight over these sandy bluffs and crumbling ravines—Goths, Huns, Lithuanians, Tartars. You name them, they've been here. The Russians take the town away from the Turks in 1794 and soon Czar Alexander gets the bright idea of getting a foreigner to help create a modern port. So he comes up with the Duc de Richelieu, then temporarily unemployed, a refugee from his hometown, Paris, where people like him are in danger of having their heads lopped off. The Duc is smart. He knows on which side his matzo is buttered. To Odessa he invites anybody and everybody who knows from business: Greeks, Italians, Armenians, Germans, Jews. His reward: more pages in our history books than in those of his native land. And a statue, the famous statue at the top of the famous steps, the Duc in a toga facing out to sea. Why this direction? Now you ask a question that we never tire of debating. One school says say he is looking for the ship to take him home from exile. Another thinks that only by facing this way can he keep the dust of the steppe—and until you know our dust you don't know from dust—out of his eyes. Me? I think that nobody in his right mind could spend eternity facing the heart of this land of perpetual chaos and tragedy.

Jews are not always in their right mind. To Odessa we were invited, to Odessa we came, in Odessa we stayed. We who wanted to get away from the shtetl, with its long coats and the rabbis always telling you what to do. In Odessa we cut our hair and took off our yarmulkes and went to work, and soon some of us were wearing suits of English wool and giving money to build hospitals, and schools, and magnificent synagogues like the Brody. We began to publish newspapers in Yiddish and in Russian, and we sent our kids for violin lessons, and in school they learned how to read French, and we all went to the opera. We loved the opera.

To live like a god in Odessa. That's what they said all over Eastern Europe in the mid–nineteenth century. It was the only place in the whole Russian empire where there were no restrictions. We could own land, attend Russian schools, work as traders and union leaders. In Odessa there were Jewish city councilmen to make the laws and Jewish gangsters to break them and Jewish policemen to arrest them. We were one-third of the population by the time of the first pogrom.

You thought Odessa was free of pogroms? Think again.

History is history. Always there was some tension between us and them. As we did better some of them began to feel that they were doing worse. So every once in a while somebody punched somebody in a bar, somebody threw a rock through a window, a small group of somebodys set upon another group with clubs or bottles, and a few noses and fingers were broken. That was the extent of the damage. But in 1871 things got back to normal. History with a capital H returned. The night before Easter the usual mob of Greek sailors are gathered in the courtyard of the Orthodox church at the corner of Trotsky and Catherine, which due to shifts in the population now happens to be smack in the middle of a Jewish neighborhood. These Greeks have just ended the annual forty-day fast—forty days with no alcohol! So they are drinking and whistling and yelling and breaking bottles. None of this is new. What is new is the rock that comes sailing over the wall, strikes one of the sailors and knocks him to the ground.

Was there really such a rock? Does it make a difference? Out of the churchyard comes a mob, throwing stones, breaking into stores, setting fires, beating up everyone who gets in the way and quite a few who don't. All the police have suddenly gone on vacation, so there is nothing to stop the sailors from spreading out through the city and continuing the party. Three days later when the governor-general steps out on his balcony to deliver a speech, a stone conks him on the head. An hour later, one of those miracles for which our land is justly famous occurs: the police are suddenly back on the job, mounted Cossacks appear, hundreds of people are hauled into jail. The disorders, as the newspapers call them, end. By standards of the next century, our century, the toll is small: Six dead, twenty-one wounded; twelve hundred houses and businesses damaged or destroyed. No world record for a pogrom, but not a bad first effort.

I'll skip the later pogroms because already I can see you are wondering about me. Is his mind wandering? Why the history lesson? What does this have to do with the end of Benya Krik? What is this long-winded shammes trying to tell us that we don't already know? Where there are Jews there is money being made and where there is money being made there are pogroms. This is worthy of a story?

If you will listen and try to remember what it was like to have summer in your heart, the point is simple. We are what we were and making things different is a lot more difficult than pickling a cucumber. Benya is the King because he lives the promise and the dashed hopes that are Odessa. He always puts aside for his mother and for our mothers too. He always buys bicycles for friends who can't afford them and never forgets that the Vera Slobodnicks, whether they are ten years old or eighty, need rings on their fingers and sweet words in their ears.

It is attitudes like this that get him in trouble. It is attitudes like this that lead to the end.

But I see you are tired. Hungry. That you have to go home to your mother or wife. When you come again another day, I'll get on with the story. Right now I'll give you just a hint. The end will come in 1921. Right here in Odessa after the

Whites have gone and the French sailors with their colorful uniforms have van-ished from our streets and the reign of the commissars has begun. A time when pogroms are over and we don't need Ducs anymore because Russia, after cen-turies of tears and prayers, is at last run by people who know that all people, Christians, Jews, Muslims, Hindus, suffer and hope, laugh and cry, work and steal, live and die, alike.

22

$\mathcal{S}$ilence. A very long silence when I finish reading. They are wondering about the voice. So Yiddish. Wondering about the history. Trying to figure out what I am doing. So am I.

Eventually someone starts clapping. Someone else joins in. The applause becomes general and the shouts begin: *Is that all? More, we want more. What happens next? You can't stop now.*

I bow. Hold up my hands for silence. Explain that if they want to have me back next year, then maybe I can read them a completed story. Besides. There are other writers in Odessa who have much to say and say it well. Young poets and story writers who understand today's realities far better than a relic like me. The new generation must have its chance. So I have invited some of them to fill out the evening.

Soft groans from the audience as four young people climb onto the stage. In the book trade, the term for what I'm doing is bundling. All too common these days. You want to purchase something popular? Something that has been published in a limited edition? The only way the store will let you have it is as part of a bundle that includes the sort of books nobody really wants. Books issued in huge press runs by the state publishers. Books that are good for you. Marxist theory. The Boss on the history of the Party. Academic economists on the depredations of the kulaks or the need for better management of collective farms.

A few brave people slip away. Lucky them. I refuse offers of a seat and lounge against a wall at the back of the room. Only half listen to the words and phrases that describe our glorious present and even more glorious future. The turbulent smokestacks of shining Magnitogorsk. The churning coal mines of deepest Donbass. Gaudy sledgehammers dancing on Turksib rails. Love triangles on state farms: a man, a woman, a new creamer for the collective.

Eventually we get to the polite applause. Chairs push back, feet scrape, people clear throats, stand up, move toward the doors. I catch Potato Face for a moment, whisper that we must meet. She nods, says *Check the post office tomorrow,* and turns away. Nadja takes my arm, glances toward the retreating stocky figure, and laughs: *Should I be worried?* At the reception a crowd swirls around tables laden with vodka, wine, hors d'oeuvres, cheese, fruit. No shortages in Odessa. Not for famous writers and their friends.

The scene is too familiar, the conversation more so. Everybody needs to ask me something, tell me something, share a question, a memory, an opinion, a fear, a hope. With the local writers, I praise the remarkable clarity and vigor of their images, the precision of their tone, their ability to so well capture the dynamic spirit of our times.

Dubinsky bores in on me: *You call this poetry? This is what the tradition of Pushkin has come to? Let me remind you, young man. The synagogue is where you will hear real poetry.*

I'm sorry. I've been busy.

When aren't young people busy? You think my own children are any different? Always too busy to visit. Never enough time to hear the word of God. Remember, I tell them, none of us lives forever. Not me. Not you.

Across the room, Nikitich touches hand to eyebrow in mock salute and disappears. Jacob tips his hat and does the same.

Moishe complains: *From you we need a history of Odessa? For history we've got books by professors we don't want to read. Now you're going to give us a reason not to read you?*

Josif complains: *Don't kill Benya. It's a mistake, I'm telling you. You'll be sorry. Odessa needs him. The world needs him. The Revolution needs him. Let him lie low somewhere. Hide out in France or Canada for a while. Then appeal to his sense of pride. The Boss's sense of justice. Have him come back to take part in the five-year plan. Even gangsters need a production quota.*

Writers need another set of eyes and ears.

Across the room, Katya and Nadja huddle in a corner. It's always a mistake to let the women in your life meet. Sisters, mothers, wives, girlfriends, always have more to say to each other than you can imagine. They always cast knowing glances your way.

I don't have to hear them to know the words.

So you're the one who's been spending time with our Isaac? We never see him anymore. What good is a nephew if you never see him? Bring him to dinner some night, we'll get acquainted, you and me. He's a good boy but he works too hard. I'll cook a meal you won't forget. In Odessa everyone knows my brisket!

He's told me all about your cooking. Don't think I keep him away. Isaac seems to keep himself quite busy.

Just like his father. Next week maybe?

I'll try to get him there.

Bagritsky in my face. More to the point, Bagritsky's wife. Hair piled high. Jewelry blazing. Eyes ferocious. Her jaw must hurt from a smile as wide as the Volga.

Marvelous, simply marvelous. Isn't he marvelous, everyone. Izzie, may I call you Izzie, you're marvelous. You're Odessa. Isn't he Odessa? What would we do without him. If Odessa didn't already have Isaac Babel, we'd have to invent you. We'd have to invent Benya Krik.

Nadja looks slightly seasick, the way I feel. I hold her tightly by the hand. A Packard whisks us to the London Hotel. Up we go to the rooftop dining room with a view of the harbor. Crowded as always with elderly Americans who speak both Russian and English in loud voices with equally heavy accents. The menu is two feet tall. Twelve pages long. It features thirty-five kinds of appetizers, eighteen salads, twenty-six main courses.

Bagritsky takes it out of my hand as I am counting the desserts. Tells me to stop, they don't have 98 percent of what they list. Leave everything to him. From a waiter wearing a tuxedo he demands caviar, smoked salmon, beefsteak, champagne.

Mrs. Bagritsky takes me by the arm.

Call me Yevgenia.

She turns to Nadja. Leers.

Let me borrow him just for a while, dear. You have him every day and every evening, don't you? Isn't that enough?

What does she want from me? What do people always want from writers? The secret. That special something they think we have. The stuff we know. Our fascinating lives. Our adventures. They never accept that there is nothing fascinating about sitting at a desk most of your life. Adventures happen to the characters you create. Writers sit and think until our heads hurt. We push a pen along paper. We wonder if anyone will care about the words that reach the page.

Other than the censor.

In that way, we Russian writers have always been lucky, perhaps the luckiest writers on earth. For centuries we have always had at least one reader who pays very close attention to every word we publish and even to a great many of them that never get beyond the stage of handwritten scribbles on crumpled sheets, tossed into wastebaskets.

Bagritsky likes alcohol. He orders champagne, wine, vodka, cognac, then keeps trying to top up our drinks. I sip and smile and begin to hold my hand over the glass. Yevgenia laughs a lot and shows her white teeth. She leans close, strokes my forearm, and whispers things not really meant to be heard. It's only the husky, suggestive tone that counts. I respond with equally incomprehensible murmurs but resolutely refuse to stroke her arm or touch any other part of her. When sometime between the main course and dessert she puts her hand on my knee, I stand up and stalk off toward the men's room. Bagritsky lumbers after me. Annoyed at the way his wife has been acting? Not at all. We stand next to each other and both sigh the way you sigh at a urinal after a certain age. He goes into a semicoherent ramble about Nadja and Yevgenia, how beautiful they both are, how luscious, how lucky I am, how lucky we are. I busy myself with my zipper and try to figure out if this is only the alcohol speaking or if he has, as I fear, something racy on his mind for the rest of the evening.

I cough, clear my throat, don't respond. He gets the idea that whatever it is, I'm not interested. Over the washbasin he takes me by the arm, puts his face close to mine, and words tumble out with passion:

Izzie. You don't mind if I call you Izzie? I like you Izzie. You're a good guy. And we have to stick together, right. We Jews have to stick together. So I have to tell you. Be careful. Something's up. Zirinovsky's been talking about you on the phone, and I saw a file on his desk with your name on it. It was not one of our files. He put it in his briefcase and took it home. Zirinovsky's a real apparatchik. He's lazy as can be. He never takes things home.

I throw my arm around him as we go out the door.

Thanks, my friend. I doubt that it's important. There's always something up. But I'll be careful. Thanks a lot.

At two in the morning, Nadja and I walk on the beach, our heads crowded, our stomachs heavy and distended.

I can't do that ever again. I can't ever do that again. You don't know what it steals from my soul.

Nadja runs ahead. Twirls around. Bubbles over with words:

Steal? Steel smokestacks against a Lenin-red sky. Steal the thunder of Thor. Steel yourselves against the stealing of exploiters' stolen souls. Souls? The marching soles of proletarian boots will trample the stolen souls of our corroded class enemies.

My expression must encourage her.

I speak in silent tongues to deaf ears. I am an engineer of silence. You hear only what cannot be said. That here in this glorious land we are free from freedom.

She puts her hands on my shoulders.

I never would have believed it. You have a rare talent for speech making. A unique way of turning a phrase. Anyone who can speak such words should go into politics. Join the Party. Give the masses what they want. Better yet: convince them they want something else.

To convince anyone of anything I would need a ghost writer. Are you looking for a job.

She shakes her head.

Not at all. I'm too busy with my own work. Not just on the film. I'm writing a screenplay about a woman who has taken to hanging around with a famous writer. She's an experienced actress but this is a role she hasn't played before. Here's the interesting twist to the plot. He's not a Muslim but he already has two wives. Maybe more.

Is she in love with him?

That's the part I haven't written yet.

23

The morning after. I am groggy, full of aches and pains, but what can you expect at this age. Face it. You are forty-two and feel older. Vulnerable. Not the person you sometimes imagine you are or would like to be, the one who walked the streets of Petrograd two decades ago ready to take on whatever life had to offer. That feeling of what you might call immortality vanished about the same time as your ambition. But who can remember exactly when that was?

Long after the summer of 1915, that's certain. Twenty-one I was and ready to pawn my soul in order to gain success. I put my diploma from business school into an envelope and mail it from Kiev to my father in Odessa, buy some crudely forged papers in the market place, and head directly to St. Petersburg. An engineer friend lets me use his couch as a bed, feeds me when I have no money. Which is most of the time. During the day I hang around morgues, police stations, libraries, and editorial offices. During the evenings, turn out short essays and stories about morgues, police stations, libraries, and editorial offices. When I get fed up with the frozen, foul-smelling streets of the capital, I begin to write about Odessa. The homesickness that gnaws at my stomach turns into a literary manifesto. Twenty-one and virtually unpublished, I predict that soon, from the sunny southern steppes washed by the Black Sea, will come a literary Messiah whose words will make the chilly wastelands of Russia bloom with the warmth of the south. You don't have to look very far beneath the lines to understand that the author of this manifesto sees himself in that heroic role.

What I have forgotten to remember is what happens to Messiahs.

Provincial journals have begun to print some of my trivial stuff, but the day Gorky opens his arms to me is the day my career begins. He puts my sketches into his publication, the *Chronicle*. Finds me a place to hide away when the police come looking for the author of a story deemed pornographic. The resignation of the czar saves me from prosecution but plays hell with my sex life. In the winter of 1916 and 1917 I am earning money by helping the wife of a rich attorney translate the short stories of Maupassant for a new edition. We work in her enormous living room with contemporary paintings on the wall and antique pieces of Sevres and Capa di Monte set on pedestals. Her low-cut silk dresses slide over nipples that seem to be perpetually erect. One night when we are drinking old muscadet, she calls me a funny one and takes my arm. An hour later I am wondering for the first time about the origins of the strange scars on her back that seem luminous in the dark, but over the next two months I never get up the nerve to ask about them. Each frosty night I walk home through tunnels carved in fog by street lamps, singing aloud in a language I am in the process of inventing.

The February Revolution ends plans for the edition of Maupassant. The October Revolution ends everything else except excitement. I linger in Petrograd in the spring of 1917, watching the birth of what some people call a new world. Some new world! The windows along the Nevsky Prospect are dark, or broken, or boarded up, and the pavement is lined with the carcasses of horses, legs in the air. Men in bowler hats use slices of bread to strike bargains with hookers. The factories of the Vyborg are all closed, cold, empty. People fight over garbage heaps, poke holes in each other with knives, throw themselves or each other off bridges into the Neva River, bleed to death in the streets. But no police come to investigate, no ambulances arrive to pick up the wounded and dying because there is no gasoline. Not a bus, a truck, or a private auto moves through the streets. The horses that might pull wagons have all been carved into steaks at the slaughterhouse.

For months I am hungry and cold, in danger but never afraid. Not even that day in an alley off the Morskaya when a heap of rags, with a red star on a filthy army cap, holds out a hand. I grasp it, pull him to his feet. He smiles, presses a knife against my throat, uses the most polite form of speech to ask for everything I have. Okay. But there's not much. A pen, a hundred rubles (enough to buy a single cigarette if you're willing to bargain for a long time), a crust of stale bread, a piece of hard cheese. He is delicate enough to refuse the handkerchief, sensitive enough to let me keep the notebook and pencil. Touching fingers to his cap, he wishes me a good day, sinks back into a heap.

Were those really the days I remember, or is it all only another story. To take more pleasure in the past than in the future is to admit your age. Maybe it's time I do so. This is certainly a morning when I can't shake the past. Ghosts keep demanding recognition. On the trolley ride into town, Aunt Bobka sits beside me, points to huge, elegant villas (now windowless and crumbling) with huge formal gardens (now wild and weed-choked) and warns me to be careful when choosing my friends. Hurrying toward the post office, I see a distant figure, Schloime Roten-stein, waving from the park table where we used to sit to play marathon games of chess on Sunday afternoons. He always beat me. He's still beat-ing me. Schloime knew what he wanted to do and did it.

At a traffic light, an ethereal Stolyarsky looks at me like I'm the one who is a ghost.

Babel? Isaac Babel?

It's no vision, but Stolyarsky in the flesh. Grayer and more di-sheveled than ever. Wearing a flowing necktie and spats. His long arms wrap around me. He delivers kisses on both cheeks, then smack on the mouth.

My Izzie. It's been too long. How I've wanted to see you, to tell you that as bad as you were on the violin, you are that good a writer. Better. You are a credit to us. Thank God I was never able to teach you a thing.

I mumble the kinds of things you say, then ask about his current stu-dents, his health, his family. He ignores the questions.

Not that I am fond of your portrait of me. The crazed music teacher. Do I really shriek and fling my arms about? No. Do I bob and weave? Not at all. Sure I move a bit, I admit that. I feel the rhythm of life. You exagger-ate, but I understand. That's the prerogative of an artist.

He is shrieking. Flinging his arms about. Bobbing up and down like a prizefighter ducking punches.

You must come see me. Hear my new students. Have you ever heard Oistrakh? He's a genius, a master, a credit to us all. Odessa. What talents we have. Come visit. You tell stories and I'll play. Promise. Come soon.

Waiting in line at the post office, I tap my foot. In honor of Stolyarsky and my own musical career that never was. The clerk hands me three envelopes. On a bench in nearby City Park, I open the one that has no return address.

Potato Face. Laconic on the page as she is in person.

Today. Thursday. The Jewish graveyard. Four o'clock.

An envelope with Nina's precision handwriting. Good news. Work on the subway is ahead of schedule. She will get the entire vacation and be able to join me in the Crimea for the full two weeks. Yalta, Massandra, the vineyards, the scenic drives are calling to her. Best of all, we'll be able to do it together. She already has her train reservations. I must remember to arrange a car. She can hardly wait.

The third envelope is covered with the huge, messy scrawl you would associate with a disturbed person in an institution or a diva who has no time for common things. Kashirina! After so many years. The envelope is thick, stuffed with pages. When I tear it open, two small photos fall to the ground. One of them shows the two of us side by side, my arm around her, my eyes squinted against the flash. I am wearing a white dinner jacket for the first and only time in my life and looking suitably stiff and uncomfortable, and I have more hair than I can remember. She is radiant in a tiara and the low-cut gown of a princess or an expensive hooker. It's a reception after one of her triumphs, but I can't remember the name of the play. The other photo shows her holding hands with a serious-looking child. My son, Misha, perhaps three, four years ago. He looks about five, blond as any Russian, light eyes staring solemnly into the camera.

On the way to the cemetery I remember Bagritsky's sweaty face close to mine in the washroom, then push the memory away. What he said is not pleasant but not surprising. Can it be true? It may as well be. If not Zirinovsky then someone else. Secret dossiers fit nicely with the headlines of these summer days. The demands of factory workers, farmers, aviators, scientists, and athletes that we smash the Trotskyist spies. Save the motherland. Get on with the heroic task of building socialism.

Hard to believe anyone is going to let K escape. Yet you never know. Stranger things have happened. Trotsky got away and lives to tell the tale, but you have to wonder for how long. An enemy abroad can be useful for the Boss. It's one way of getting the country to rally round the leader. Give some substance to the notion that the counterrevolutionaries are getting ready to return. Strike first. Don't let them take away everything we've gained.

I walk beneath the huge stone portals of the Second Jewish Cemetery, push open the wrought-iron gate, pass the empty guard box, soon see Potato Face in the distance, standing by my father's grave. Even from a hundred meters away it is clear that Odessa is affecting her style. A print dress falls close to her ankles. She wears summer shoes, a hat with a wide brim that puts her face in shade. I approach, resisting the impulse to call out. There is a large bouquet of flowers on the grave. I stand next to her, bow my head. She saves me the trouble of mentioning them.

Men never remember flowers. Her voice has less edge.

We stroll and I tell her about Jacob and the two thousand dollars we need to get the job done. It seems like a lot of money to her too. Isn't there any other way? I stall, then reluctantly I tell her about Nikolayev. The guys in jail. She nods from time to time.

You lived in Nikolayev when you were a kid, right? Your father had a business there. When's the last time you visited there?

Thirty years ago.

Maybe it's time for a short trip? Time to meet a chief of police? You like policemen, right? You find them fascinating.

I find lots of people and places fascinating. Somehow I doubt that the chief of police in Nikolayev is going to be one of them.

Maybe it won't be necessary. She'll check a few things out. Contact some people. Make some calls. It won't take long. She'll be in touch.

I ask if she happens to know a guy named Zirinovsky who works in the local housing office. Potato Face shakes her head. No. How could she? She's a stranger here. This is her first time in Odessa, remember? I'm the only person she knows south of Kiev.

She turns away, then turns back. I think again of that micrometer. Something very like the beginning of a smile is playing about her lips. The only part of her face not shaded by the hat. Her lips in the sun are nice, shapely, full. They speak words that startle me.

Mr. Babel. You're rather enjoying all this, aren't you?

127

24

My dearest dearest darling Manuilych,

    I know, I know, I know you very well, my yiddishe *babushka. I know exactly what you are thinking at this very moment as you read these very words you are thinking why the photographs what does she want. Have you looked at the photographs? Do you remember that night after all the champagne in the hotel room at the National you were feeling so rich? Always the grand gesture, you were grand at that, taking the honeymoon suite for a night, the royalties were rolling in then, they couldn't keep* Red Cavalry *in the bookstores no matter how many they printed and the Germans gave so much for their edition, the whole world was at our feet. I wouldn't let you undress me, remember, I wouldn't undress myself, I wanted us to make love with me in my gown, a queen and her slave and I wouldn't let you use your hands you had to take my panties off with your teeth and you kept complaining it was hot under the dress and the petticoats. You were always good at complaining too, heritage we used to laugh, we laughed so much, what happened to all the laughter we used to laugh. I wouldn't let you come up for air for the longest time until your jaw was sore and your tongue and I said alright, my slave is a prince, come to your princess and you came we both came like it was the first time anyone ever came like we invented coming. God is my witness, nobody ever had a tongue like yours, in all these years no other like it that is what I miss, can still dream about your head between my legs, my sweet babushka, your lips, your tongue. Okay so I like to talk dirty, I always liked to talk dirty and you liked it too even if you always sounded like a monk, an old rabbi when we were out with others and I asked someone about the size or smell of their lover's genitals and did they like it doggy style and you drew back with the look of someone who wanted to run away or to kill me as if you couldn't decide which and later you would sulk or criticize or both but never once did you reach out and hit me, I wouldn't have minded, really, a good smack now and then from my lover, not too hard just enough, it would have turned me on even more it still would, but you were too Jewish for that, too much under the thumb of your mother still, are you now? How is the old lady? I chased her all the way to Belgium, lucky her. She owes me some thanks, is she still there? She couldn't stand me and your sister not to mention Zhenya, the frozen one. What I rescued you from, what we taught each other. I chased her too. People tell me she is still in Paris and you are still telling people you want her back all the while you are living with another woman and sniffing out how many others? But I want you to admit I was the best. Better than the best. I saw* Sunset, *not the best of your works and the production was rotten, but that was me, I know it, Mariya was me, so Russian, so blond, the kind of woman for whom you will give up everything, lose your life. But only fantasy. In real life you give me a child, you make promises, and you leave. Just like that, I couldn't believe it. Okay so it wasn't just like that. I can admit it now I had Misha on purpose, it was a way of keeping you, or so I thought, you talked so much about wanting children, worried that Zhenya would never have one not after six years and no pregnancy but then again not much sex either. Or were you lying about that? Izzie you are such a storyteller, you don't know what is fiction what is fact, it's like it's all just words to you. God knows what you tell people about me, about us, not that you are one to gossip but I can hear your voice talking about Moscow in the twenties and saying yes, that Kashirina, a beauty (give me that, babushka, you know it's true, you could never get over it the little Jewish boy has his Russian queen), how could I resist. She pursued me everywhere, didn't care that I was married, stalked me with the relentlessness of a bounty hunter. Your wandering eye, your endless tales of travels and war, your oh so innocent seductiveness, your cute Jewish ways, do you mention those, do you wonder what's a straight-up Russian girl to do. I was twenty-five. Twenty-five! With a husband, a child, a career, and bored, oh so bored when you came along. The world lit up, babushka, for three years life was written in flames. I leave my husband and you leave me, I could have died. I think I did die. When Zhenya left for France and your sister who also did not like the sight of me and your mother I thought you were through with your all-absorbing family problems, I thought the time had come at last to take care of us. It was a fatal mistake, for only then did I come to realize that for you us did not exist.*

You existed and I existed but separately, there was no we. I remember the excuses well, commitments, family, you need space, you can't be tied down, you have to travel you have to write you have to see things but you meant you had to be famous and run around the world and some of the things you see are other women, women without children, women who don't love you so much and don't think that I don't know about Yezhova in Berlin and I have right here one hundred and seventy-one letters from you that I will keep forever, and this includes the two from Berlin when you and she are Russians abroad, getting acquainted with a foreign capital and each other. Yes I wrote to break it off. I got tired of your lies, the way you would say one thing and do another, so I remember what I wrote, Leave Me Alone and Never Write to Me Again. And you haven't. God knows, I didn't mean the words forever. We have a son and never once in ten years have you tried to see him. He is our son, even if I am remarried and Ivanov agreed to adopt him, even if he does not have your name he is Our Son. If you are still wondering why the letter let me tell you that I am wondering too why I write after so long. Except I don't have to tell you about the times, the way the world is closing in even on someone without politics like Ivanov, I worry for him and I worry for Misha and me. People tell me about you, you are as secretive as ever, always on the go to various places in the country even if you are not writing so much anymore, at least not anything we ever get to read. I know you see Sergei, know you are working on some film with him, I meet him from time to time but tell him not to mention me to you. He is the one who told me you were in Odessa this summer. That's one place we never went to together, it was a mistake, I remember how you talked of the town, how you loved it, how you had hopes that the summer sun of the Black Sea would spread north, warm this whole country, make it sunnier, a more hopeful place. I know lots of that was your ego, your hope that your words would do that for us all, make us all a little Jewish perhaps even though you did not like to use that word, and maybe you did that for us for a while but not now. Sometimes I would like to talk to you again, you always had a way of explaining things, saying what we could learn even from all the things that were happening we did not like. More of them, so many of them are happening now I don't have to spell it out for you but remember me sometimes, look at these pictures and remember and write or call and come to see

your son. Ivanov won't mind, he is the best of husbands and the best of fa-
thers but blood is blood and we have mixed ours in Misha, he is the future
we did not have together. Will you read this and say she is crazy and long-
winded as ever, I know you well don't I even after all these years. Okay there
is a favor I want if you have the connections that everyone seems to think
you have. Tell them to keep away from Ivanov. Sometimes he shoots off his
mouth too much but he is a harmless sort and I need him. Misha your son
needs him too so for old time's sake talk to the people you can talk to. Life is
difficult enough already it would be impossible without him trying to deal
with a ten-year-old and a career when nobody seems to want to hire me
much anymore. Some part of my heart all these years and in the years to
come belongs to you. Take care of yourself my yiddishe *babushka. Think of*
me sometimes. Think of us.

Yours forever, Kashirina

25

*W*aiting. Not my favorite pastime. Nor a skill I have ever perfected or wanted to perfect. Hurrying has always seemed the natural way to live. As if there was never enough time for all the going, seeing, doing, and then turning it all into words. But this is clearly a new stage. A summer of waiting—waiting to be cured of asthma, waiting for K, waiting for Benya Krik to let go of me, or me of him, waiting for a passport to go abroad. And now, waiting for Potato Face to tell me what to do.

In theory, waiting should be a good time to push forward on the Benya story, but it's slow going. My mind is too much on today and tomorrow and next week. And on the issue of how to survive, a skill long honored in this country. We have to keep our options open, stay light on our feet while the world keeps changing around us and the Party line shifts. We have to be ready for almost anything in this era, when the unimaginable can so suddenly become the real.

What was less imaginable than what happened to writing, the glory of our culture. Who could have imagined the sudden rage for finding and promoting real proletarian writers. Militant Party members insisting that the words of any coal miner, steel worker, sheep shearer, or lumberjack were inherently poetic and truthful, and certainly more valuable than those of any longtime professional. What a mad belief—that by holding a shovel, plough, hammer, sickle, or by driving a tractor or a truck, you have earned the right to have your words published, the less poetic and less grammatical the better.

Ending that nonsense was one of those rare acts by the Boss you can wholeheartedly applaud. Even he, with his tin ear, couldn't stand the unspeakable drivel that ended up on his desk. They say he still reads late at night, still scrawls a poem now and then as he did in the old days. Nothing about love or building dams or harvesting wheat or digging coal. The Boss specializes in satires of government inefficiency, caricatures of members of the Politburo, acid criticisms of himself. Aides secretly get them into circulation and they are widely enjoyed, memorized, repeated, and finally overheard by informers who report them to authorities. The poems get inserted into dossiers and are used in trials of wreckers and Trotskyists as evidence that they hope to overthrow the government.

A leader with a sense of humor. Just what every country needs. The Boss as prankster. We all laughed for months at his public pronouncement earlier this year: *Life is merrier.* Lately it seems less funny when we see the phrase plastered on banners hanging over the entrance to every public space in the land.

Give the devil his due. For some people life has been getting better, merrier. No longer is it a crime to have middle-class parents, grandparents, great-grandparents. Or to have been born in a home where there was a piano in the parlor and untranslated foreign authors on the bookshelves. The new constitution gives everyone, even the children of the bourgeoisie and the detested kulaks, the right to attend universities, work at decent jobs, vote in elections. Not that it provides for any choice in those elections, but you can't have everything.

Another sign of the times: free love is out, marriage is in. No more instant weddings in registry offices. I was as shocked as Zhenya at the abruptness of our ceremony.

Just sign here, said the clerk.

We did.

You are now husband and wife. Next.

Is that all? Zhenya asked me. *No blessing? No congratulations?*

The harassed clerk waved us on and called the next couple to his desk.

Today we have Wedding Palaces. Speeches that invoke the name of the proletariat. Champagne toasts. Men in dark suits and women in white dresses, who sport gold rings. Women who talk of fixing up kitchens and buying rubber plants for their living rooms, who dream of refrigerators, radios, and bedroom suites made of birch. Some can even afford them. Some in the Party now have kitchens that don't have to be shared.

This is not the world I remember. Not the world we foresaw. It was not for refrigerators and rubber plants that the son of the rabbi of Zhitomir braved his father's curses to join the godless Bolsheviks, sneaking away to enlist in a unit of the Red Army under the name Bratslavsky. Not that I had time to ask him about kitchens or anything else. He was long past voicing thoughts when we pulled him out of the mud near Kovel, a pale figure without trousers, his genitals as open to the elements as they were on the day he was circumcised. We eased him into our cart, gathered up the scattered contents of his pack, tried to make him comfortable, but his flesh was torn in too many places for him to survive more than a few hours. Fifteen years later, I can't remember exactly what I packed back into his kit. The actual items have long been replaced by what I later wrote. It's a choice moment in *Red Cavalry*. The belongings of the dead rabbi's son become an emblem of the crazed strands of our Revolution, an emblem of redemption and hope. Did I believe in that redemption? Who remembers? But the image was touching enough to draw more than its share of tears. I always found it difficult to understand how something so metaphoric could be taken so literally. That readers could believe the boy's pack could actually contain all that I described: small portraits of Lenin and Maimonides, leaflets by Trotsky with marginal notations in Hebrew, published resolutions of the Sixth Party Congress bookmarked with a strand of female hair, a notebook with lines copied from Kropotkin, Mark Twain, and the *Song of Songs*.

Children. Marriage. Families. In this one area I have fulfilled and overfulfilled my production quota, comrades. Call me a Stakhanovite of women and give me an award: not the Order of Lenin but a trip to France. Evidently I'm not yet through. But this is not the time of life to fool oneself about someone named Nadja. Can we still believe in something called love? An emotion at once too easy and far too difficult to feel. Yet something tugs me toward her despite our first two meetings, in the theater and then in the Moldavanka. Or is that the attraction? The erotics of the unknown, the seduction of suspicion.

By now it's far too pat. Nadja has so many days off camera that we are free to do whatever we want to do together. Some nights she stays over. I find her sandals in my closet, a lipstick on the bathroom shelf.

If this were a work of fiction, I would have to flesh out this relation-ship, provide more details about her life, desires, beliefs. Recount the funny incidents she relates about the things that happen in the studio and on the set—the arguments with the director, the repeated delays when the power fails and all the lights go off just as the camera is begin-ning to turn. I would have to share our intimate moments—the feeling when I open my eyes to the storm of Nadja's hair spread across the pil-low, the passions, the looks, the wonderings, the intimacies. On these pages, writing for myself, I don't have to do that, don't have to describe all those things we have lived too many times and know too well to be-lieve unless they come to us as words on a page.

Just as well. This new voice I have chosen, the voice that has chosen me, is not one in which you can speak of sex or love. Not without a touch of irony or a tidal wave of self-consciousness. I never have been able to write about love, unless that word can be used to describe the longings of a child for a world he'll never understand. Some people read moments of love into *Red Cavalry,* but if love is there, it's only because in that world it was being murdered daily. To write of love you have to use adjectives that make everyone uneasy these days, choose metaphors that died peacefully in their sleep decades ago. The atmosphere of this century has become too thin to sustain the language. It's a wonder any feelings can survive so long after the words for them are gone. Can they?

Somber this morning as I wait for Nadja to awaken. From the writ-ing table, I cannot see the sea. Dense fog shrouds the bluffs. A hint of seasonal change. Summer cannot last forever. When she calls to me, I re-turn to her arms and we hold each other quietly for a long time, then climb down the rickety wooden staircase to the beach for a swim. Back in the house, I am suddenly tired of caution. I want to share something, so I bundle her into the car and we head off toward the end of the Foun-tains, top down, sun pouring onto our heads, dust billowing around us. At the Sixteenth Station I turn up a steep dirt road and roll to a stop high on an embankment overlooking the sea. We stand on rutted earth, barren save for a few yellowing weeds. Below us a jagged path that leads to a small cove, a beach of stones. The nearest villas are barely visible.

Breathe deeply, I say. *Take in the air. A unique fragrance, full of the dryness of the steppe, the salt of the sea, the powder of the hillside, the faint aroma of dead plants. It's a smell you find nowhere else on the coast. Nowhere else in the world.*

Nadja sniffs. Looks puzzled.

Deeper. Take it into your lungs.

She inhales with an expression that says: What's he talking about? What's so special?

I tell her what I have told nobody else, including Nina. The smell is special because this plot of land belongs to me. I bought it three years ago as a place to retire. Here in the sun I will finally escape the gloom of Moscow, the directors who always want quick rewrites, the assignments from magazines that have me staying in awful hotels from the Donbass to the Ukraine to Magnitogorsk, gathering material for stories whose titles, assigned by ambitious editors, make me retch: *Building a New World of Steel. Building the New Man. Building Collective Farms for Collective Happiness.* Here I will be calmed by the stillness of the countryside, live out my days to the rhythm of the sea. It's an old tradition. Russian writers on the land. And now it's possible. Water lines from the city reached here last year. I can build a house, plant trees and a garden. Write stories about country life.

Nadja giggles. It's not what I expect. She apologizes, then giggles again.

What's missing from the picture is the family. The patriarch needs a family. An aging wife, children, grandchildren, holiday dinners. But which family? In your case, there seem to be two, three, who knows how many? You'll need a very big house. Separate wings. A palace.

Women know when you are talking about love. If that's what we are really talking about. If we can really talk about it anymore.

Nadja knows I am thinking things I cannot say. But she doesn't want to hear them. Not now. She knows it's necessary to divert me, get my mind onto something else. So it's her turn to tell me she wants to share something too, something just as precious to her, the story of a screenplay on which she has been working for years. One she cannot seem to finish. A story about the forgotten priest of a small church in a far-off valley in the Ural Mountains, so remote that he never has any contact with the church hierarchy. A priest sworn to celibacy who is, the villagers think, quite mad because he hears voices, talks aloud to himself, delivers sermons so crazed, so incomprehensible, that people no longer attend the Sunday services or have anything else to do with him. One stormy night a half-naked peasant girl with a starving child arrives on the doorstep of the church. Voices speak to the priest, tell him this is a holy woman whom he must help and cherish. He takes the mother and child in and feeds them. He ministers to the child. He forces the mother into modest dresses. He makes her attend mass three times a day. He storms around the church at night chanting prayers aloud. But she proves to be rebellious. A lustful woman who sneaks away into the huts of male villagers at night and sleeps with them. The priest finds out and locks her up, but she escapes, enters his room and climbs into his bed. Raging with desire, he tears off her clothes. Just as he is about to enter her, the voices call to him again, say that this is his chance. The woman is Mary, mother of God. If he makes love to her the resulting child will be Christ reborn. So he will be the father of God, but he also will be damned to eternal hell for the sin of violating both his vows and the girl. The priest hesitates, but the girl, her face beneath him twisted in passion, reaches out, wrestles him down to her burning body, moves against him, takes his throbbing penis in her hand and pulls it toward her vagina.

Nadja stops.

That's all?

That's all.

What happens? How does it end?

I don't know. Maybe you can help. Say, for example, you were the priest. What would you do?

26

*A*t the post office in the morning, a small package and another note from Potato Face. Unsigned, but I recognize the neat handwriting. Good news. The deal is done. All that I must do is to meet with the police chief of Nikolayev and Jacob's boys will walk. The expenses for the boat will be covered. There is no explanation as to why the chief needs to see me, but at the bottom of the page the final phrase suggests there is more to this woman than you see on the surface: *Bon voyage!* Maybe the explanation for the trip is the package. Attached to it is a note addressed to me: *Give this to the chief in Nikolayev. Your colleague, friend, and fan—Jacob.*

Potato Face and Jacob know each other? Work together? Why should I be surprised? Stranger things happen these days. What is stranger than the charges that K and Z are the murderers of Kirov, in league with Trotsky, saboteurs of the Revolution—the Revolution to which they have devoted their entire lives? Does anyone believe such things? No doubt plenty of peasants and workers are convinced, even delighted. Now they have somewhere to direct their anger over the end of the bread subsidies, the hard currency stores that they can't enter, the apartments and cars that people like me get to enjoy. K and Z are symbols of hopes that have been betrayed, of fat cats at the top, of Moscow, the Party, Jews. Getting rid of K and Z will no doubt make a lot of people feel really good.

Not me. Not even if I were not one of the supposed betrayers. Revenge is an emotion I have never understood, and destruction has never given me much satisfaction. What makes me feel good is writing, travel, touching the hearts of women. Not as isolated acts but as part of something larger. Revolution is the word we once used for all this. How we discussed it for years in school rooms and cafés, desired it the way you desire an exotic lover, even if we had never read Marx, barely knew the name Lenin, had never heard of Trotsky. One thing we knew for certain:

the old world was rotten. Change had to come, and the word for that change was *revolution*. We did not know what it would mean, but we got it, with all its painful lessons about the difference between reality and desire. The lessons took a while. During the February and October Days, in 1920 and even 1922, it was possible to believe that beyond the violence, stupidity, and growing terror, some great idea was yet about to unfold. We would live to see an end to exploitation, hunger, and disease, a world in which equality, justice, and works of great art would go hand in hand.

I hurry to the station, catch the train for Nikolayev for a long, dull ride through a dull, yellow countryside. An anxious ride, too. For once the words of Maupassant cannot distract me, so my notebook gets filled up. Writing is a good way of turning gloom into humor.

And really. This whole business is funny. Ridiculous. The notion that a political prisoner will escape and that I am going to help him. If I were writing this as a story instead of living it, I wouldn't dare put a character like me in the position of having to take action in such a situation. I'm the kind of character who dreams. Writes. But I certainly don't take action. Not really, even though I have long been fascinated by power and have hung around those who do. But only as a spectator. Mandelstam kept asking me about this last year when he was scurrying around Moscow, trying to find a way to end his exile, and I was giving all sorts of useless advice.

It's about the smell of power, not the taste. That's what I told him. *I like to see what it does to people who exercise it. How power makes them feel. How it gives them pleasure or pain. Maybe both.*

No secret that I am close to important people in the Kremlin. That I feel a certain odd thrill in seeing how they act. This has been in part a matter of chance, along with a way of using chance to my own advantage. Russia may be big, but Moscow is a small world where sooner or later you meet everyone. Friends, acquaintances, people you run into here and there, at the Writers' Union or in restaurants or at private parties: everyone has an agenda. So why not the guys at the top? Dzerzhinsky, Yagoda, Zinoviev, Radek, Kaganovich—I've been approached by each one of them, asked by each to open my eyes and ears for them. Always I put them off by pretending that I don't understand what they are asking. Some come at it obliquely: maybe I could just let them know if anything unusual is going on. Others are more pushy, direct: my observations would be worth something, perhaps a great deal. I never bother to ask what sorts of things they mean by unusual. I keep them wondering. Hoping that sooner or later Babel will be of help.

So far it has been they who have helped me.

I get around. I overhear things and ask questions. I pass on some of what I learn as warnings to friends and to friends of friends. Sometimes I visit a friend in an office to try to help someone. Last year I got Mandelstam bedded down for a few days before they caught up with him and sent him back to Voronezh. It's always like that. Whatever you do can be no more than temporary. People run here and there trying to buy a little extra time, but in the end they all go quietly. A dark sedan parked outside the apartment in the wee hours, a knock on the door. If you're smart, you already have a bag packed with the essentials. They never give you much time. People have been dragged away wearing no more than pajamas and a coat. Five years later in Siberia they are wearing the same pajamas but the coat is gone.

Father would not be surprised. He knew better than any of us. He had a single question that applied to everything: Is it good for the Jews? War, peace, a good harvest, a constitution, a duma, a new model tractor or automobile. All judged the same way. If no Jews were involved in some enterprise, he worried. If too many were involved, he worried even more. That was his complaint about the Bolsheviks. Too many Jews on the Central Committee. It was bound to come back to haunt us.

They can change their names. They can call themselves Trotsky, Kamenev, Zinoviev. They can claim to be atheists and close down churches and synagogues. But everyone still knows that they're Jews. The Trotskys can make the Revolution but the Bronsteins will have to pay for it.

Old-fashioned. Reactionary. An oppressor. It's embarrassing to recall the things I said to him. The names I used. But he always had an answer that was full of certainty.

You'll see. One day you'll see, but it will be too late. I won't be around. So tell it to your children. They won't believe you either. See how it feels.

Not that he was religious. He wore a suit and tie, cut his hair short and had a neat mustache. He went to synagogue three days a year and tried to fast on Yom Kippur, but he made such a fuss about the ensuing headaches that Mother went off to the rabbi and obtained a special written dispensation: owing to a serious medical condition Emmanuel Babel is allowed to eat a snack on Yom Kippur and still be considered an observant Jew. For the seder on the first night of Passover, Father used a Russian Haggadah. He cut so much from the original text and hurried through the rest so quickly that Mother's brisket was not yet fully cooked when he finished and said: *Bring on the food.*

In Nikolayev I learn another lesson about waiting. The police chief is busy today. For two hours I have to sit across a desk from him while he talks on the phone, signs papers, whispers to orderlies who rush in and out. Everything about him is big: head, nose, shoulders, hands, elbows, smile. So are the tattoos on his forearms. A naked girl on the left. A Star of David on the right. He makes sure I see it when we finally shake hands. He smiles, winks and nods knowingly, and becomes effusive.

Isaac Babel in my office. Welcome. What a red letter day. It's not often we get famous people in Nikolayev. To what do we owe the honor? I know. You must be looking for material. You want to hear about some of my tough cases. You're going to bring Benya Krik to Nikolayev. Put us on the map.

It's an act. He knows it. I know it. A convincing enough act. He takes the package, slips it into a drawer without really looking at it or even hefting it for weight. He doesn't want to talk about our deal or even about police work, but about writing. His great interest is literature. No doubt this surprises me. Have I ever known a cop who dreamed of becoming a writer? He tells me he's the first. Do I want to know why? Police work has its limitations. Besides, you can't stay on the force forever. So he has begun to write stories. About cops, Jewish cops. Nothing has been published yet, but just wait. His talent will soon be recognized. And since Isaac Babel seems to have bowed out of the cops and crooks business, maybe there is room for someone to take my place. Not that his stories are like mine. Not at all.

Here's my angle. You'll pardon me for saying so, but nobody's interested in gangsters anymore. Not even Jewish gangsters. Sure. Ten years ago your vision was a breakthrough. Who knew? Who even suspected? Jews cheat, they swindle, but they don't stick a gun in your head. Why not? No balls. Jews don't have balls. So you were right. For then. But people are fickle. They get tired of the same thing. Besides gangsters are passé in this day and age. Why? Because we live in a world filled with gangsters. The government is run by them. People want to feel safe. Protected. They want to hear about cops who can take care of the gangsters that threaten us. So if these cops are Jewish, that's the real news. Everyone knows that Jews bargain. They argue, they write books, they pray, but Jews don't arrest people. They don't beat people with rubber hoses to get confessions. What a surprise. It will shake up the Black Hundreds and all the other anti-Semites. Here's the message: watch out or we'll arrest you. We who are wearing yarmulkes and prayer shawls will bust your ass. Imagine this. My hero is Orthodox. Every morning he puts on tefillin. Every afternoon he arrests a drunk, a dope fiend, a robber, a rapist. He has connections with jewelers, special insights into the ways of diamond thieves. Believe me. This is what the public wants. They'll eat it up.

I know what's coming next. It comes.

Isaac. You don't mind if I call you Isaac. I'm doing a little favor for you and your friends, so is it too much if I ask for a favor in return?

He opens a drawer in his desk, pulls out a thick folder, hands it to me.

You can see it coming, Isaac, can't you. This must happen to you all the time. So you know these are my stories. Do me a favor. Take a look at them. Let me know what you think. Give me a few pointers. One Jew to another. That's how we survive, right? We're a people who help each other.

I take the folder. Do my best to smile.

One more thing, Isaac. A very small favor for me that will be a favor for you, too. My guess is you haven't been to a synagogue in a long time. So for me, and for yourself, go next week to the old synagogue on Masterskaya and give this to my friend Rabbi Lubovsky.

He sticks a hand in his pocket and pulls out a tiny box, flips it open to reveal a beautiful silver mezuzah.

Give it to him personally. I know you'll enjoy meeting him. Hearing what he has to say.

He ushers me toward the door, his arm around my shoulder. I'm a great guy. He always knew that. Always knew he would like me if we met. A worthy representative of my people. More than worthy. As for his stories, don't worry or think about them too much. Just read them. Don't make notes. Don't send a letter. He'll find a way to get in touch. Nothing could be more important to him than the opinions and advice of Isaac Babel.

27

*T*wo Jews. Three congregations.

The old joke is now outdated. Call it another accomplishment of the Soviet regime.

The Brody Synagogue has been closed by order of the Ukrainian government. That pride of the wealthy and the nouveaux riches, that huge nineteenth-century structure on Pushkin Street with its Moorish windows and pipe organ that lots of pious folk thought belonged in some cathedral will soon be home to the state archives. Its longtime rival, the Ha-Gadol, is also boarded up. Thus ends a hundred years of struggle between the Reform and the Orthodox over the question of whether the Torah allows you to sell seats for the high holidays (the Brody) or insists that you must admit everyone who shows up (Ha-Gadol).

Nobody believes the official explanation: not enough people are attending services to justify the cost of keeping such places open. For this ignores what everybody can see before their eyes, that all the other synagogues, large and small, are packed Friday night and Saturday morning—from the tiny temple in Peresyp, with its retired stevedores and plumbers, to the congregation in Moldavanka, where Hasids whirl themselves into a state of religious exaltation, to the old shul on Masterskaya to which the police chief has sent me. I have to wonder: is it only coincidence that this is the temple Dubinsky attends?

Years since I last went to a service, but the atmosphere on the sidewalk in front, the noise, confusion, the loud arguments and shrieks—it all feels strangely familiar. Except that everyone seems so aged. The wrinkled women full of smiles. The stooped men with thunderous voices. Wearing a suit and necktie, I enter with Lyosha and Katya. People break into smiles, clap me on the shoulder, kiss me on the mouth, pinch my cheeks as if I am a bar mitzvah boy. The yarmulke feels alien on my head, perhaps because when last I wore one it didn't rest directly on bare scalp. An old man takes a prayer shawl off his shoulders and drapes it over me. Honored, I bow.

The service begins. The rabbi chants, the cantor wails, old men bob and mutter, then scramble to kiss the Torah as it is carried through the aisles. It's like being caught in a once familiar dream now long forgotten, a dream whose meaning is elusive, full of messages conveyed in a language I have never learned to understand. Some strange emotion presses up through my stomach, emerges as a quiet heaving in my rib cage, moisture in the corner of my eyes.

In a small meeting room after the service, I approach Rabbi Lubovsky, introduce myself, hand over the small box with the mezuzah. He looks like an actor who has been cast in the part—long white beard, twinkling eyes, powerful voice that grows gentle when he says: *Ah, so you're the one the police chief mentions? What a good man is our police chief. He cares for his people. Watches out for us. These are times when we need good men who care for their people.*

He opens the box, holds up the mezuzah, remarks on its beauty, says a prayer over it while making a gesture with his right hand of the kind that reminds you of a wizard. He replaces the mezuzah and hands me the box.

It's for you. Keinahora. *Put it over the door of your new house. It will bring you luck. No, better than luck, it will bring you blessings. Blessings are more important than luck.*

The elderly folk crowd around us applaud the sentiment, then pull me away to discuss my family.

Your mother, oy oy, *could your mother cook. Her blintzes were one of the wonders of the world.*

A mensch. Your father was a mensch, a real mensch! He only came to services on the high holidays and sometimes he was too busy even for that. But he was still a mensch and we still miss him.

Manny was here when we needed him. For the building fund, for the hospital fund. You could count on Manny.

Fenya. They don't make them like her anymore. She could knit. She could sew. She could run charity events. Raise money to buy new books for the cheder. What a woman!

Not religious, but he was a Jew. No doubt about it. Manny was a real Jew. He knew who he was.

You know what a Jew is, don't you? Someone who would never trust a Russian. Your father was a smart man. He did not trust Russians.

It's not only because of Nadja and my past. They are not talking of the father I remember.

No, not at all. My father didn't hate Russians. He insisted we are all God's children.

Mutters from the crowd. One man throws up his hands, tilts back his head, and looks toward heaven with eyes wide open.

We shouldn't live in the past, I say. There's nothing special about Jews. Today Jews are the same as everyone else.

Arms fly about. Hands make extravagant gestures of disbelief. People drift away, talking to themselves.

Emmanuel Babel knew, he knew plenty. Sons. They don't know from nothing. Sons! They never learn. What can we do with our sons?

What else is new?

At dinner nobody mentions this encounter. Maybe because Nadja has joined us. Lyosha is on his best behavior. He keeps refilling her wineglass, leaning over and telling stories that aren't very funny. Katya bustles about, heaping food onto our plates, bringing more and more dishes to the table, ignoring my repeated complaints.

Stop. Sit down. Eat. You remind me of Mother.

She relaxes over dessert. Fresh-baked strudel, honey cake, two kinds of melon, blackberries, coffee from Latin American beans that Lyosha nabbed as part of some shady deal. Katya holds out a pack of cigarettes, American cigarettes. She's the only smoker, but each of us takes one. She tries to grab mine back.

I won't inhale. Anyway it's a poor substitute. After a good meal I really miss a cigar. Getting healthy isn't all it's cracked up to be.

A surprise to see Nadja light up. A bigger surprise when she answers Katya's questions about her background with a different story about her family.

Cossacks. That's her background. Horseback warriors who settled near the River Don centuries ago. Fierce, proud people with their own land and governors. Traditional defenders of the czar, the status quo, privilege in all its forms. But it's a mistake to think all Cossacks are alike. Some go to school, some think about justice, some even support social change. Her father was one of those. Early on he took up the banner of the Revolution, volunteered for General Budyenny's cavalry, fought for two years in the Ukraine and Poland, and was wounded three times. But that didn't stop him. He rode into battle covered with bloody bandages, one arm in a sling, a blazing carbine in the other.

Red Cavalry is the reason she is sitting in this room. It was his favorite book. He would say: *Babel got it right. He's the only one who got it right. The complexity. We were revolutionaries and barbarians. Angels and devils. We committed atrocities and heroic acts. Killed people and liberated them. Such things are never contradictory. Quite the contrary. You can never separate good and evil.*

When Budyenny denounced *Red Cavalry,* her father became furious at his former chief for oversimplifying, for not understanding what his men had experienced, for his thinly veiled anti-Semitism. Her father always said that Babel was a man he would like to meet. He wanted to shake his hand, tell him that Budyenny did not represent all Cossacks, that he, for one, was damn glad someone told the truth about the Civil War. Jew, Gentile, Muslim. It made no difference. All shared the same land, the same God, the same Revolution.

He died a few years ago. A decade after her mother had succumbed during the typhus epidemic of 1920 and two years after the family land had disappeared into a collective farm. Nadja's inheritance was tiny: some furniture, his saddle and books, and his desire to meet the author of *Red Cavalry.*

Katya beams, claps her hands.

What a wonderful story. How romantic. You should write it up.

Lyosha has doubts about such a story getting published. Lyosha always has doubts. But on this issue he's correct. The moment for personal heroism is long gone. Socialist Realism demands a third-person narrator, a modest someone who doesn't dwell on the past but looks to the future. Someone prepared to tell us how to live together in the new world we are constructing.

Between the main course and dessert, Lyosha drags Nadja into the other room to show her the album of family photos. Me as a schoolboy without glasses and with hair.

Are they right about Father? I ask Katya. *The old men?*

Manny hated one thing and it wasn't Russians. He hated injustice. It comes in many forms.

I tell her something happened in synagogue today. During the service, I felt something I can't describe.

Maybe I'm more Jewish than I think.

Now you sound exactly like Manny. I don't know much about God, he'd say to me. But we need to believe in something greater than ourselves. So since we already have synagogues. . . . He wouldn't finish the thought. Instead he would open his hands wide as if to ask for a blessing. Or maybe to confer one. I never knew which.

28

*I*n the cemetery I ask Nadja about her father the Cossack, a rather different figure from her father the kulak. We have just put fresh flowers on the grave of my father, the merchant, on one of those sunny August days when even a cemetery can seem full of promise. She kneels down and says hello to him out loud. Thanks him for raising a son who is so generous and has given so much to the world and to her, then stands up to deal with my question.

Isaac the Literal. Who would have believed it? I seem to remember a character named Benya Krik getting married twice without ever divorcing or converting to Islam.

I think it's a mistake for you to read my stories.

How about the author whose childhood stories have him being raised by an aunt, his grandmother, his parents, all at the same time but in different locations?

We stroll toward the exit. Nadja skips a couple of steps, twirls like a ballerina and almost bumps into Professor Kalina. We stop. Everyone seems a bit flustered and out of breath. Except for the painfully young girl who hangs on the professor's arm. She wears a tight skirt, very red lipstick, high heels. He nudges her away, but she smiles broadly all through the awkward introductions. Nadja. My friend, Miss Kornilova. She's a new patient, new to Odessa. Needs to get out and walk as part of her treatment. I'm showing her around. Trying to give her a feel for the town.

Babel, where have you been? You've been missing appointments lately. Are you feeling okay?

He looks directly at me for the first time.

You look good. You look fine.

His right eyelid flutters slightly.

The treatments must be working. Something's working.

Another flutter.

Don't be a stranger now. We're not done with you yet.

I promise. We start to go our separate ways but he stops, excuses himself to Miss Kornilova and Nadja, and pulls me aside to say he almost forgot. There's something I should know. A woman came to him about me a couple of days ago. Not a very attractive woman. A woman with a lumpy face. She showed him some sort of credentials from a government agency and insisted she had to see my medical records. When he refused, she got pushy, then threatened him. If Professor Kalina did not cooperate, who knows what might happen to his sanitarium? That made him angry and he threw her out. But then he began to worry. Am I in any trouble? Should he have cooperated? But this would be immoral. The doctor-patient relationship is sacred.

Thanks so much. Don't worry. This sort of thing happens to my associates all the time. It's probably a spy from one of my publishers, wondering if I am really sick or just malingering. Publishers are ruthless.

We go our separate ways. Nadja can't refrain from looking back. She reports that Miss Kornilova is leaning against his arm, nuzzling his neck as they disappear behind a stand of trees. How interesting are the treatments at the Lermontov? I should tell her more. What do those nurses do with me? Do I get an erection when one blasts me with the fire hose?

We head into town, toward Fanconi. A small crowd swirls around a signboard outside a newspaper office on Pushkin Street. Everyone is staring at the headlines of the latest edition. The trial is over. It took one day. Kamenev and Zinoviev were given the death penalty. It was immediately carried out.

Others hurry away. I stand and stare.

Nadja takes me by the arm. Tugs. I stare some more. Stare through the headlines and through the blank wall. She pulls strongly, leads me to a trolley, but I am not here, in this car. I am somewhere else. In the past. Another city. A courtroom. A jail cell. A muddy street during a pogrom. My father kneels in the road. Behind him, a mob is looting and smashing his store. Breaking windows, tossing out through the smashed glass boxes filled with nails, papers, small cabinets, anything they can lift. A photo of me in a school uniform lands in the mud. The building goes up in flames. Father kneels at the feet of a horse. Above him, a Cossack officer, staring straight ahead. Tears run down my father's face. He begs. Captain, see what they are doing. It's my entire life, captain. Help me. Stop them. The officer looks straight ahead. Do what I can, he says, then raises his arm to signal the troop behind him. They ride down the street and around the corner.

Nadja leads me to the bedroom. Takes me in her arms. Touches me until my blood moves. I kiss her neck. Bite her shoulder. My teeth sink into flesh. She pulls away. I leap from the bed, roaring:

It's too much. Too fucking much!

It's nothing new. Just what you would expect.

She's a stranger. I turn away. Storm out of the room and into the kitchen. Yank open drawers and cabinets. Slam them shut. Nadja follows. Stands with arms folded across her chest.

What are you looking for?

There was some vodka somewhere.

You're not supposed to drink vodka.

They're not supposed to kill them. Zinoviev. Kamenev. I knew Kamenev. He was harmless as a fly.

I find the bottle, wrench it out of the cabinet, yank off the top, tip it up for a swallow. Nadja shrieks and tries to grab it out of my hand. I don't let go and we are wrestling over it, struggling, bumping, pulling at each other, grunting, swearing, two ferocious animals clawing back and forth until the bottle flies out of my hand, smashes into the sink, and shatters into pieces. Silence. We look from the sink to each other and back to the sink. Burst into laughter at the same moment and, heaving with emotion, collapse into each other's arms.

29

A morning alone with my own dark thoughts. How to assess the news? It is true or has some elaborate game begun? I hurry into town with the aim of finding out what is going on. But how? The newspapers and the conversations in the marketplace are full of stories about conspiracies. Trotskyists, wreckers, saboteurs are apparently hiding in closets all over the country. More trials of Party leaders, other Old Bolsheviks like Bukharin and Radek, are rumored to be in the offing. Just about everyone except the Boss seems to be under suspicion. Except for Z and K. Now they are history.

No messages for me at the post office. Potato Face has never given me an address or a phone number, here or in Moscow. I don't even know her name. So I put in a call to police headquarters in Nikolayev and get through to the chief immediately. His voice booms through the receiver.

You've read my stories already? What do you think? Am I a worthy successor to Isaac Babel?

No. Not yet. I've been busy. I'll read them soon.

So what can I do for you?

You know that woman who sent me to you?

Woman. What woman? It wasn't a woman. I got a call from a former colleague in Moscow who said you were coming to Nikolayev. That you had something to give me from him.

I promise to read the stories and hang up. My impulse is to phone people in Moscow. Perhaps Shtainer, to see if anything has happened at home. But this is no time to talk to a foreigner. Better would be friends in the Writers' Union, but there's nobody there I fully trust. Sergei would be a possibility, but he's somewhere on the road and will arrive here in two days. Yezhova is another, but her husband no doubt has the phone tapped. The ones who would really know what's going on are the hustlers on the Arbat. But they don't have private phones.

I hurry to the Moldavanka. Jacob said never to call on him, but there's no harm in strolling along the street. By the fourth time I march past the sign S. KRAPOLINSKY. HAULING, MOVING. YOU NAME IT, WE CARRY IT FOR YOU, Moishe and Josif put in an appearance. Today they wear suits, ties, hats, gleaming shoes. They treat me to a glass of wine at a café that looks out on the marketplace. A ship must be in from the Caribbean. The stalls are selling pineapples, even those normally devoted to antiques, clothing, books. Vendors grab customers by the arm, yell into their faces, undercut each other, and drive the prices so low that one thing is clear: the pineapples have to be stolen goods.

The guys confirm this, brag that an entire shipload of cargo was lifted from the docks. A job worthy of Benya Krik. The old spirit of Odessa is alive and well.

Moishe wonders when was the last time I had a pineapple. Not in years. He crosses the street, takes half a dozen from a stall without paying, crosses back, puts them on the table in front of me, pulls out a knife, and cuts one open. We all eat.

To help the creative juices, they say together.

And how are my juices flowing these days? is what they want to know. Not too freely. Too bad. But Josif and Moishe are happy to suggest a few ideas that may help. It's important to make Benya's love life more active. People are more interested in sex than in crime. Get him into bed with two women. Or three. Women of different colors, shapes, sizes. Describe the smell of their silky cunts, the soft wetness of moist tongues sliding along swollen genitals, the feeling of sharp, polished nails, raking Benya's back.

Their breathing is getting heavy, their faces red. Not from the pineapple.

You guys should give up this life. Join the Writers' Union. God knows we need some new talent. But before you do, go and tell Jacob I need to see him. He'll know what it's about.

Next day at the post office I receive a plain envelope with my name and in it a single typed page with no signature. Only the message: *Don't believe everything you read in the papers. There will be a delay. The plan is still go.*

What plan? asks Jacob.

Our plan, I say. *Remember?*

We are sitting in the same café across from the marketplace, breathing the stench of rotting pineapple. Crushed skin, hacked-off tops, trampled slices cover the ground and fill the gutters. All the merchants look a little queasy. On the table before us, the note.

I don't know from any plan that involves stuff in the newspapers. The only plan you and I have made has to do with a cruise. A sea voyage for someone's health. Everything is ready. There are many possibilities for vessels. It will take only a few hours to arrange things once you give us the word. But you need to hurry up. Even the best plans don't last forever.

Does he know anything about the trials? Anything that didn't make it into the papers? He plays coy. Trials? What trials? The Moscow trials. The trials of Zinoviev and Kamenev. Oh, those trials? No. He only knows what he reads in the newspapers. What about his friends in the capital? The ones who checked up on me. They must know lots of things. Is he in touch with them? What things? he asks. Things about the sentences. Were they really carried out? Are K and Z really dead? Am I implying, he wants to know, that our deal may have something to do with the trials of Trotskyists? He's shocked and dismayed. Certainly he would not want to undertake anything that might be unpatriotic, anything that might help an enemy of the Soviet people.

I'm not enjoying this and I tell him so.

Listen my friend. Some things I can talk about and some things are best left unsaid. There's no percentage in gabbing about them. So let me subtly change the subject and give you a big thanks. My boys are free. Back on the job. They wanted to be sure that I thanked you. So did their wives. Their children. Their parents. Their brothers and sisters. Their grandparents. Their friends and neighbors. Their cats and dogs. Their landlords. You did a good job with the police chief. We're all grateful.

Job? What job? I handed him a package. Agreed to take his stories home with me.

That's what did it. The package is one thing. But Isaac Babel agreeing to read the stories, that's distinctly another. That man would do anything to have his stories read. To have them published. Have you read them?

I shake my head.

He's always calling me. Wanting to know about illegal activities. He's into the criminal mind. Wants to know what makes us tick. Tradition, I tell him. Everyone needs to belong to something and for some of us this is it. But he thinks, No. There's a type. A psychological type. He asks questions. Lots of questions. Do I love my mother? Do I beat my wife? It can be annoying. He doesn't listen. It's poverty, I tell him. An unfair distribution of wealth. Here in our Socialist society based on the glorious slogan, From Each According to His Ability to Each According to His Needs. Follow that like you follow the Golden Rule and even the great tradition of criminals will vanish. But no. In this country we're like everywhere else, only we add hypocrisy. In other countries they're more honest about their dishonesty. In other countries everyone knows there are the rich and there are the poor, whom you always have with you. Here we are all equal. Only some are more equal than others. Far more equal. Look at you, Isaac. A house, a car. You shop at private stores, you go to restaurants in hotels, you travel around, you go abroad. Okay, you used to go abroad. Past tense. But you're not even that high on the ladder. You're not a Party member. Imagine if you were. The private clubs, the Turkish baths, the stables, the masterpieces on the wall, the sterling silver, the suits from England, the shoes from Italy, the buckets of champagne, the mansions in the Crimea. So you don't have to think about a criminal mentality, that's what I tell our friend the police chief. Think about people like me as some of the few trying to live up to the ideals of socialism. Redistributing the wealth. Working for the common good. You wouldn't believe how many people we help support. The hospitals, the synagogues, the Hebrew schools, the old-age homes. You think they get along on the pittance the government provides? The government wants to do away with all of them. Wants us all to forget our traditions, to die of disease, to get out of the way so they can have it all. But without us, what would be left? A bunch of goyim stealing from each other, putting each other in prisons, sending each other to Siberia, killing each other in the name of a bunch of ideas they don't even understand, ideas created by one of us, a nineteenth-century Jew named Marx who had his head in the clouds of German philosophy and who never had to work a day in his life. The only thing he ever suffered from was carbuncles and a wife who refused to go down on him. This is a man whose ideas we should live by? You'd have to be a crazy to think so.

30

*P*oetic justice.

You could call it that. Maybe cosmic irony. At the very least, a sign of change. A signal that time is running out.

Father's gold watch is gone. Chain and all.

I reach for it in the railroad station, where every wall clock seems to show a different time. The inside pocket of my jacket is empty. I do what you expect. Pat the other pockets, turn them inside out, look wildly about as if I expect to see someone running away. I check the impulse to call out, throw a tantrum, swear aloud, and instead punch my right fist into my left hand.

It must have happened on Catherine Street. At home I checked the time more than once. Saw it was late. On the slow trolley I looked at the watch again and saw it was even later. The downtown streets are crowded. I struggle toward the station. Faces are a blur, bodies no more than heavy obstacles to my haste. Desperately I try to remember a shove, a bump, a remark, a face, a pair of eyes. Anything out of the ordinary. Any clue as to who got it away from me.

A hand touches my shoulder. I jerk around angrily, ready for a fight, and look directly into a smiling face surrounded by wild tufts of hair that stick out in ten different directions.

Don't bite, says Sergei, stepping back. *I'm not that late.*

They just stole my watch. The sons of bitches. My father's watch.

Sergei kisses me on both cheeks and on the mouth.

They're picking everyone's pockets these days. Getting away with more than watches. Maybe it's your old friends. You're the expert on thieves in this town.

We go directly to the steps. Sit together at the top. Behind us, the Duc on his pedestal. Below lies a white church, huge warehouses, a harbor full of freighters, the gray hulls of naval vessels at anchor. People alone and in couples and groups climb up and down the esplanade. They pose for photos. Mothers with children and the elderly fill the benches in the park on the nearby bluffs.

By now this is a ritual. Every time Sergei comes to town, we sit here. Every time we have the same conversation. Only it's really a monologue. He talks. About these steps. How much he has come to hate them. Sure they made him famous, but they ruined him too. Ever since 1925 everybody has been waiting for another sequence as brilliant, stunning, innovative, and world-shaking. But inspirations like that come once in a lifetime. In your twenties when you aren't afraid. In our twenties when the world was not afraid. Remember when people cared about revolution and the new visions it would bring? Now it takes two directors to make an old-fashioned melodrama like *Chapayev* and everyone calls it a masterpiece. A Hollywood studio hack could make the same thing a lot more entertaining and it wouldn't carry such an ominous message: *Listen to the Party, comrade, no matter how smart you are, it always knows better than you.* Put Sergei on one of those destroyers in the harbor and he'd turn the big guns toward the steps and blast them to hell. Then he'd burn all the prints of *Potemkin* and everything that had been written about it. He'd destroy his past and everyone else's at the same time. Start all over. Invent film and montage all over again. Invent a new world.

I raise the issue of the trials. Obliquely. Beginning with a story that I have never told him. About the party at Gorky's, not so long before his death, when I asked Yagoda how one could resist an interrogation by his men. It is long past midnight. Long after all the vodka and wine with dinner and vodka and brandy afterward and more vodka. A typical scene with Kremlin jockeys late at night. Nobody is sober, not even me, and nobody is drunker, or laughing more hysterically or shouting more bad jokes aloud than Yagoda. I mean my tone to be playful, but the question seems to sober him up. He looks directly into my eyes and for a moment sounds deadly serious.

Deny everything. Keep denying everything no matter what we say or do. No matter how much we threaten you, deny, deny, deny, deny it all. Without your own words, without your confession, we are helpless.

He raises his brandy glass, roars with laughter.

Helpless, helpless, helpless. Imagine it: the NKVD totally helpless.

Yes, you have to have quite an imagination.

Sergei sounds gloomy.

What's the word in Moscow? I ask. How did they get Z and K to confess aloud in court to crimes they could never have committed before an audience of people who knew they could not have committed them?

You are forgetting how forgetful people have become. These days memory has become most inconvenient. I've been told the whole process was simple enough. The Boss sent word that if they confessed and if they implicated some other leaders and if they repented of their actions, he would let them go. So they confessed and implicated others and repented of their actions and were taken out and shot that night. Now there's justice worthy of a film!

Have you heard any rumors? That they weren't really shot. That the story is just for public consumption. That they are really hidden away somewhere. That they may be allowed to get out of the country.

Sergei gives me a look that says he knows such a story has to be a fishing expedition. But he's too good a friend to raise questions about the bait, the species, the water where I'm doing my angling. All he does is raise one eyebrow.

These days I would believe almost anything, but that's stretching it a bit far. The Boss is not exactly known for his generosity of feeling, least of all toward former colleagues. Remember what he told Krupskaya when she took a stand against him: You think you have something important to say because you are Lenin's widow, but you better keep your mouth shut or you won't be his widow for much longer. I'll get someone else for the job.

An old story, but one that can still make us both smile. These are times in which you need things to make you smile.

It's worse than you think, my friend. Worse than you think. You like to hide away in the Caucasus, in Odessa. You think you can get out of range. But you can't. We're all dancing on the edge of a grave. Hey! Not a bad image. Maybe we can work it into the film. After the mob tears the icons from the walls of the church and everyone dances on the altar. A bunch of peasants, drunk as can be, still moving in rhythm while they dig in the mud. Up to their knees, up to their waists. They sing aloud, they tumble one by one into the grave. A flight of white pigeons rises from the ground and swirls to-

ward heaven. Like it? You are coming to Yalta with me. You have to. There's no way I can finish the film without you. Hell. No way I can finish it even with you.

Sure. Nina is meeting me there. We're going to take a vacation.

Sergei holds his palms toward me, shrinks back in a humorous double take, and promises to be on his best behavior. To keep his pockets free of incriminating images. Not to let Nina into his room.

We smile together, remembering the first time I brought Nina to his place in Potylikha. My knock on the door is answered with his muffled request that we wait a moment. When he lets us into his large room with the huge writing table, many of the framed pictures on the walls are turned around so you can't see the images. It's an evening devoted to the souvenirs from his Mexico sojourn. Primitive pottery, bright serapes, carved wooden figures of peasants, skulls, demons. Most startling: the flea circus. In a box tinier than one for matches, a flea bride complete in a white gown and veil and a groom in black suit, shirt, and bow tie. I am looking through a magnifying glass, Sergei at my shoulder, when we hear a loud gasp. Nina has turned around one of the frames and is staring at a large photograph of a fat, hairy, naked man. She looks pale. Sergei shrugs and offers to turn around all the frames so that she can see his whole collection. She shakes her head vigorously and on the way home keeps saying, *So fat, so revolting, so immoral.*

This is not Siberia, I explain. Not the fifteenth century. Men or women, fat, thin, bald, hairy. It's only a matter of taste.

The next few weeks I catch her glancing at me suspiciously. Asking lots of questions. That story about the young man and the hooker in Tbilisi? The young man who says he is a virgin because he has been the prisoner of a homosexual older man for years. Is that based on me? Does it have any truth? Have I ever been with a man? Have I wanted to be with one? Sergei, for example. How long have we been friends? We spend lots of time alone together. Don't we ever do anything but write?

He's not my type, I tell her. Too short and stocky. Too disheveled. Too excitable. Too Jewish. Hasn't she noticed? I like slender blonds with long legs. Cool, self-contained women. Quiet sorts who can take care of themselves. Who don't ask too many questions.

Sergei chuckles.

Bathing beauties. Your were right, my friend. Better to have brides than Cossacks marching down these steps. Izzie, you should have come with me to Hollywood. Chaplin's pool was full of fifteen-, sixteen-year-old girls. Boys too. He has many talents, that man. A great eye.

I gave up on young girls a long time ago.

Oh, oh. I hear that old familiar tone. That serious rabbinical voice tells me there is a woman nearby. Why not? There always is. Let me guess. A midget from Ceylon. Doesn't have to get down on her knees. No, I've got it. A giantess from the Congo. Black as the ace of spades. Beautiful as Cleopatra. More limber than Pavlova. More acrobatic than Nijinsky.

An actress. A pretty good actress even if I've never seen her on the stage. I like the reality of her. Even though she's deeply unreal too. The way I figure it she's spying on me for someone or other. I'm not sure who or why I'm worthy of the attention.

Sergei throws his arm around me.

An actress and a spy. Double trouble. That's you my friend. Where did a good Jewish boy get such a taste for excitement? In Hebrew School? Did they make you read the kabbalah? Or is it just that Odessa weather you always talk about here? The mystical spell of the Black Sea?

Nothing mystical in this case. She's real enough.

My friend, you are one person who wouldn't recognize reality if it flowed over you like hot lava. You want to know reality, go to Mexico. Why did I ever come back? That's what I keep asking myself. I could have lived on a beach. In a hut under a smoking volcano. What beautiful bodies they have there, full, juicy, muscled. You wonder why I could never turn off the camera? Never begin to edit? Because of skin like you see nowhere else in the world. Michelangelo should have spent time in Mexico. It would have been a different Renaissance. Everything in brown marble. Thighs, butts, calves, backs, genitals huge enough to fill the Sistine Chapel.

We are silent, gazing at the scene below. Each of us preoccupied with genitals of a different sort.

Sergei. Let me ask you something I've never asked before. If you loved it so much, why didn't you stay? What brought you back? You had friends there, people who love you and love the Revolution more than anyone here.

Siquieros, Rivera, other artists. You could have made the films you wanted and lived your fantasies with none of the troubles you have here.

Another pause. He sighs.

It's something I wonder all the time, my friend. But there's no real answer. Slings and arrows are the closest I can get. Hamlet's right. Desdemona's wrong. The best I can figure out is that fantasy has to be kept away from reality if we want to keep it fresh.

$\mathcal{T}$he day before I am to catch the boat, Lyosha bangs on the door.

The mezuzah looks good, he says when I open it. *Another sign how the world is changing. I never thought my nephew would be taking a rabbi's advice.*

With Lyosha I always fear the worst, but the worst today is not so bad. Just a little unsettling. He has come with a message from the police chief of Nikolayev. He knows the chief? Not personally. The message has come through Jacob. It's a simple message. Don't go to Yalta. This is a time to stay put. Going to Yalta could be dangerous.

Thank the chief. Thank Jacob too. But I have a living to earn, and some obligations to a good friend.

For a farewell dinner, I take Nadja to the last remaining private restaurant in town: the Black Sea. Specialty of the house is bluefish. Nobody knows how this place manages to stay open. To get a reservation you have to use pull or foreign currency. The Writers' Union comes in handy. *Of course, of course,* the secretary says. *We'll be happy to get you a table.*

We order champagne. Real champagne, not the local imitation. I find myself talking a lot. About Eisenstein the genius, Yalta the beautiful. The villa I plan to build with tiles imported from Italy for the roof, floors, bathroom. A place like Gorky had in Sorrento, with big sofas and chairs, a huge writing table, windows that open to the sea, and pine trees and cypress to shield us from the wind of the steppes. I can see her in charge of the lush garden. Bougainvillea climbing the walls in three colors: white, purple, orange. Wisteria to sweeten the springtime and shade the terrace. Arbors loaded with green and purple grapes. We will stretch out in the afternoon. Read, dream, make love, sip iced tea. Chew on sunflower seeds and spit the shells into the bushes.

A nice fantasy, she says. *An idyllic picture, but for whom? Or is this a marriage proposal? I'm flattered but you seem to have forgotten a few problems that stand in the way.*

Problems?

Me, for instance. I'm married. Remember? I have two kids. Are you planning separate bedrooms for each of them? One for my husband, too? Or can you find a bed large enough for all of us?

I tell her that I don't mind kids, quiet kids. Husbands are somewhat less to my taste. But she can't fool me. She's not in love with Boris. That's been clear since our first night together. She likes him. She admires him. But we all have to be adults: a mistake is a mistake. He's happy where he is and she's miserable. Kazakhstan is no place for an actress. We can let him visit the kids once in a while, say every year or two.

Odessa's not much of a place for an actress either. Besides, love is not the issue. Boris is great with the kids. Unlike some people sitting at this table. You don't have a great track record as a father.

A blessed interruption prevents me from answering. One that turns out not to be blessed.

Monsieur Babel. Jacques Dupont, journalist. Our mutual friend Boris Souvarine introduced us in Paris last year. At Le Dome, remember? What a pleasure to see you again. On your native soil.

For him, maybe, but not for me. Not at all. I don't feel like looking at his small mouth, speaking French, his pointed face, nose, chin, ears, all sharp, intrusive, inquisitive. Dupont's round glasses reflect the light of the chandeliers. I wish we had never been introduced. He is one of those foreigners who finds Russia and Russians fascinating. The kind who used to talk about the depths of the Slavic Soul but have, more recently, shifted to joys of the Great Experiment. The future of socialism. But he is French. Profoundly suspicious of everything and everyone but himself.

Without being asked, he sits down. Barely acknowledges my introduction of Nadja and gets right to the trials. What do I think? Were they fair? How well did I know the accused? Did I suspect them of Trotskyism? Were the sentences just?

Foreigners will be the death of us, always full of questions you cannot possibly answer without making trouble for someone, usually yourself. With such types anything you say may be published, embroidered with colorful details, no matter what they promise. My first lesson in this was with a Polish journalist who cornered me in Nice in 1927. My first trip abroad, my first time basking in the glorious sun of the Riviera. At the sumptuous bar of the Hotel Negresco he plies me with Pernod until I can hardly remember my name and asks questions about the Party, freedom to write, discipline, terror—who knows what else? My answers vanish into a fog of alcohol. No doubt I nod my head at the wrong time, murmur yes to something said by someone who seems for one drunken minute like a fellow human really interested in understanding the contortions that are becoming necessary for artists in the Soviet Union.

My reputation was a bit shaky at the time. It's only been a year since the second attack by Budyenny. Only two years since the public criticism of *Sunset* for morbidity and decadence. So it doesn't exactly help to have the lead essay on the front page of a Polish literary review depict me as a man who loves to lounge on beaches in the Riviera sun and hang out in the bars of swank hotels, denouncing Soviet policy toward the arts and artists and proclaiming how nice it is to breathe the free air of France. Russian newspapers pick up the story, spread it across the land. Babel is a decadent. A danger to the regime. What follows is the usual. Cries by apparatchiks that I have betrayed the trust of the motherland. Letters to the editors full of charges and countercharges. Months of investigations by the Party. Two lengthy inquiries by committees of the Writers' Union. It takes more than a year for me to get a full clearance, and after such accusations no clearance is ever exactly full. The Polish journalist is found to be a well-known anti-Soviet propagandist who hoped to discredit both me as a famous Soviet writer and the whole regime. But this judgment hardly ends all suspicion. Doubts continue to surface in journal articles or speeches at meetings of writers and Party officials. Whatever dossiers are being compiled on me in whatever offices grow thicker.

Memory makes me ready to be rude. I am about to tell Dupont that of course the trials were open and fair, in accordance with the provisions of our new constitution and our code of laws, when he drops his voice and cuts in with another question: What do I know about the rumors that Kamenev and Zinoviev weren't really executed, that someone spirited them away? That maybe Stalin let them go? What do I think about the idea that they weren't even in the courtroom? Foreign colleagues at the trial swear that the defendants didn't look quite like themselves. A Dutch journalist was certain they were doubles. An Italian insisted that years before he had seen the one who was supposed to be Kamenev in a minor role at the Marinsky Theater.

Dupont looks expectant. For a moment I can't find my voice. When I do, the words come out on their own, for my mind is elsewhere.

Haven't you been here long enough to learn that rumors are one of our chief products for export? We create them for gullible foreigners. It's a way of raising hard currency.

He objects. *Be serious, monsieur. These are serious times for your country, for the world. If those two were allowed to get away, it must mean some great change in policy.*

My turn. I ask Monsieur Dupont something I have been wondering about for years. How is it that foreigners who spend a few days or maybe even weeks in our country, with all its different cultures, regions, and ethnic groups, foreigners who don't speak our language or understand our customs, become such instant experts on everything Russian? How come they ask questions to which they themselves are ready to supply the answers? And how come if we don't tell them what they already know they act as if we are imbeciles? But maybe we are imbeciles in the eyes of foreigners. Is that true, Monsieur Dupont?

His retreat is flustered, angry. I turn back to Nadja.

Fame. It's wonderful. That's what you're after.

An actress needs to act. I might be willing to give it up for directing. Get me a job at the Odessa Studio. Tell them they need a woman to get behind the camera. That might be an incentive.

She puts her hand over mine, says she has to tell me something. If I want to see her again, I must hurry back. Three, four more weeks and the shoot will be done. She has obligations. A home. The villa is a dream, a very nice dream. But it's my dream. She likes the villa and she likes the dream and she likes me. She might even use the word love if one could use that word without complications. But there are complications enough in her life without me, and in mine without her. If I am honest.

Quelle surprise, as Monsieur Dupont would no doubt have put it. These are the sort of words that usually come out of my mouth. When I get around to using words. More often in the past I've just slipped away, then followed with a letter full of sentiments far easier to express on the page than in person. Women go for letters in a big way. They trust the written word far more than the spoken one. Or maybe it's just the mixture of the practical and the romantic. Letters can be reread, relived every day. For me they have been a way of avoiding the inevitable: the tears, the clinging, the back-and-forth, the heated arguments that always follow.

The villa was, after all, only a kind of test. A provocation, just to see how she would respond. But I am surprised at the feelings that take hold of me after her announcement. They are not feelings I care to describe.

I don't tell her that I will be meeting Nina in Yalta. For all the reasons that you never tell one woman about another. Plus one more thing. Whatever happens or does not happen, something with Nadja has made me understand that the time has come to explain to Nina that the time has come for us to go our own ways. She is smart. She will know I'm right. I have long warned her that we could never be permanent. The difference in age is one thing. But it's mostly a matter of lives at different stages, on different trajectories. When the subway job is finished, a hundred opportunities will await her. She may well be asked to join the Party. But not with Isaac Babel in the wings. Use me, is what I always told her. You can learn a lot that will help you. But do me a favor: don't ever confuse learning with love.

32

*Y*ou with the glasses on your long nose. You're still hanging around? Still waiting to hear about the end of the King? So come close. Don't make me shout. Not that I am not proud of the story and my part in it, but my voice is not what it used to be when I witnessed the rise and fall of Benya the First. Okay, okay. So you know about the rise already. I promised you the fall and the fall you will get. Sit down on that tombstone. It's nice and comfy but not so comfy that you will fall asleep while I talk. A fitting place from which to watch the follies of mankind. And womankind, too, for let's not forget we are only half of this business of living, and not the fairer half. You don't agree? Let me tell you something: Benya would. From women he knew. Give them a flower, a ring, a hug and they will help you get to Paradise. Don't and you remain forever outside the pearly Gates of Eden.

Like with more people than you would imagine, it was the Revolution that led to the end of the King. But before you get to the end you have to start at the beginning of the end. Which is the War. The one to end all wars. Our King was, you should believe it, a patriot. He loved his hometown and he loved its people, and as long as the government left them and him alone to make a tidy profit, he loved it too. The war, like all wars, was good for business, better for business than for the government, but that's another story. An army needs wheat, uniforms, guns, boots, ammunition. All these things have to be shipped from one end of the country to the other in long, long trains, and if a boxcar or two gets shunted onto a siding, who will notice or care? The train is still longer than any train you ever saw before the war, and if a few bellies are empty at the front or a few soldiers have to march through snow in bare feet, well, you can be sure that the law of the conservation of energy is still in force. Somewhere else in the country a bunch of someones with very full bellies are walking around in nice new boots.

On the docks it was the same. Benya had the stevedores tied up, so that freighters from England and France were always unloading much more stuff into the warehouses than ever made it from those same warehouses to the railroad station, let alone the front lines. This new branch of foreign trade was thriving so well that Benya grew bolder and his assistants careless. With the result that one bright afternoon Benya, while climbing the outside stairs of Mrs. Mugenstein's apartment, was seized by four French sailors holding carbines and an officer who wore a hat with a plume on top and had a sword hanging against his striped right leg.

At least let me pay my respects, *said Benya. But this reasonable request was ignored. What a shame! Benya's visits were the highlight of Mrs. Mugenstein's social calendar. Regular as a clock, he had arrived at her place once a month for the seven years since her only son was accidentally killed during a robbery by one of Benya's thugs. Benya—who knew?—did not believe in accidents. To even things out, he took care of his thug and the two men were buried on the same day, not far from each other in the Second Jewish Cemetery, each with a single bullet hole in him. Over Mugenstein's open grave, Benya delivered a moving funeral oration. But it was the splendor of the event, planned and paid for by Benya, that earned him his title. The black coaches, the white horses, the crowds of well-dressed mourners, the members of the Society of Jewish Salesmen, the groups of attorneys, physicians, midwives, chicken pluckers, the marching bands, the elders of the Brody Synagogue, the sixty boys of its choir, the mountains of flowers—all these led my friend Moiseka the shammes to turn to me, right here on this very wall where I now sit, and nod in the direction of Benya, who was at that very moment driving away in a black sedan with the horn of a phonograph sticking out one window playing an aria from* Pagliacci. *Moiseka leaned against my shoulder and whispered in my ear the immortal phrase:* That man is a king. A real king. At last we Jews of Moldavanka have a king!

For seven years, Mrs. Mugenstein and Benya drank tea together, and ate slices of her strudel, and she reminisced about the old days when her son was still alive. How much better things were before the war brought so many foreigners to town. Ukrainians, Austrians, British, French, Bulgarians, Romanians. Odessa was crawling with Romanians, with their sad dark eyes and their gold teeth and their women who wore such bright lipstick and way too much of it. Many more things than usual were disappearing from the stands in the Greek market, that's what all the merchants said, and who was to blame but the Roma-

nians. It's part of their tradition, explained Benya. It was their only tradition so far as Mrs. Mugenstein could tell. What a problem, she said to Benya. Can't you do something about the Romanians?

If he mumbled words that sounded like a yes, it was only to please Mrs. Mugenstein. Benya, you should know by now, was not a man who had any quarrel with Romanians or anyone else. He was a businessman. He knew very well that a certain amount of stealing was the lifeblood of the economy. Good, too, for diverting eyes from his own activities. Besides, for all their poverty and furtive reputation, Romanians were an upbeat people. They opened nightclubs and cafés on Greek Street with gambling tables in the back room. They sang aloud, banged cymbals, danced and drank all night, and were always willing to handle hot merchandise, no questions asked or answered. They were, in short, very much like Odessans writ large, so why should he do something about them?

A couple of hours after being seized, Benya sits in the cabin of a French destroyer anchored outside the port. In one hand, he holds a glass of brandy, in the other, a good cigar. Across from him sits the captain of the ship, Jean-Pierre Bonnard, a man who looks so surprised and pleased you know that he must have expected the king of the waterfront to be a thug, not this elegant, handsome figure in a dark suit with a flowing necktie. A translator hovers above them, but he doesn't have much to do because Benya—wouldn't you know it?—has for years been sneaking away from his boys to attend language classes at the Alliance Française. He knows French well enough to express his innocence. To say to the captain: You are an officer from a republic with a great tradition of liberty, equality, fraternity. You are a man of the world. So you must know how it is in Russia. Something goes wrong and whom do they blame? The Jews! They can't help it. Old habits are hard to break. But as a businessman who has long honored France, who considers your country my spiritual home, I would never condone the theft of wartime gifts from our great ally.

So happy is he to deal with a civilized man, a man who can, no less, speak French, that Captain Bonnard gets confidential. Personally he doesn't give much of a damn that the entire contents of two or even twenty freighters have vanished from the warehouse. But the home office has been getting touchy and is ready to roll a few heads. Benya understands. Nothing must tarnish the reputation of the French military. That is why he accepts such a small payment, not much really, a few thousand francs and a small sack of bullion, as a guarantee that no more stuff made in France will disappear from the warehouses. This he does in the spirit of the Duc de Richelieu. The great tradition of Franco-Odessan collaboration. So up stand the two men, and they clink glasses and together shout Vive la France! Vive la Russie!

There's an old saying in Odessa—for all I know it dates from the time of the Duc: get along with the French, you can get along with anybody. The King, you might say, could get along with anybody. That was his charm. So much charm that during the war Benya was able to go international. The British, the Americans, the Czechs, he did business with everyone who could afford him. So much business that the King was already a rich man when the first Revolution came along in the winter of 1917, and richer still when the second one happened in October. Nobody knows how rich. He didn't have an accountant and he didn't have a bank account and nobody ever confessed to knowing exactly where he stashed his money or the rest of his loot. But everyone knew that those anonymous gifts that helped to keep open the Jewish Children's Hospital, the old folk's home next to the Second Jewish Cemetery, the cheder, and the Talmud Torah all came from the King. Give the man credit. He might not be honest but he was smart. He understood the world was wider than our little community. He knew that what was good for all of Odessa, not just the Jews, was good for us. So the Opera Association, the Greek Sailor's Fund, the Home for Orthodox Foundlings, the Relief Fund for Refugees, all these—and who knows how many other worthy organizations—shared in Benya's growing wealth.

What goes up must come down. It's a law of nature we always hope to cancel. When things are good we don't let ourselves think about it, because what we don't know is how or when things will fall apart. Maybe if we are lucky, it will be after we are gone. So like all good things, the boom years had to end. The second Revolution was not like the first. In October there was a mind at work. A plan. A vision. A sheyner vision, but who knew that? Some people did. Benya's wife, Tzilya, for instance. She wasn't the daughter of Zender Eichbaum for nothing. He who owned sixty milk cows and more rental units than you could count, and who sat in the first row at the Brody three days a year. Tzilya had wanted to go to college, but it was hard enough for a Jewish boy to get in, let alone a girl, so she stayed home and read books. Not love stories but serious novels and history and philosophy, Tolstoy and Dostoyevsky and Marx and an obscure revolutionary living abroad named Ulianov. From her Benya heard for the first time that this Lenin character was dead serious about making real changes in Russia.

Bolshevism, Benya said. It's just another racket.

History will have to judge whether Tzilya or Benya was right. Judge in the short term and the long term and the in-between term because judgment is all a matter of where you sit. Like this wall in this cemetery. From this vantage point nothing much may seem to change except that every year the neighborhood is a little more crowded. Not that this matters much. The newcomers are like the old residents. Nobody yells, nobody tries to tell you his troubles or asks for a loan. From here you can still tell a lot about what's going on outside the walls. You watch people and you learn. Do they sob for a long time when they kneel by the graves? Do they forget to bring fresh flowers? Do they come regularly or do they fail to come at all, and when they come do they cover their eyes for a long time or do they hurry away?

Some impatient American—what other sort of person would dare?—wrote a book that gave an instant label to the Revolution: Ten Days That Shook the World. A label just nonsensical enough to stick and stick good. Ever since, all over the world, everyone thinks that's it. Ten days. Capitalism is out. Communism is in. Lenin is a genius. Tell me another. For we who had to live through it, for we who lived in Odessa, those October Days were the beginning not the end. Of turmoil, upheaval, disease, starvation, death, and worse. What is worse than death? Mutilation. Humiliation. Degradation. Anywhere else a huge social revolution would be enough to occupy the time of day. Not in Russia. We need pogroms too. The Civil War that follows those ten days and goes on for three years and then some is, you might say, a festival of pogroms. Cossacks, Poles, Ukrainians, the beloved workers and peasants of the Red Army—all compete to see who can, when nobody is looking and sometimes even when they are, kill the most Jews.

Put it this way. The four years following October are a nightmare. A mishmash of events, experiences, suffering. So confusing that no recollection, no story, no work of history, no novel, even were the great Lev Tolstoy alive to write it, could give you more than the tiniest fraction of what we endured. Invasions and counterinvasions, occupation by foreigners and by Ukrainians, by Cossacks, and by Soviets. We had a blockade and a famine, epidemics of typhus and typhoid and scurvy and a dozen types of lethal influenza. We were the headquarters for a German army, a British navy, a French expeditionary force, and more White Russian regimes than anyone can remember. One week you would see German sentries with spiked steel helmets guarding the door of army headquarters in the London Hotel, while officers with sabers in nickel-plated sheaths stand at a bulletin board reading mimeographed communiqués signed by Field Marshal von Ludendorff. The next week Red Guard patrols tramp through the streets and armored cars thunder past with sailors lying on the mudguards, pointing their Mausers every which way. Next week some Ukrainian Hetman captures the city and on every street corner stands a peasant lad in a ragged great coat who demands your papers, but if you don't have any, he tugs his forelock and lets you go on just the same. Shall I mention the cheerful British marines who kick a football back and forth as they trot down the street? The French soldiers in blue coats and gaiters with double-necked aluminum flasks that hold both wine and water?

With every new regime, the money changes. So does the street life. Everybody prints bills that, the moment they come off the presses, are worth exactly what we used them to wipe away. Some weeks it can seem like the Revolution has never taken place. Elegant private coaches roll down Catherine Street, money changers haunt the corner of DeRibas and Preobrazhen, the marble-topped tables at Fanconi and Robinat are filled with men in suits discussing the stock market. Cabarets do a booming business, the Opera House is jammed every night, private yachts from the Black Sea Club sail out past the white stone lighthouse, military bands give concerts in the parks. Then the Soviets or Ukrainians arrive and the streets grow quiet, the banks close, the rich huddle behind the locked doors of their mansions. Life centers around the street markets. Not the old ones with stands where you can share a glass of tea and enjoy a chance to gossip and bargain. The new ones are fugitive places in alleys, places where you no longer need money, where books, fur coats, furniture, jewelry, antiques, heirlooms are exchanged for jars of pickles, cans of fish, half-kilos of wheat crawling with weevils.

Regimes come, regimes go, but one thing they all have in common: the troops steal everything they can get their hands on. So in the years following the Revolution, Benya Krik has plenty of competition in what is a shrinking market. Shrinking? Vanishing! Vanishing? Vanished! By the time the last Whites flee in early 1920, a meal, a good bowl of soup, or a piece of fresh bread is a distant memory. Along with a warm room. The empty villas out in Arkadia have been stripped of their wooden doors and mantels for firewood. Once you burn your furniture and books, there is nothing to do but huddle together and wait for spring. By then even the wharf rats are starving, roaming about in the daylight over the counters of empty food stores, while our famous Odessa cats lie around watching them, too preoccupied with their own empty stomachs for a chase.

Considering what's been going on, Benya does better than you might expect. During the time of the Germans and Ukrainians, he transforms his gang into a guerilla band that specializes in raiding ammunition dumps and supply trains. Sometime during these years he realizes the Soviets are going to defeat all the Whites and all the foreigners and take control of the country. Sometime during these years his wife realizes the same thing, with the result that one day he comes home to find that she has departed with all her clothes and jewelry. Her goodbye note gives no destination but its explanation of her action, it must be said, devotes pretty much equal time to Bolshevism and other women.

Alas, it's true. Benya loves Tzilya as deeply as he can love, but love is no guarantee against a wandering eye. Not that Benya ever felt, from the day he got married, a moment of real affection for anyone other than Tzilya. His flings are hardly serious. They are only momentary passions, brief physical attractions. But try to tell that to a wife. The word only, it will turn out, is not an excuse but an unforgivable crime. Why? Here is another of God's deep mysteries or major mistakes. Two sexes with such different ideas about the nature of love. This is a reasonable way to create a world? He does make mistakes, you know. Like His mistake of putting all the Jews in Russia, a country filled with meshuggeners who torment them and a climate so cold it can make you long for the tortures of Hell. While He was creating the rest of the universe, would it have been so hard for Him to put the Jews in Switzerland, where they could enjoy the lakes and the good mountain air and take vacations in France?

Some people say that Tzilya's departure changed the King, made him lonely and bitter. Some say it turned him toward the cause of the people. Some say he didn't care, but those are the ones who didn't know Benya, for if we know one thing, it's that the King had a very big heart, and if it bled for others, wouldn't it also bleed for himself? Long before the Whites pull out, Benya has begun to call *himself a Bolshevik. His boys learn about it one morning when his chief lieutenant, Froim Grach, arrives to find the King staring at himself in a full-length mirror, wearing not one of his classy pink or dark purple suits with a flowing tie but a well-tailored military outfit, tall riding boots, a military cap with a prominent red star above the brim, and a holster with a pistol on his hip. Froim whistles and asks,* Where's the costume ball? *Benya tells him to wake up.* There's a ball going on all over the country. They call it the Revolution and it's time for us to join the dance. *Froim can't believe what he hears.* We're joining the Bolshies? Those crooks? They're doing away with private property. Don't worry, *the King tells him.* Don't believe rumors. Bolshies are like everyone else. They need help. They'll cut a deal. And if there's a deal to cut in Odessa, who better to cut it with than us?

33

I live here like in the bosom of Christ. I eat grapes, swim in the sea on sunny days, work for my own pleasure, enjoy all my hours in this lush Garden somewhere East of Eden.

Four postcards. Each with the same picture of waves beating on the rocky seacoast off Massandra. Each with these same opening lines. But the rest of the message is different. To Mamma and Mera: that our Lord bestow his blessings upon them by transferring some of the Yalta climate to rainy Brussels. To Zhenya and Natasha: that they will someday be able to come with me to Yalta to enjoy the sandy beaches, rose-scented breezes, palm trees against the vivid blue sky. To Nina: that she not forget to bring wool sweaters for both of us just in case the weather changes. To Nadja: that I miss her.

My palatial room at the former Hotel Russia has a glorious view. Fifty meters away people sunbathe, kick footballs, splash into the warm sea. In cypress groves on the hillsides what were once the summer palaces of aristocrats are now sanitariums and rest homes, crowded with workers on holiday. Young Pioneers with red scarves march along the Lenin Embankment and through Seaside Park singing hymns to Our Great Leader. The central market overflows with bounty such as you never see in Moscow: ripe tomatoes, fragrant melons, huge grapes heaped into astonishing mounds and all on sale at bargain prices.

Yalta is a town in which to indulge the senses.

Unless you happen to be with Eisenstein, a madman when it comes to work, and with him it always comes to work. For a week I am stuck inside a hotel room, arguing over the script of *Bezhin Meadow*. Sequences, images, plot, dialogue—everything is at issue and every issue is jumbled together with a dozen other things, Eisenstein's life, his art, his craft, his imagination, his need to redeem the failed *Que Viva Mexico*, his desperate desire to complete a film after a break of seven years. All our words are spoken under the shadow of Boris Shumyatsky, current czar of cinema, who dislikes artistic innovation and Sergei in equal measure. Shumyatsky has forced Sergei to toss out virtually all the footage shot last summer and has demanded a complete rewrite. Why he okayed me for the job remains a mystery, unless it's as a kind of perverse insurance that the film will never reach the screen.

The subject matter is touchy enough. Sergei is trying to do the impossible: create a film that will satisfy both Russian tradition and the Party line. The title is from Turgenev, but the story is strictly Soviet. It's based on the case of ten-year-old Pavel Morozov, hailed across the country as a martyr for socialism. This member of the Young Pioneers put the interests of the state ahead of his own blood. He denounced his father as part of a conspiracy of kulaks who planned to burn the wheat harvest rather than share it with the collective farm. Enraged at learning of his son's betrayal, the father slaughtered Pavel with a butcher knife, then dumped his body into the village square. This act insured the youngster immortality. In schoolrooms they now hang his picture and point to him as one of the great heroes of the Soviet state.

Typical of where his mind is these days, Sergei's approach is more Old Testament than Party line. The year in Mexico has stoked his religious tendencies, particularly his mystical streak. One of my jobs is to talk him out of wild scenes that will certainly get the film banned. Like the one in which a peasant woman who is making the bombs that will set the grain on fire sits in her hut staring at an icon until she begins to feel that the Lord will punish her for this act of destruction. At that point Sergei wants to have the ceiling of the hut split open, the heavens crack apart, the face of God appear in the clouds, and the woman collapse in fear and trembling.

I object. The idea is a trifle, shall we say, unrealistic.

Of course it's unrealistic comes the answer. That's the point. Don't I know him well enough to understand how he hates the real? The actual. Don't I know how much he prefers the imaginary, the things we cannot see, the things that are not there? After all these years, don't I realize that his great love is not the is-ness but the isn't-ness of things?

I have to remind him of the is-ness of iron bars. Tell him there's only one face in the country that can qualify for that of the Almighty. Is he planning to give the Boss his first screen credit?

We avoid the Yalta Studio, our so-called Hollywood on the Black Sea, with its tourists, snooping Party officials, and spies. Sergei has always preferred the outdoors to soundstages, and he has found two great locations in the foothills. A nineteenth-century church filled with icons and crucifixes and jeweled goblets and other treasures that peasants, in a climactic scene, will strip away and toss into a bonfire. And a farm with an old tractor station that will serve as the storage place for the harvest that will be burnt to the ground for the final scene.

The rushes are stunning. The chaos of the day transmutes into the beauty of images upon the screen. The shouts, the tantrums, the quarrels, the raised fists, the shrieking voices, the dust, the broken cables, the lights that collapse, the bruises, the upset stomachs—all are gone. What remains is pure movement, sumptuous shadows in black and white, the swirling choreography of crowds, white horses racing against a sunset, muscled arms raised, hands holding tools, faces scarred with age, suffering, madness, passion, love of man or God.

Late at night we talk in our rooms. Two veterans, similar enough to understand each other, different enough to find each other interesting. Both of us the sons of fathers who sent us off to get a practical education. Both of us endowed with strong artistic ambitions and blessed with early success. In the twenties we swam in the turbulent maelstrom of Moscow, a sea of new ideas, publications, theories, films, art forms. *Potemkin* shakes the world in 1925; *Red Cavalry* in 1926. We are toasted at home and abroad, in Berlin, Paris, London, New York. For a year or so the triumph is pure enough, then the troubles begin. *October,* shot for the tenth anniversary of the great Ten Days, raises the question: Whose ten days? Rumors have it that the Boss himself came into the cutting room and looked over Sergei's shoulder to make sure he removed every offensive frame. A thousand meters on the floor, including almost every frame in which Trotsky's image was visible. Sergei refuses to corroborate or dismiss the story.

My own *October* is Budyenny's attack on *Red Cavalry.* I win the battle but lose the war. But there's nobody to blame but myself. Creativity has its own demands. My desires and imagination take me in odd directions, back toward childhood and gangsters. Publishing becomes more difficult. Editors let me know that I am increasingly out of step with the times. This becomes absolutely clear two years ago at the First Congress of Soviet Writers, when a new doctrine is officially enunciated—Socialist Realism. Not that it is really new. It's hardly any different from bourgeois realism, just old-fashioned storytelling and traditional morality but with working-class characters. At the congress, silence was no longer allowed. The powers at the top were beginning to demand more than conformity; now they wanted open affirmation. That's why I spoke of not yet knowing how to write for this new world. That's why I joked about my mastery of silence. But soon even that ploy may not do the trick. Our leaders may be getting smart enough to understand irony. Silence itself begins to seem eloquent.

Okay. We all adjust to life. It's not a conscious process. You have to eat, work, live, so you do what you can and hope for the best. Since returning from Mexico Sergei has been teaching at the film institute instead of making films. I live by writing the kind of stuff I would choke to read. He is the more vulnerable. A taste for women, young, old, even under age, is okay, like a taste for too much vodka. Boys are another matter. Sergei's drawings are well known by now. No doubt you can find them in the files of the NKVD and in the Boss's desk drawer, ready to be pulled out when they want Sergei for something important. One day they will ask him to make a film showing the Boss as the modern version of one of our great czars like Peter the Great or Alexander Nevsky. Ivan the Terrible would be more to the point.

All this is the subtext of our evenings. Out loud we do what old friends do: reminisce about the wild nights in Moscow, the parties, art openings and premieres, the many moments that seemed transcendent or insane. That talented fool Mayakovsky—whose suicide in 1930 would be like a bell, sounding the death knell of our dreams—leaping into a fountain on a freezing mid-February day in the twenties to show how artists disdain comfort. Mandelstam with his long face, at a writers' meeting, worrying aloud about the state of the Russian soul, and someone shouting from the back of the room, *Since when does a Yid have a*

Russian soul? The Boss, standing in a formal reception line, when he forgetfully put a lighted pipe into his pocket and smoke began to curl upward and nobody had the courage to tell him, and suddenly his coat is on fire and he starts to flap his arms and tries to struggle out of the coat but nobody dares reach out to help, for everybody knows how much he hates to have anyone touch him, and as the flames begin to engulf the coat he hurls himself on the floor and rolls around until the fire is out. I remember the horrified faces. Everyone looking in the other direction, staring at the walls, not daring to move, as finally Lazar Kaganovich helps him to his feet. The Boss looks around the room with the blackest stare in history and stalks out the door.

Now we can laugh. But you have to wonder: How many unsuspecting souls paid for that mishap?

At least not us. Not yet.

34

*N*ina. Antonina Nikolaevna Pirozhkova. Steps down from the train in Simferopol and I see her again as if it is the first time. Clear as a Siberian stream. Clean as a new snowfall. Free of shadows as the steppes in the midday sun, with a radiance that lights everything around her. Even the gloomy lunchroom at the Donbass Miners' House on Petrovka Street in Moscow.

That's where we met four years ago. I am there at the invitation of an old friend, Ivan Pavolovich, president of the Eastern Steel Works in Magnitogorsk. He and I have shared drinks and dinner in more than one city, and shared a few late-night adventures too. Ivan has heard my complaints about Zhenya staying on in France. He knows her just well enough to understand what I will never admit. To say to my face:

Never. No matter how bad things get in France. If she's starving to death. If she has to walk the streets. Never will she return to Russia. Not with a daughter. And who can blame her, my friend? She'd be crazy to return to you and your wandering ways. That's a high-strung woman. She has opinions. A mind of her own. Sure you think you miss the child. I understand. But how much can you really miss her? You've never even seen her. You don't know for certain that she's yours. Anyway. You can always have another child. With another woman. Someone who will put up with your ways. You'd be far more miserable with Zhenya here than you are with her two thousand kilometers away.

I arrive late to lunch at the Miners' House direct from the foreign office. Ready to share happy news. After months of application forms, affidavits, sitting in offices, undergoing interviews, making promises, nagging friends and Party members, asking editors, publishers, and low-level officials to pull strings, I have at last received permission to leave the country for a while. To visit my family in France. To see my daughter for the first time.

Over Ivan's shoulder, I see a young woman who makes me think of pilots and athletes. Attractive but not stunning, with an inquisitive sort of intelligence to her face. Some distant resemblance to Isadora Duncan of a decade before, when she was hanging around in Moscow cafés with the poet Sergei Esenin, trying to interest the minister of culture in the revolutionary potential of modern dance. But sleeker and cooler than Duncan, a bulky type who always looked like she was about to wrap a scarf around her head and begin leaping across the room. This one is self-contained. She looks as if sitting at this table, eating lunch, and staring up at me is the only thing in the world she is supposed to do at this moment, and she is doing it with all her being. Like breathing.

Ivan does the introductions.

Isaac Babel. Writer. Raconteur. World traveler. Meet my friend Pirozhkova, the construction engineer. In the profession we all call her Princess Turandot. She'll have to tell you why.

Nina neither blushes nor explains. She does look very like an ice queen, but looks are deceiving, and I soon enough learn she left most of the frost behind in Siberia. Nina holds out her hand and acts not at all surprised when I bring it to my lips. Nor does she make the sort of tiresome remarks you are liable to get from other women these days. Comrade, such aristocratic gestures are no longer necessary. Men and women—we are equals now.

I call for a bottle of vodka.

You are the first female construction engineer I have ever met. It's true, I don't know many engineers, but the few I do know have taught me one thing about the profession: engineers love vodka.

All through lunch I keep filling our glasses. We toast the triumphs of Soviet engineering, past, present, and future. The Siberian Institute for Transport Engineers, where Pirozhkova was trained. The Kuznetz Construction Project, where she met Ivan. The Metropolitan Project, where she is trying to get a position. The subway that she hopes to build. May it be lovelier than the Paris Métro and more efficient than the Berlin U-Bahn and the London Tube combined.

Nina matches me drink for drink. Toast for toast. We raise our glasses to the future of Soviet literature. Gorky, our national treasure, may he live forever. *Red Cavalry* and Benya Krik and the Duc de Richelieu. The Odessa climate and the Black Sea. My coming trip to France. My wife. My daughter.

Only later do I learn from Pavolovich that Nina normally drinks no more than wine. One result of all our toasting is that she spends the rest of the afternoon and much of the evening heaving up lunch and suffers for the next three days from a splitting headache. Only to uphold the honor of the profession did she drink so much with me. Despite the bravado of her toasts, she knows my works only because Ivan has mentioned them. She is a rare being, the first woman I have met in years who has never read a single word I set down on a page.

A few days later I invite her over for the special lunch of *vareniki* with cherries and show her around the impressive apartment I share with Shtainer. Two floors, six rooms. I open a bottle of wine and launch into the story I use as a litmus test for new friends. The one based on the name of the street where I live: Great Lane of Nikola and the Sparrows, a name taken from the old church right across from my house. To raise money for its construction, my story goes, the parishioners joined together in a business venture: catching, cooking, and selling sparrows. It took them two hundred years to pay for the building.

A line crosses her brow. You can see her doing sums in her head. A church must cost so much. Which means so many sparrows at so many rubles for so many years until she erupts into laughter like a volcano. Tears sputter and flow. She laughs more and chokes out the words: *Five hundred billion sparrows. There wouldn't be a sparrow left on earth. There haven't been that many sparrows since the beginning of time.*

I like a woman with a sense of humor. A woman who plays along when I offer her a ruble for every private letter she will let me read by immediately pulling one out of her purse. I reach for it. She opens her other hand. I search my pockets, find nothing less than a ten-ruble note. She accepts it as a down payment on the next nine letters. This one from her mother is full of warnings: wear warm clothes and watch out for the men in Moscow. They are all sharpies. There's only one thing they want from a pretty girl like you.

We see each other several times before I leave for France. At my apartment, at restaurants, and at her place, where she makes weak tea and responds with merriment to the Can-I-Look-in-Your-Purse routine. The weekend I have to wind up my affairs in the country, I invite her to Molodenovo. We ride around all afternoon in a horse-drawn cart, visit my sunny room at Karpovich's house, talk with trainers at the stud farm, wander along the river where spindly colts graze alongside mares with huge bellies, ready to foal. By nightfall I have lived a unique experience. An entire day with a woman who has not asked me a single question about writing or made a single comment about literature or wanted to know what I am working on now.

On my return from France in the fall of 1933, Nina is between jobs. So I ask her along on a research trip to the Caucasus. *Pravda* has hired me to report on the progress of the Cossack settlements and other collective efforts in Kabardino-Balkariya. More than money takes me there. Ever since my Tbilisi days, the Caucasus, with its wild horses and wilder landscape, has called to me. As it has to so many writers—Lermontov, Tolstoy, Turgenev. All have fallen in love with its heady air of freedom that even this regime has not been able to dampen. Much of this was due to one leader, Betal Kalmykov, first secretary of the local branch of the Party, a thickset mountain man and defender of the poor. Like any Soviet chief he was a boss, but at least a boss with a sense of rough justice. Betal was a kind of cliché, just the kind of cliché we need. If I had to write on collectivism, he would do better than anyone else. My desire was to turn him into a large figure to match Benya Krik, but one with no cynical edge, a leader capable of instilling hope that change for the better is possible. At least it still seemed possible in the Caucasus three years ago. But nothing stays the same. Last year Betal was summoned to Moscow. We spent a night at the bar in the National Hotel just before he was to attend a meeting at the Kremlin. That was the last time I saw him. Typical. Betal never left the meeting, never went home. His end is clear enough, but not even my best sources have been able to tell me exactly what happened or why. As if why ever makes a difference.

Nina and I travel well together in the Caucasus. We enjoy the seashore, the mountains, the marketplaces with fatted calves and sheep, the hunters who bag deer and wild pigs, the mineral springs, the horse races in open fields, the country dances with people in traditional costumes, colorful full skirts, embroidered shirts, high boots. We love the foods you don't get anywhere else—deer, boar, and game birds cooked over a spit, potatoes roasted in the ground, jam made from wild mountain fruit. Our accommodations are primitive, but neither of us cares. We sleep in leaky rooms above filthy taverns or in shacks on farms, but neither of us wants anything else. In the mornings I am so productive that in three months I finish work on *Mariya*. Nina tiptoes around me and never complains. She is the first woman I have known who is entirely self-sufficient. Practically and emotionally. In Khabarovsk, while I write, she volunteers to work on the carrot harvest, then in the afternoons tutors mathematics at the high school.

Early in November she must return to Moscow to begin a new position with the Metropolitan Design Office. On New Year's Eve, 1934, I ask her to share my apartment, but only on certain conditions: that she promises never to read a word of any of my unfinished manuscripts and that she never asks where I am going or where I have been or when I will return.

God knows why: she agrees.

35

*S*imferopol to Yalta. A white road winding through mountains, the convertible top down, cool wind ruffling Nina's hair and chilling my scalp. The driver takes the curves fast, throws us against each other. She bubbles with delight to be away from Moscow with its gray skies and cold rain. But the weather has helped keep them focused on the subway project, and they are way ahead of schedule. Two new subway stations will open next month. The trials have been exciting, too. Everyone is talking about the confessions. Didn't I used to know them? she asks, Zinoviev and Kamenev? How could they have done it, turned against their country, betrayed the Revolution. But men like that wouldn't confess to something if it weren't true. Would they?

Her sharp gasp at the sudden view of the sea saves me from having to answer. A broad blue vista sprawls before us. I point to the white town of Tesseli, where Gorky had his last villa. Down we go toward Yalta, to palm trees, beaches, the faint smell of orange blossoms, the grand lobby of the hotel, and our room with its balcony where we sip Massandra wine and watch the sunset.

Something odd happened a few days ago, Nina says. *I didn't want to tell you by letter, but I have to let you know because it may be important and I don't want you to think I broke my promise not to touch your stuff.*

She went upstairs to my office to find the sweater I had requested and found instead, inside the locked door, papers scattered all over my desk and the floor. The trunk, which holds my manuscripts in neat folders, had been dragged out from under the table and the lock ripped from the hinges. It's odd. How could someone get in? The window is still closed tight. At first she thought of saying something to Shtainer but didn't for fear it would come out sounding like an accusation.

Don't worry about it. It has to be one of my editors. My voice is as light as I can make it, given the sudden weight on my shoulders. *They won't take any of my short stories. No one wants them. But they must be even more desperate than I thought for that manuscript on collective farms. Damn. Someday soon I may actually have to write that thing.*

I change the subject, tell her we have to meet Eisenstein for dinner.

Listen. Don't order anything too expensive. In your honor, he's treating. But he is on the stingy side.

She gives me a familiar look. The one that says, I don't know if you're kidding or not but I think you are.

Honest. It's his Jewish heritage.

I thought he's only half Jewish.

The lower half. Below the waist. Where he keeps his wallet.

As soon as we sit down at the Ukraina, up jump a bunch of tourists from Italy.

Viva Eisenstein! they shout in unison. *Viva Babel!*

Heads turn all over the room. They surround our table. Fire questions.

Are you shooting a film? Are you working together?

We smile. Gesture. Wave our arms. Point to our ears as if we are deaf. To our mouths as if we are dumb. We babble Russian nonsense syllables. Sergei throws in a few words of Japanese. I add some Yiddish. Their enthusiasm slackens. We all shake hands. They go away.

Other directors sulk or rage when they are making a film. Not Sergei. Work always puts him in a good mood. Tonight he is in great form. Entertaining Nina with stories about his months in Hollywood. The producers with cigars who would lean back in leather swivel chairs and say sure, you can make an American *Potemkin*. Why not? People love ships. They love sea stories. *Mutiny on the Bounty* was a hit, so why not *Mutiny on the Black Sea?* Only he needs to cut down on the common sailors. Focus more on the officers. Dashing men in uniforms. Add a love story. Create a few characters you can identify with. Beautiful babes. Palm trees. Romance on the beach.

Sergei puts on the white fedora he has been sporting this summer. A trophy, given to him by Chaplin. The great comedian has a reputation as a radical. So when all else fails at the studios, Sergei goes to his house to ask for money to make a film. One about the gold rush. Nothing like

Chaplin's comic masterpiece about Alaska. This one would be a California tragedy. *Sutter's Gold.* An exposé of the greed that lies at the heart of the capitalist mentality, that leads to dishonor and death. Chaplin takes him out onto his private tennis court and beats Sergei in three straight sets, calls him the greatest director in the world, and then presents him with the hat. No money. No support. Just a hat.

The monologue gives me time to watch Nina. Two months apart and she looks different. There is a subtle light in her eyes, a slight widening of her cheeks. Maybe the Metro's dining room is serving better meals. Maybe she has found a way to indulge some secret vice involving sweets. My speculation ends when we climb into bed. She is definitely thicker around the waist. I don't have time to ask. She beats me to it. With a smile, a hug, a huge explosion of joy. She's pregnant.

Talk about mixed emotions.

I do my best to appear pleased, but my best isn't very good. Nina doesn't notice. Or doesn't let on that she has noticed. Her enthusiasm is more than enough for two. So are her plans. The usual plans. Doctors, clothing, schools, a house outside Moscow. Of course she won't give up her work. We can easily afford a maid. Child-care centers are too crowded. You can't trust them. And with a new child, I'll surely want to stay at home a lot to watch him grow.

Right.

Next day Nina wants to do the town—the Lenin Embankment, the city garden with its rare trees from all over the world, the artist's Yalta. So many writers and composers have lived and worked here. Gorky, Rachmaninoff, Stanislavsky, Bunin. The great Nekrasov once sat in room 68 at the Taurida Hotel, composing odes. Fifty years later Mayakovsky insisted on using the same room to write a celebration of Lenin. Chekhov's White Villa is the top attraction. Everything has been preserved as it was at his death thirty-five years ago. Or so the guides say. The furniture, his books, spectacles, and notebooks. Even the desk on which he wrote *The Cherry Orchard.*

So jammed are the rooms with tourists that I can sneak a quick sit in his chair without the guard seeing me. When I stand up, Potato Face is staring my way from across the crowded room. Why am I not all that surprised? A small gesture says we need to talk. When Nina goes off to find the restroom, we meet on the crowded hillside between the villa and the museum. No greeting beyond a quick nod. I don't even have time for the obligatory question: What are you doing here? Her words are urgent.

Trouble. Yagoda is on his way out. Yezhov will be taking his place. Very soon now. Our whole arrangement may be in jeopardy. You have to return to Odessa right away. Things could happen quickly.

Or not at all?

She puts her finger to her lips, shrugs.

You have to be there. You've made arrangements. If this is going to happen, you're the only one who can do it.

Nina takes me by the arm and smiles up at us. I introduce her as Antonina Pirozhkova. Potato Face saves me from embarrassment.

Svetlana Kripinskaya at your service. So strange to bump into Comrade Babel here. In such a lovely resort. I've never seen him outside the walls of the passport office. He's always bothering us for one thing or another. He gives us more trouble than a hundred other writers.

Isaac specializes in giving people trouble.

Really, does he give you trouble, too?

Not when we're on vacation.

The conversation turns to the usual. The weather, the museum, the blossoms, the sea. Nina holds me by the arm as we stroll back toward the hotel.

She looks like someone who really does work in a passport office. Where else would that face get a job?

Next day, we see that face once again. On the trail up to the summit of Ai-Petri, a mountain famous for the view of Yalta and the sea. Not that we have actually climbed it. My lungs and Nina's condition put us into a studio car, which takes us up a winding road to a meadow in the shadow of the summit. Sheep graze nearby, and climbers rest after the ascent from the beach and before the assault on the peak. In her summer dress, hat, and sandals, Potato Face has not been doing much climbing either.

Again we talk tourist talk.

The bus, she says, waving toward the road. *I just couldn't miss this. But I didn't have time to climb.*

Yes, the view is wonderful, says Nina. *Do you have to leave soon? Work,* says Potato Face, nodding. *My time here is finished. Was it everything you expected? A good vacation? Very good. I think the effects will linger for months and years to come.*

Odd, says Nina. We are back in our room. *That woman. Kripinskaya. Turning up again. Do you think she could be following us?*

Not likely. She was there before us, remember? Maybe it's the other way around. Maybe we are following her.

36

*C*he sun rolls on the knife-edge of the sea. Long shadows of church domes spill across yards, fields, fences, the milling crowd. Eisenstein rushes through the confusion of a crew, dashing this way and that, giving orders. Nina and I hang back at the edge of the activity. It is her first time watching a shoot. We have not spoken much these last couple of days. Not seriously. Not about the major issue we suddenly share. My hesitation and fears are the reason. Is this a suitable moment to bring a child into the world? But any questions I have don't much matter. She has already made the decision.

Lights come on against the darkness. Cameras roll into place. Soundmen check equipment. Assistants herd local peasants together into the yard. Sergei addresses them.

Remember. You have collectivized the land. You have decided to turn the church into a recreation center. You are taking it apart, piece by piece, men and women together, stripping the inside clean, pulling the icons from the walls, dismantling the altar, dragging it outside piece by piece and heaping everything up into this pile. Now you are going to burn it all. Burn the past in favor of a better future. But it isn't easy. You have gone to church all your lives. You love the church. You hate it too. To prepare yourselves to do what you are going to do you have been drinking. You are drunk. The men will drag the huge cross onto the pile. Set it on fire. Challenge God in this way. So you are afraid. God may punish you. Hurl a bolt of lightning. And you are angry at yourselves for being afraid. You drink some more. You set the fire. You dance in drunken ecstasy. You shriek like maniacs. Okay, does everyone understand?

Yes, yes, yes. They nod and gesture. They know what to do.

Sergei calls *Action.* The cameras begin to roll. The extras suddenly shrink in size, appear meek, sheepish, cowed. They tiptoe back and forth, gently remove icons from the walls, carefully hand them to each other, politely carry them outside and place them on the pile. They smile as if to say: *This is only acting. We're not really doing this.*

Cut!

Sergei grabs a middle-aged man by the blouse and shouts directly into his face: *This is not a tea party. You're drunk, remember? You're full of rage.*

The man pulls back, protests. *But these are real icons. They're from the church.*

So what? You hate the church. You hate the goddamn icons and the goddamn cross.

The peasant nods. Sergei turns away. The peasant crosses himself. Assistants hand out bottles of vodka. Everyone takes a few belts, including Sergei. *Action,* he shouts, and keeps on shouting while the cameras roll.

By the fifth take the peasants have worked themselves into a proper frenzy. They hurl objects onto the pile, shriek at each other, pound their feet in a drunken dance around the burning objects. One plays an accordion, others beat on tin gasoline cans as if they were drums. Four squat, red-faced women, faces twisted in painful ecstasy, drag a heavy cross toward the flames. A huge, bearded man stumbles into the circle of light carrying a body. Everyone draws back as he tosses the bloodied mass onto the floor.

My son! My son betrayed me! Revenge is sweet. Betrayers must be slaughtered like dogs!

Cut!

Sergei hugs the actor. Tells him in a stage whisper: *More violence. Much more violence. You have killed your son, not a dog. Your son! Your only son. You've destroyed your own future. You've destroyed the world!*

The scene becomes more disturbing with each take. They go on and on, until we've lost count of how many times the actor has lurched into the circle of light, raised the dripping body for all to see, shrieked his lines, hurled the bloody mass to earth.

A subdued feeling in the car back to Yalta. I try to cheer things up by telling Sergei it was brilliant sequence. It's a brilliant film. Sure, sure, he knows that. Knows, too, that it will never be screened for the public. Shumyatsky will see to that. Six months from now he'll no doubt be forced to stand up in public and denounce his formalist and ideological errors. Again. Or maybe I haven't heard the news out of Moscow: we are supposed to leave the church alone. After two decades of abuse, it turns out we were all wrong. Priests aren't so bad after all. What goes wrong these days is not the fault of religion. It's the fault of the kulaks and their allies—artists who remain sentimental about the old monarchy, Old Bolsheviks who have decided to follow Trotsky, along with various sorts of malcontents and other wreckers. And all the other people who refuse to accept the brilliant successes of the new Soviet world.

Nina looks stricken. By the violence of the sequence? A touch of pregnancy? Twice in the night her sobs wake me up. I put my arms around her, calm her back to sleep. Over a breakfast of rolls, fresh cheese, strong tea, she starts to weep. We are sitting on the balcony. She gets up, lunges into the room, heaving with emotion. Tries to speak, gasps, sobs out a confession.

The truth, Izzie. I have to tell you the truth. I love you too much. I have to tell the truth.

What truth?

Hesitation. More sobbing. Her voice choked.

The baby may not be yours.

Relief is my first feeling, but it's followed by something unfamiliar. Tenderness perhaps, mixed with a touch of outrage. But I never get outraged, certainly not about women. This doesn't happen to me. I clench my jaw. Try to keep emotion from showing. But when the words emerge even I can hear the tension in my voice.

Whose?

Nina looks away. Her voice grows soft. She hesitates, then stutters:

Ma-Ma-Malraux. I think Malraux may be the father.

André Malraux? No. Really? Why not? It's not that much of a surprise. Not at all. Or is it?

My good friend, Andriushka. L'amour, toujours l'amour. The charm of the French. L'amour, surtout, l'amour.

I take her in my arms, kiss her on the forehead. She presses against me, then pulls away. She needs to get it out. There are, after all, priests in her family. People of conscience. She needs to explain.

Last spring. When Malraux came from France to see Gorky, full of plans for a new international encyclopedia. One that would do for the working classes of the twentieth century what the original one had done for the middle classes of the eighteenth. A book that would be an intellectual weapon in the struggle of humanism against fascism. Together André and I went in a special train to Tesseli, he and I alone in a single car. Gorky was already ill. I served as translator. The meeting was a disaster. The two men agreed on nothing but the general idea of the work. On most big issues they were centuries apart. Gorky was fast succumbing to his heritage. When André talked at length of protecting individual rights, the old man looked distracted, puzzled. Liberty, equality, fraternity? Surely today these are outworn ideas. Today we must protect the rights of the collective. Keep the masses from exploitation by those traditional elements that wish to keep them in servitude.

The spirit of the engineer slowly returns. Nina grows more composed, better able to explain. She tells me that it began after André and I returned from Tesseli: *Malraux hung around the house a lot, remember? Very disappointed at the failure of the project. You hardly noticed. You expected the failure and were off, running around as usual. He doesn't speak Russian, doesn't feel very comfortable with Russians, so he spends a lot of time in your room, at your desk, writing or pretending to write. I bring in tea, cakes, make sympathetic noises over the failure of the project. He smiles. His hair falls into his eyes and he brushes it away. The gesture is meant to be cute. He knows it. So do I. It is cute.*

We communicate in broken German, with a few words of French. He says things about my hair, my smile. I don't understand them all, but the tenor is clear. He's different from the man you know, a different man from the public André, who always seems so high-strung, who talks so fast. Now he speaks slowly. Softly. I ask him what he thinks of Moscow. Trop de Métro, *he says.* Too much subway. *I understand enough French to get the joke. We laugh together. It's true. All we ever talk—no, it's me. All I ever talk about these days is our glorious subway. He says I'm beautiful when I laugh. He says I'm beautiful when I don't laugh. He says I look like Isadora Duncan when I move. I turn my head away. He says he knows I am shy. Inexperienced. He asks about Siberia. What do people do all those long winter months? How do they keep warm? Do they have lovers? Did I ever have lovers before meeting his good friend Isaac?*

He asks if you are a good lover. I don't know how to answer. I don't answer. He asks if I ever made love to a foreigner. With someone who wasn't Siberian or Russian or Jewish. With a black man or an Asian. Asians are wonderful lovers. He tells me stories about his time in Cambodia. The sensuous women of Phnom Penh who never wear anything above the waist. Curious women who tore away his belt and pulled down his pants in order to see what a European man had between his legs. Don't I ever wonder about other men? Western Europeans? French men?

I must be blushing but I don't leave the room. He says he understands. I am loyal to Isaac. This is a touching sentiment, but amusing too. Such proper bourgeois morality in this revolutionary culture. But certainly not a morality that touches Isaac. Babel, he says, is one Russian who has freed himself from the old moral strictures. Don't I know how famous he is for amorous escapades? This is not to say Isaac doesn't love you. Of course he loves you. He's loyal in his own way. But when he is in France, well, you know how French women have always loved writers and have always loved revolutionaries, and when they find a man who is both at the same time, voilà! We men are weak creatures. How could Isaac refuse their advances? More than once he has quoted to me a passage from the Talmud: you will answer in the next world for all the pleasures you refuse in this one. André has known many women, but Russians are new to him. They are a mystery. I am a mystery. Cool, but he senses depths of hidden passion. I drive him mad with the desire to know what is beneath that cool surface. Who am I? What do I want from him?

Nina stops. Hesitates. Afraid the details may hurt me.

I shouldn't be telling you.

Emotion has made her forget that details are the lifeblood of the man who looks inside purses and reads private letters. Pleasant, unpleasant, both, neither. The world is made up of details. I insist she continue, but there really is no need. I already know the story. Have lived it. We have all lived it and written it, too. Enjoyed it and felt guilty and done it again.

One day André puts his hand on hers, and she pulls away. The next time, or the time after that, she does not. One time their eyes meet. The next time it is lips. Then bodies. One time their clothes stay on. The next time a blouse or a shirt comes off. Then pants, skirts, underclothes. The third time or the fourth, they begin to talk, but words raise issues that bodies can never fully resolve. What follows is the awkward phase, the phase of vague promises and splendid rationalizations. Later come the regrets, the partings, the bittersweet afterglow. She doesn't mention those to me. You don't mention regrets when you are telling a story as a way of seeking forgiveness.

$\mathcal{R}$eturning to Odessa ahead of schedule creates complications. Nina still has one more week of vacation and she wants to come with me. Normally I would say no, blame it on important business. But this time an excuse would be inexcusable. She already is doubly disappointed, in her own behavior and in my response. A betrayed lover should have blood in his eye. Not be full of the comforting sounds that I keep making, assuring her that these things happen.

Sergei and I hug goodbye at the studio. A long bear hug as if we fear we may never have a chance to hug again. Maybe we won't. An aide hands me a letter in Nadja's handwriting. The postmark is a week old. The message is simple. *Hurry back.*

A stormy crossing has me stretched out in the stateroom, feeling miserable, sucking on a lemon, my face a vivid green. So says Nina. She doesn't mention my color once we get to Odessa, but it can't be much healthier. On the odd chance that Nadja may be using the key to the villa that I left with her, I tell Nina I have given my seaside manor to a friend. We take a room in a small hotel, just off Primorskii, close to the Opera House and the Duc, and arrange for board in the same building. Except for breakfast. Nearby is the best bakery in Odessa. Every morning Nina slips out for warm, poppy seed bagels. No matter how many she buys, the bag is empty by nightfall.

Morning hours I claim for writing, but the moment Nina leaves to do the usual tourist things—the art and archeological museums, the Opera House, the grand parks, the Sailor's House, the glass-roofed Passage with its elegant nineteenth-century shops selling less than elegant contemporary merchandise—I hustle out the door to try and find out what is going on. At the post office there is a terrifying heap of correspondence, but I know the contents of most of the envelopes without having to open them. Demands from publishers, threats over missed deadlines, inquiries from editors of newspapers and journals, requests from story editors, proof sheets for an article, gossipy notes from friends in the Writers' Union about who is sleeping with whom to get what published. Nothing important. Nothing from Potato Face and nothing about K.

I bang on the gate of s. KRAPOLINSKY. HAULING, MOVING for a while, but the tough-looking guy who opens it has no idea where Jacob is. How about Josif and Moishe? He scratches his ear. Josif and Moishe? Josif and Moishe who? Never heard of 'em. In the marketplace, talk of trials, past or future, seems to have died down. It's melon season. Huge cantaloupes are on sale at outrageously low prices. I buy one and take it back to our room.

Afternoons present a problem. Nina expects us to do things together, and I can hardly explain my fear of a chance meeting with Nadja. Fortunately, the season begins to cooperate. We are suffering something Odessans call *that weather,* gray rainy days with chill winds. This becomes an excuse for me to purchase a new hat and coat and to avoid the usual public places in the center of the city. One afternoon I treat both of us to long mud baths and massages at the Lermontov. Another, I take Nina to the old cafeteria in the fishing port where guys I have known for a quarter century entertain her with tales about huge catches and great storms at sea. Once we take Nikitich out to dinner. Nina loves every exaggerated story he tells of Odessa in the old days. Especially the details of my enormous difficulties learning to swim.

We spend one afternoon in the Moldavanka. Walk together through the old market and stop at the stalls where my mother used to shop and where I once bought pigeons. Visit the sites of the whorehouses and gangster lairs of my stories and the apartments where my family lived. I pull my hat down low, hunch into the coat, keep looking over my shoulder, rehearsing the stories I will tell if we run into Nadja.

Lyosha is the unexpected answer to my prayers. His somber face appears just as we are strolling away from the fruit stalls in the market, munching on pears. I make an elaborate introduction and pointedly mention the place where we are staying. For once he is discreet. Perhaps because I am raising my eyebrows and making extravagant gestures behind Nina's back.

Ah, this is the Nina I've heard so much about. He asks appropriate questions: Is this her first time here and what has she seen and how are things in Moscow? He laments: Too bad Katya is out of town, I'm sure she'd like to meet you, have you over to dinner. He wishes her a good stay, tips his hat, and pulls me aside to whisper: *We've got to talk. Get in touch with me soon.*

Next morning in the post office, two envelopes with no return addresses.

The purple writing on the thick envelope is unfamiliar. Pages and pages of a letter covered with what seems to be one long sentence in a hand that begins neatly enough and deteriorates until it becomes large and barely legible. The scrawly signature, *Yezhova,* stabs me with memories.

The thin envelope is covered with now familiar handwriting and a now familiar kind of simple message. This time she provides the address of a rooming house near the beach at Arkadia and specifies a time and date for a meeting: two days from now. This time she signs the bottom of the page: *Svetlana.* Seeing the name written out on the page destroys something precious. Will I ever again be able to think of her as Potato Face?

Her note leaves me one problem and one opportunity.

She has chosen as a time for the meeting the hour when I will be putting Nina on the train for Moscow. I could beg off that duty. I could send a note changing the time, but something in me wants for once to get ahead of this game by taking action on my own. I want to surprise Svetlana. Maybe I can learn something important.

A twenty-minute trolley ride and I am in Arkadia. The rocky beach is deserted, lonely without the bronzed bodies and striped umbrellas of summer. Out beyond the breakwater, the size of the whitecaps says fall is here. So do the boarded-up cafés. An elderly man points the way through the botanical gardens toward the rooming house. I stroll down winding paths past flowers, bushes, trees from all over the globe.

Just past a stand of waving bottlebrush a pond comes into view, and my heart plunges from the roof of a tall building and hurtles helplessly toward the ground.

A hundred meters away. Their backs to me. Sitting on a bench. Side by side. Facing the pond. Talking. Gesturing. Moving their heads. In the body language of two people who know each other well.

Nadja and Svetlana.

I quickly step back behind the bottlebrush and watch, while my mind races back over various encounters, meetings, conversations, moments in and out of the bedroom. The two women continue to talk, toss bits of bread to the ducks floating and gabbling on the pond, lean close to one another from time to time. Eventually they stand up and shake hands, kiss on the cheeks and mouth, and walk off in opposite directions. Nadja turns back and her eyes pan across the bush where I am hidden. I shrink into the leaves. She calls out something to Svetlana, who half turns and answers her. They wave goodbye and go their separate ways.

Back at the post office, I send a telegram setting the meeting for the next day but two hours later than the suggested time, and insist that it be in the botanical gardens. In front of the duck pond. I can't prevent myself from indulging in personal irony by adding: I'm certain she won't have difficulty finding the place.

Nina's last night I take her to the dining room of the London Hotel. For two days she has been doing something uncharacteristic: moping around with a long face. No wonder. I have hardly been a decent companion on this vacation. The pregnancy, the affair, any mention of us— all have become the excuse for my distance. Over the last week she has tried to edge toward talk of the future. Each time it feels as if words like *permanent, commitment,* or *marriage* are about to enter the conversation, I change the topic. Invent another cute childhood story. Like the one about my grandmother chasing me into the yard and, in front of my friends, prying a stolen lamb chop right out of my mouth.

Someone who will believe that will believe anything. Including the sweet talk of an André Malraux, a man for whom language is a kind of religion, a man always bubbling over with words about literature, politics, art, and his favorite topic: himself. His own precious ideas and romantic actions. A hundred million women in Russia, and he picks Nina. But who can I blame? I am the one who invited him into the house. I am the one who left him there with her.

The linen, silver, crystal, and the good wine, the waiters in starched white jackets, all these help Nina to grow bright, open up, and begin to talk of *us*. The collective us. A family.

Yes, it was wrong. She knows that. Knew it at the time. It was a mistake. She's not that kind of woman. It won't happen again. But he was so winning. So, somehow, wounded. Beneath all the clever words he is lonely. So was she. Be honest, she says. You are always going away somewhere. She never knows about me. What he said is right. Right? About the other women. She has known, sort of. But she has never asked about my present or my past. She knows I had a life before her. I am a writer, and writers are people who claim special privileges. She has never interfered. But it is different with a child on the way. It may not be mine, but then again it may be. Either way, a child needs a father and a father needs a child. You're a man who needs to father a child. You have two children, but you still need a real child you can hold in your arms every day. Not a child in some other country. Not a child with someone else's name. A child at home. To call your own. A child we can call our own.

She may be right. I tell her that. She is probably right. But I need some time alone. I have to think it over. These things are never easy. I have obligations. I have family abroad. I have complications. We can't decide right now. We have to wait until I get back to Moscow. It's only a few weeks. We can decide then.

What I am thinking while I do this dance of avoidance is what a rare human being this woman is. What I am thinking is how mysterious are our hearts. What I am thinking is that if I were smart, I would love her. Take her in my arms and say, Let's get married, I want the child to have my name. What I am thinking is that there is no cause for guilt. With Nina as with all the others. What I am thinking is that my entire life has been centered around my creativity. My precious creativity. It has gotten me everywhere and nowhere. Brought me travel, women, privacy, secrecy, an interest in the police and their doings. For years all I have done is watch others going about their lives, except for those few times I have tried to help those in trouble, and even then I was watching myself acting in a noble way. Trying to understand what it is when one acts, what one does in the name of selfish altruism. What I am thinking is that creativity is as much an excuse as anything else. For doing what you want when you want. For refusing to take responsibility. For not having much faith in God and even less in human beings.

38

Izzie, Izzie, Izzie my friend, my love,

Where are you now that I need you? Izzie, he has gotten what he has always wanted always plotted and schemed to get and it will kill me, Izzie, if I don't kill myself first with vodka or drugs or both of them together. I know you always warned me as long ago as Berlin, you said enough was enough, but it was the twenties and enough was never enough, not on those glorious nights—do you remember the full moon above the Brandenburg Gate, the smell of the Tiergarten, we were riding in a carriage and drowned in the smell of new-mown grass and dung, how we laughed about the heaps of dung we never saw but smelled, dung from giraffes and gazelles and lions and elephants, they were the funniest, huge mounds, we imagined and laughed, you too, and you have never been much of a laugher not out loud, you smile secretly at some joke only you know, but did you ever know our lives would become dung, our country, that new world we believed in would all become dung. To tell the truth we always preferred Berlin or Paris, but you got to Paris not me, three years in Berlin and then back to Moscow, if I had stayed in Berlin I would never have met him, married him, and now he's head of the secret police, he knows all the secrets now and those secrets are going to kill a lot of people, me included and you included, for he has always hated you, you know that, ever since he found out about us and I have to say this, Izzie, I have to say why did you let me do it? It was your fault for being married already before Berlin. I was married too but you know how I hated my husband, that's why I was in Berlin, and I said I didn't care, what kind of a woman doesn't care? but I said I didn't, I was free, it was the 1920s not the 1820s and I was from the most progressive country in the world, the one with the future when we would all write novels and live in a city that was smarter and more modern than Berlin and we would call that city Moscow.

Why is this woman writing to me now? I can hear you say. Do you

think of me as that woman, your Berlin lover, like in one of your stories, re-
member I never asked you to leave your wife but then I knew you wouldn't,
and what do I know but that we are carrying on very nicely at my hideaway
in Kolkova, and then you begin to make excuses and suddenly are never
there from one week to the next and all of sudden it is someone else, it is al-
ways someone else, isn't it? who lets me know that in fact you have left me
for that crazed vampire Kashirina, not only left but you have a child with
her—did anyone ever tell you that you too need a good examination of the
head, always did, oh you were so crazy in Berlin, me too. How did we get
over that, how does a woman get over that, maybe I never did but I did
enough for the years of friendship, a decade or more, you never believed did
you that lovers could become friends, I never believed it either, but I need to
tell you this, it has been so good having you all these years while he has got-
ten stronger. You know how often I have wanted to leave him but he won't
let me, Izzie, he terrifies me, you have never seen him in his rages, no, in
public he is polite as can be but you have seen the scars, you have mentioned
the black and blue marks, but I won't talk about them, I never talk about
the way he cuts me with the buckle of his belt sometimes oh you cannot can-
not imagine how many times, yes, you have seen the scars, you know I have
tried to leave him, I will try again but I want to see you before that, just one
more time for old time's sake if you could just hold me and Berlin could
come back to us again. I know things are not so good for you these days, I
know you can't leave either, it's getting harder and harder and with him in
charge nobody will be leaving soon, the whole country will be cutting its
wrists or he will be slitting them for all of us, not only wrists but throats as
well. So you wonder about this letter. I want to say be careful my lover, you
were the one that got away—how did you do it? and all these years, coming
to my office, editorial meetings and sometimes at my house, when he would
insult you, you would notice I am sure, but never said anything, but where
did you think the insults were coming from? Tell you the truth I let on that
maybe things are not over between us, maybe we are seeing each other
when he isn't looking, doesn't that drive him wild, he who can barely get it
up unless there is a big picture of the Boss on the wall, smiling down on him
or he is using his belt or his fists to get out the pain that now he will have
others to work on, a whole country and not just me. Take care of yourself,

he will go to whatever ends are necessary. People tell me that he used to be okay, Nadezhda Mandelstam once said that before we married he was a perfect gentleman, but I ask you why then did he have so many wives? I don't even know how many even though he admits to three, well me, three husbands, so we are even only I am not a danger to anyone not to my ex-lovers and he is a danger to all of us to the country to everything, he is the master of the dung heap so be careful and call me when you get back into town.

   Yevgenia Yezhova

39

I arrive late on purpose. Approach on the same path as the day before. Step behind the same bushes for a moment. Watch Svetlana sitting on the bench, tossing bread crumbs to a small flotilla of ducks, quacking and pushing each other aside to get closer to the food.

Summer is over.

She wears the same olive-drab suit, the same masculine shoes as the first time she walked into my room three months ago. Shows the same coolness as I approach, sit down next to her. She glances over, nods, puts the bag of breadcrumbs between us. I take a handful. Join in the feeding. Let her make the first move.

Nina got off okay? Her voice is low. *She's nice. Your friend.*

I grunt something that could be taken as assent or a sign of severe intestinal problems.

I like Odessa, she says. *I'll be sorry to leave.*

I remain silent. For a while only the ducks talk. They have nothing interesting to say.

A shallow sigh.

It's over. Her voice is still low.

It?

The whole operation. Something has changed. Someone lied. I don't know the details. K is dead. Your job is over.

Dead? Since when?

Days. Weeks. Maybe they killed him right after the trial. I don't know.

How long have you known?

Known for certain? A few days. Suspected? A bit longer.

And me? What am I supposed to do?

What you have always done. Nothing has changed. You can go back to writing screenplays and stories and giving public talks about how your story-writing skill is not up to the needs of today's workers. Maybe you should finish that story about Benya Krik. The beginning was promising.

And you?

She doesn't want to answer that question. Doesn't want to carry on with this conversation. So I turn. Lean toward her on the bench for the first time. Clamp my right hand on her left wrist and hold tight. She jerks around and our faces are very close together. The lumps vanish. I am aware of the gray eyes, wide open and for the moment, unguarded. Well-shaped lips that quiver slightly.

Tell me. My voice is urgent. Angry. Insistent. *Who sent you? What has this really all been about?*

Her eyes grow wider, then she turns her head, tries to pull away. I put my left hand on one shoulder, shift the right one to her other shoulder. She struggles. I tighten my grip and we are pushing, rocking back and forth, and the demon of desire is rocking with us. She utters a gasp, a cry, a bleat like some animal and then her lips are against mine, her body heaving, her tongue pressing into my mouth, and I respond with all the pent-up frustration of the summer, the not-knowing, the wondering, the worrying, and even as we kiss, a corner of my mind refuses to acknowledge what is happening and keeps insisting that this is not desire but some sort of strategy, a way of getting her to tell me what is really going on, what role Nadja has been playing, who else is watching me, what's going to happen now.

We break apart as suddenly as we came together. Sit side by side once again. Toss bread to the ducks. Neither of us trusts words right now. Eventually the bag is empty. The ducks quack for a while, then paddle away.

Useless to ask questions she can't answer. Useless to share worries that are mine alone. Not until this moment do I begin to sink toward the deepest depths of knowing. Not until this moment do I understand how much I have been counting on that passport to France to see my daughter. On the chance, too, for a definitive break with Zhenya. A face-to-face break, once and for all. A break to leave me free. For what?

Nadja?

Right.

Odessa?

Right again.

Maybe I do need to have my head examined.

She breaks the silence. Speaks in a tone I have not heard before. Warm is one word that comes to mind. Apologetic another. It's the longest speech she has ever made.

She is sorry to have raised hopes that will not be fulfilled. She knows how much I want to go abroad. Need to go. But it is beyond her control. She too is disappointed. More than disappointed. This was not just a job. What happened to K and the others was wrong. A travesty of justice. A betrayal of too many hopes. Things are getting completely crazed. Too many innocent people are going to suffer.

She wants to tell me something else. About her own involvement. I was not just a random name picked by someone higher up. She was the one who suggested me. That first day when she asked if I was Isaac Babel the writer, it was all she could do to keep from giving me a big hug. She knew very well who I was. Has been a great admirer of my writing for many years. Of my courage, too. Does that surprise me? Her office is close to the inner circle. She has access to certain files. She hears lots of things. Things she knows I never speak about to anyone. The many times I have gone to Gorky or Yagoda or some other official in the Kremlin to ask them to intervene on behalf of a colleague who's in jail or who has fallen under the suspicion of the secret police. Even the Boss heard that I was trying to have them end Mandelstam's exile on the grounds that a great country cannot let a great poet freeze and starve to death in Voronezh. He asked Yagoda to repeat the poem that led to Mandelstam's arrest, and when he finished, the Boss ordered him not only to keep Mandelstam in exile but to lengthen his sentence. Then he said: Who is this Babel to think he can make such demands of the Party leadership just because he wrote a popular book or two and has become so well known in the West.

Yids, said the Boss. *They stick together.* He began to chuckle. *But you have to give Babel one thing: he seems to have balls, bigger balls than all the others. Who ever heard of a Yid with balls?* Then he laughed out loud. There is nothing more frightening than the Boss laughing aloud. Especially when he isn't drunk.

Svetlana stops. We look at each other for the first time since our kiss.

I shake my head in wonder and thank her on behalf of my grandchildren. Won't they someday be pleased to learn that the great leader of our country once thought so highly of Grandpa's genitals.

We stare at the pond again. There is nothing more to say. No words to finish this oddest of all encounters in a life of odd encounters. What can you call our relationship? Were we partners, associates, friends, colleagues, conspirators? No single word seems quite right for our meetings and our shared disappointment.

The ducks return to see if we have something more for them. We stand together, shake hands, avoid each other's eyes, perform the ritual of departure. A kiss on both cheeks. A final hug. As we begin to turn away, she stops and grips my arm with passion. I take a step backward.

Isaac. You've made all the arrangements. For God's sake, now use the boat yourself. You're being watched. Be smart. Use it before it's too late. Go see your daughter. Get away. Go live in France and write the truth about what's going on here. In the next few years we're going to need a lot of people to tell the truth. You're not safe here. Not anymore. Not even in Odessa.

She turns away. I start to speak, but what is there to say? That I want to know exactly who is watching? That I need more details? She takes a few quick steps and turns around. Her gray eyes sparkle. For the first time, her face widens into a smile. Her teeth are horrible. I wish she had kept her mouth shut.

Do it. Izzie, be good to yourself. This is not a time for Jewish indecision. It's a time to act.

Then she winks. Potato Face winks. And walks away.

40

*G*oing back to the villa I expect the worst. My stuff trashed, my things stolen, my manuscripts shredded. It only shows I've been reading too many detective novels. Everything is just as I left it: papers in place, tea stored in airtight containers in the cupboard, clothes in the drawers and the armoire. Only the next morning do I notice that one thing is missing: the silver mezuzah has been stripped from the front door frame.

When I see this, there is no time to think about what it may signify. It's very early. I have been wrenched from my bed by an urgent knocking on the front door and yank it open to find Katya. A different Katya, not my normally self-possessed aunt. This is an old woman, haggard, disheveled, her eyes red. She collapses against me. Even before I get her into a chair, the words are spilling out. Lyosha is in jail. The police barged into the apartment in the middle of the night, turned everything upside down, tore up closets, ripped into mattresses, broke through the backs of cabinets and dressers. Lyosha cowered in the corner, screaming he had done nothing, until he was dragged away.

I try to calm her. Take her home and say I will see about helping to get him out. Promise to check back later, then head directly to the Moldavanka. Jacob is happy to see me, but I stop him before he can begin his usual patter. Oddly, my news doesn't much surprise him. Pretty routine, he says. The police periodically need to look as if they are making attempts to clean up the city. Usually they let Jacob know in advance so he can make it easy for them. Set out the right kind of stuff for them to pick up. Cases of American cigarettes, sacks of wheat, cartons of German radios. Sometimes Jacob has to sacrifice one of his guys for a few weeks or months. The victim gets well paid. The police are happy and Jacob's guys are happy. Things go back to normal.

I must look surprised.

It's Odessa. Nothing changes. But picking up Lyosha is a bit different.

He sounds more worried than he lets on. For the first time he doesn't ask about what I'm writing, doesn't want to discuss literature or the declining quality of Soviet life. He will check with the police, see if there is a way of getting Lyosha out without any fuss. But not directly. You can't do these things directly. He'll start with my friend, the police chief of Nikolayev.

Jacob reaches into a drawer. Pulls out a wad of ruble notes. *Give these to his wife. Tell her Lyosha has friends. Tell her not to worry. I understand she's quite a lady.*

I wonder aloud, Could this have anything to do with changes at the top? Yagoda out of power. Yezhov taking his place. New trials that seem to be on the way. Jacob shakes his head. People can give all the orders they want in Moscow but someone has to carry them out here in Odessa. This is something local. Besides. Between Yagoda and Yezhov there's no difference. The organization remains the same. They all have to do business.

He leads me across the courtyard and we make our way to the post office. As we wait in the long-distance line, I express surprise.

You can do this over the phone?

What? Under the new constitution a citizen doesn't have the right to talk to a chief of police? We have our own way of talking. A little Yiddish, a little Ukrainian, a little code.

He emerges from the phone booth with an expression I can't read.

Don't worry. It will take a couple of days, but there's nothing special going on. He asked about you. Wanted to know if you'd read his stories yet.

I shake my head.

Jacob throws his arm around my shoulder on the way back to the office. There's something else the police chief told him. Something that confirms certain rumors in this town. Jacob understands that our deal is off. That I won't be needing that boat passage for a certain somebody. But a deal is a deal. He does not forget. If I ever need a boat for someone else I should let him know. And from what he has been hearing, if anyone ever needed a boat out of Odessa, it's me. Sooner than soon. Right away.

Tell me more.

What's to tell? Except that there are times when Odessa is not a healthy place. This is one of those times. Especially for you. From what I understand, Moscow is likely to be worse. Remember: to everything there is a season. A place too. That includes boat trips. They're good for the health.

I get seasick too easily.

Jacob takes me by the arm. Puts his face close to mine.

Isaac. In case you don't know it, you're a national treasure. Odessa will be far poorer if you go away. We all will be. But it looks like Odessa is going to be poorer one way or the other, so why shouldn't it be poorer with you alive and healthy? It's your choice, my friend. Only remember you have a duty. To your readers. To the future. Be smart. Lots of us need you.

Back at Katya's, I explain it's nothing too serious. Don't worry. Lyosha will be back in a day or two. We drink tea and eat honey cake. Far too restless to return home, I begin to wander through town, needing to think even if I'm not convinced that thinking ever helps you to make a decision. But it is a good way of passing time. I walk and concentrate on the weather. It's definitely fall. During short bursts of rain, I stand in doorways or under the trees in parks. The city comes to me in dreamy images, muffled sounds. I pass the Sibiriyalovsky Theater, the Opera House, linger on the promenade above the harbor and near the statue of the Duc, and gaze out at the ships with foreign flags. Stroll through the Moldavanka and pass the apartment where I once lived for three days. Half the merchants in the market have closed their stalls because of the rain. I put a ten-ruble note into the cup of a fiddler playing a mournful lament that originated in some far-off shtetl. I bump into a man in a full-length raincoat. For one long moment we are face to face. He starts to push past me and an image comes to mind: this is the face who tried to buy my watch, my cufflinks. A face that appeared at my reading. A face I glimpsed on Catherine Street the day Eisenstein arrived. I grab him by the arm and bark:

My watch. You're the one. You stole my watch. Where's my watch?

He jerks out of my grasp and begins to run. I follow, chase him along the street, bumping against people, shouting *Excuse me,* yelling *Stop!* over and over at the fleeing figure. Neither of us is exactly a runner, so this is almost a chase in slow motion. He turns a corner and disappears. I follow and we are moving down an alley that ends against a brick wall. I grab him by the arm, pull him roughly around, hold him with two hands, and shriek: *Where is it? Where's my watch?*

His face full of terror. He tries to pull away. Begins to shout *Help Help Help!* but I hold him tightly, shout back:

Shut up, you fucker, shut up. Give me the goddamn watch.

He struggles, again shouts *Help, Help!* I clap my hand over his mouth. He bites down. Sinks his teeth into my palm. I howl, jerk back my fist and punch him in the face. He starts to shout again and I punch him again and again until the shouting stops and his nose and mouth are smeared with blood and he collapses against the wall muttering, *Cossack, Cossack.*

Aware suddenly of blood everywhere, on his face, on my hand and sleeve, on his coat and mine. Dimly aware, too, that I have been beating a man on no more than a fleeting suspicion. I ease him to the ground, step back, pull out a handkerchief and try to wipe the blood away from his face, all the while murmuring over and over, *I'm sorry, I'm sorry, I'm sorry,* until I realize the handkerchief won't absorb any more blood and that he can't hear me because he's unconscious. I stand up slowly, walk, then run down the alley, turn the corner, head for home. On the streets and in the trolley, people keep looking in other directions as I try to wipe away the blood from the sleeves of my coat.

41

*C*wilight. I am sitting in the lobby of her hotel when Nadja enters. She's a good actress. Does an exaggerated double take. Spreads a smile across her face like a slow sunrise on the summer steppe. Thrusts her handbag toward me and says: *I can always use the ruble.*

Our embrace takes place in a realm where passion and politeness are first cousins. Nadja doesn't hesitate to accept my dinner invitation. The film has wrapped. She has no more lines to memorize. Nothing to do in this town but say goodbye to me. We go back to the Romanian cabaret. Crowded, noisy, and smoky as ever. With one new element: a balalaika has been added to the band. After the clarinet and saxophone take solos, a smiling string player plucks out an improvisation.

What gives? I gesture toward the bandstand. A waiter shrugs, makes a sour face, holds his hands over his ears.

Me, I can do without it. Who needs such sounds? But someone convinced the bandleader that balalaikas are an old Odessa tradition. Goes way back. He claims that the Turks were playing balalaikas when Catherine's troops conquered Haji-Bey. You ask me, they heard what we're hearing and they turned around and said forget about it. Let's go back to St. Petersburg.

We eat, we drink, we dance, we return to the villa and make love in a room lit with two candles. Make love as if we both know that something is coming to an end. Not until we are on the terrace in the morning, tea cups in hand, do I get to what's on my mind. Beginning with a name.

Svetlana Kripinskaya.

Svetlana Kripinskaya. Interesting name.

Interesting woman. Are you by any chance working for her?

She pauses a short beat.

It's not exactly work.

What would you call it? A rehearsal? Preparation for a new role?

In a way. She pauses. *But surely this is no surprise.*

The surprise is that it's Kripinskaya. I knew you were working for someone, but I imagined it was for the other side.

I am. For them too.

Does my mouth drop open? It must.

Don't be naive, she continues. *It's not a matter of two sides. There are a whole bunch of them. Which ones do you work for?*

Me?

You're friends with everyone at the top. Yagoda, Yezhov. Anybody else I should know? Aren't you on their payroll?

I don't know what to say. Clearly I expected something else. Something more emotional and dramatic. Remorse, perhaps. Tears. Nadja collapsing in my arms. Begging forgiveness. Giving me the chance to say it's all right. Don't worry. I understand.

I'm surprised you seem so surprised.

So am I. What have you told them?

The truth. Mostly. That you're a lousy swimmer but a decent lover. That you like to sleep late and feel guilty about liking horses so much. Nothing they don't already know. But you are a tough one to know. Even that novel or journal or memoir or whatever you want to call it that you hide away in the drawer doesn't say anything that isn't already perfectly obvious to the whole world. I read it when you were gone. Since you didn't take it with you I figured you wanted me to read it, right? I like the woman character, even if her motivation seems a bit shady. But you've got him all wrong. In life he's not nearly as hard-edged as the Isaac you depict. He worries about people, cares for them. He's gentle and supportive. All I can figure is that you're still that same little Jewish boy, trying to cover up his tenderness with the stance of a tough guy. Just like you did in Red Cavalry.

I lean across the table. Our lips meet. She tells me the story I have been waiting to hear.

Yes, she really is an actress but she has never been within a thousand miles of Kazakhstan. And yes, there's no Boris, no kids. She is from Leningrad. A decade out of acting school and still struggling with walk-on roles in the State Theater. Why so little progress? Probably for the same reason they must have chosen her to watch me. Because of the background she has been trying to hide. Minor nobility, an estate burned during the Revolution. The details of that first story of her life were pretty much true. The second story with the Cossack father was only a way of trying to let me know that something was fishy. Why? Because this started out as a job but got to be something more. I may be a rascal but a lovable one. Not that it makes any difference. She's going home to Leningrad. Waiting for the payoff. Roles in real films. Not like the one here, no more than a short subject on collectivization in Kazakhstan. Not exactly a role designed to promote a career. It was cooked up by the guys who hired her. They said you wouldn't know; they figured you would never come to meet me at the studio. A good cover story, no? The theater people believed it. Who knows or cares anything about Kazakhstan or theater there? That was the test. If the story convinced the people at the Sibiriyalovsky, then Babel would be a cinch.

Was I?

She smiles her answer.

It began when two guys came to her rooms in Leningrad. Guys who knew everything about her. Background, education, love life, ambitions, frustrations with the theater, desire to get into films. Everything. They appealed equally to her self-interest and her patriotism. Do yourself a favor. Do your country a favor. We need you to get close to Isaac Babel. Tell us what he's up to. At first she said no. This was not the sort of role she was seeking. But no was not part of their vocabulary. Money was. So were threats. Her background could get her fired. No acting, no work, no identification card, no food, no housing, no life. Besides. Where's the harm? Wouldn't it be nice to have a role in a film? Only a short subject, but if you do your job, it will lead to something much bigger. So she changes her mind. Decides to meet this character and see what happens. Have an adventure. What she did not count on was falling in love.

Svetlana showed up after she was already reporting to the guys. Just before our meeting at the theater. The guys did not know when you would come, but they knew that sooner or later you would. *Babel's a sucker for theater,* the guys told me. *It's the one form where the critics always killed him. He's a sucker for actresses too.* She had to sit through seven performances before I showed up.

For that alone I deserve a bonus.

Svetlana knew everything that the guys knew, but her exact relationship to them, if any, was never clear. She just barged in, offered money, and told Nadja to keep quiet. Not to mention anything to the guys or to me. The two of them met once a week or so. She listened to Nadja's reports. Pretty dull stuff. Babel did this, he said that, we went here, we went there. Svetlana also asked a lot of questions. What does he talk about? Whom does he visit? What is he writing? She never made threats but occasionally did hand over some cash. And she never explained what this was all about, not even after Nadja felt close enough to ask. Svetlana shook her head and said there are lots of things it's better not to know, and this is one of them.

Did she really ask about me as a lover? Us as lovers? Did she ask for details? Did you give them?

Men! Nadja faces me. She has been waiting for this encounter. Waiting to ask me a question, too.

Isaac, tell me. I don't really understand this world. Are you reporting to someone about me?

I start to giggle. To laugh with great gusto. I get up and pace around the terrace.

The critics are right. They really are, damn them. I'm completely out of touch with the spirit of the times. Just when I decide to become a materialist, the world turns in the direction of some sort of dialectical surrealism.

Silence. That moment when two people realize they have nothing more to talk about. That they are right on the edge of becoming ex-lovers. Of saying goodbye to the many futures whose impossibilities once tore at their hearts. It's a moment when you have to select words carefully because they are what will come to mind long after you can no longer recall the scent of her hair, the smoothness of the skin between her shoulder blades, her husky whispers in the night.

Silence. Dreams slip back into the unconscious. Something must be saved.

Don't trust them, I tell her. Don't go back to Leningrad. You know too much. They'll want to use you again. Make you do something similar. Or get rid of you. They won't let you get away. The film career won't happen. One way or another, they'll take you out. But I can help. Let me help you get away from here. It's already arranged. A boat out of the country. You can go to France. You've always wanted to go to Paris. You'll be free.

Izzie, you're the one in trouble, not me. You're the one who needs to get away. I can take care of myself. I'm not the only one they've sent to watch you. There are people here and people in Moscow. If there's really a boat that will get you away, you should be on it. Do yourself a favor. Me too. Go to see your daughter in France. Get out of here.

Yes. She is an actress and she isn't. Drawing on real emotions to create false ones for the stage. Or is it the other way around? Hers are the words of someone who knows what she is doing. Has done it before and will do it again. Knows what she is after. Lots of what she told me may have been true. Probably was true. But even now Nadja is not entirely what she seems to be. Sure, she is someone who has been touched momentarily by feelings you're not supposed to have in this profession. Not if you are doing this kind of job. Not if you are a real dame. However much of her story is true, and whatever else she has been or is, Nadja is certainly that.

42

My dearest darling son,

It has been a long time since I have written to you, I know that. It's not because I don't think of you, because I want you to know I think of you each and every day, all day long. It's because of the arthritis, which makes it difficult to hold a pen for very long. I don't want you to think I am complaining or to add to your burdens. You have enough of them already, and I know that Mera adds to them every time she writes a letter and has to ask for more bagels. The arthritis is normal enough when you get to my age. It's no worse than when you were here two years ago. There are lots of people in their late sixties here in Brussels who are lots worse off than I am. I see them in the park, their hands and feet looking all crippled up, hardly able to walk, on those days when I am well enough to sit in the park or the rain stops so I can get out of this apartment for a while.

How nice it must be to be in Odessa again. Is it nice and sunny? I remember it as always nice and sunny in the summer. Here it rains too much. Whoever heard of so much rain in the summer! I miss Odessa. I miss the sun and the melons and grapes and I miss the smell of the sea. And fresh fish every day like we used to have in the summer. I miss that too. Being abroad is not all it is cracked up to be. I know if I knew the language it would be easier, but it's hard to learn things at my age, and if I did who would I talk to? Belgians? What do I have to say to them and what do they have to say to me? It's fine for Mera and Boris. They are making a life here and they need to talk to people. The only people I talk to are old Jewish people, in Yiddish or in Russian. We have things to say to each other, mostly about the old places that we miss. I miss the bagels too. Are you eating lots of them? How your father liked bagels. And smoked bluefish. Do you remember how he liked to have smoked bluefish every Sunday morning, summer and winter. I never cared for it smoked myself. I liked it fresh. I liked the tomatoes, too, and the melons. Oh, I mentioned melons already. Sometimes even writing a letter I forget what I have said.

You are a lucky boy, Izzie, to be back in Odessa. You are a good boy, too, and that is why you are lucky. Are you taking care of yourself? Are the treatments at the Lermontov helping your poor nose? Be sure and dress warm. Even in the summer the breezes can get chilly later in the day so take along a sweater. Beware of getting in drafts. You are a big man, but you are still not so strong. You were always not so strong. I didn't ever know why. I was always strong as an ox and your father was healthy until he developed that heart condition. Mera was healthy too. You were the one we always worried about. Your asthma. Your nose. Your attacks of hiccups. Do you re-member the time during the pogrom of 1905 when they killed poor Uncle Shoyl and your father's store was burned down? How could you forget? Do you remember we went to the house of our neighbor, Mrs. Rubtsov, that very pretty woman who wasn't Jewish, and you came into her spotless living room all covered with blood from those pigeons you had snuck out to buy? What a day to do that! That horrible man without legs smashed your bag of pigeons against your head, and Mrs. Rubtsov washed you off, and then you began to hiccup and you could not stop for days. Maybe it was weeks. After that you were always sick with one thing or another. So take care of your-self. I hope the Lermontov helps this time.

My son, I want you always to remember how proud I am of you. Your father, may he rest in peace, was always proud of you too. We were so proud that you were one of the two Jewish boys who got into the commercial high school and we were proud when you went off to college in Kiev. I know you didn't want to go. I said to your father, He doesn't want to go. Maybe we should let him stay here. He said, And what will he do here? Enter my busi-ness? My son needs to know more than I do. He needs to be an educated man. He needs to get ahead. It is no secret Manny was not happy when he learned you were on your way to St. Petersburg to take up writing. We both were worried when you went to St. Petersburg and stayed there during the worst days of 1918 when everyone was freezing and starving. But you know what? He was secretly very very happy when you began to publish things in Gorky's journal. Manny bragged to everyone he knew. He would say, You know Gorky, don't you? He's the most famous writer in Russia and he is printing my son. Gorky has good taste.

Manny was not a worrier by nature. Not until after 1905 when he lost everything in the pogrom. It's all in God's hands, he would say, even though he did not really believe in God. But he worried and I worried during the Civil War when you were in Romania and then in the Pale and Poland. I can tell you he was not too happy about you being with the Cossacks. What's a son of mine doing with Cossacks is what he would say. But the big worry was over your safety. We thought you would be killed or maimed or worse. When your first stories began to appear, just before he died, Manny had a smile as wide as the moon. I think he thought you showed the Cossacks just as they were, and they were too dumb to realize what you were really saying.

I hope you are visiting your father's grave, may he rest in peace. Remember to put flowers on it. Say a prayer over it even if you don't believe in prayers. You are more like your father than you think you are. He did not like the Revolution. You know that. He hated the way it took away everything again and made us live jumbled up with a bunch of people we didn't know. A revolution? he said. A pogrom. There's not much difference except a pogrom doesn't last so long. He said the Revolution would not be good for the Jews. But in a way he understood why it came. He was not in favor of injustice, and he saw injustice all around him. Your father was a good man. I know you two never spoke very much after you dropped out of school. I know you argued a lot. But he loved you. I think maybe you loved him too. I hope so. He was a good man and I pray to God every night that he let Manny's soul rest in peace. Not that I believe in God any more than he did. But a prayer couldn't hurt. Could it?

My hand is beginning to ache so I better stop. I am probably repeating myself anyway. That's what happens when you get old. There is nothing new so you repeat the same things over and over. But I want you to know that your mother thinks you have been a credit to us. To our name. You have given us a mitzvah, a grandchild. What else can a mother want? Not that we see Natasha very much. I wish Zhenya would bring her from France occasionally. I wish Zhenya would write to us more often, but you know Zhenya and her ways better than I do. It is a pity we are so far apart, my son. I understand why you resist coming here, despite all the pleas from Mera. Brussels may be nice but it can never be home. For me there will never be any home but Odessa. Write some more stories about it. They help me to remember. And take care of yourself. Dress warmly and eat. All we have in the end is our health. And our love for each other. I love you. Your mother loves you. I know you will always be a good boy whatever you do.

Love and kisses from your mother,

Fenya

43

*M*orning sun. Curtains blowing in a cool breeze. The smell of the sea. A burner, a kettle, a teapot, a cup on the table before me. I stare out the window. Wait for inspiration to finish the story about Benya and the Revolution. When it doesn't come, I write this instead. Afternoons I go to the Lermontov for the heat lamp, the massages, the inhalation therapy. At my examinations, Professor Kalina tries to explain why my asthma attacks have gotten worse.

A difficult case, my boy. A difficult case. It may take us two or three years to get to the bottom of this. Could be the lingering effects of the hardships of the early years of the Revolution. Not enough heat in the winters. Not enough food. But we'll lick the problem, don't you worry. We'll get you fixed up. Just give us enough time.

Something none of us has in overabundance. Not these days. That's what everybody keeps telling me when they visit. Josif and Moishe arrive one morning with a message from Jacob.

Tell him he should get out while the getting is good. That's what Jacob told us to say. But we're not just saying it for him. For us, too. Things are getting too dangerous. We need you alive. We need Benya Krik. Jacob will arrange everything. He says it's already paid for. Just give us the word and it's done.

Lyosha says the same thing when he comes to thank me for getting him out of jail. With genuine feeling in his voice for the first time in years. They got to him this time. It wasn't like his earlier arrests. The questions were not about smuggling or other petty illegalities, but about his beliefs. Mine, too. Did he make statements about the madmen running the country? Does his nephew agree with him? What have I said about Trotsky? About the trials? About Zinoviev and Kamenev? The Germans and the Japanese? Has he noticed anything suspicious in my house?

The boys at TEPHOOSU, in their own way, pass on the same message. When I go there to ask about a building permit for my lot, Bagritsky doesn't even bother to conceal his laugh. A mirthless laugh. He sits in what was once Zirinovsky's office, in what was once Zirinovsky's chair and asks: Who would have imagined his former boss had been a Trotskyist? Bagritsky's necktie is sober. He wears a dark suit. He laughs again, a harsh laugh. *No building permits can be issued for private residences. Not these days when private residences are definitely on the way out. Even for well-known writers. Sorry but you will have to vacate the villa, comrade. We need you out by November.*

I enjoy these final mornings. The view. The afternoon swims. The visits to the post office. Editors are no longer bothering to write to me. Nor are friends in Moscow. Maybe they think I am a dead man. Maybe they know something I don't know. On the other hand, I do get telegrams from the head of production at Mosfilm. They need me to do rewrites on some film scripts. And there are plenty of notes from Nina, who conspicuously ignores the topic of pregnancy in favor of news about the subway.

Believe me. I often wonder the same thing you are wondering. Why keep on writing pages that will never be read? But in everyone who puts pen to paper there lurks the hope, however distant or remote, that someday someone will encounter his words and be moved to see the world in a slightly different way—as more mysterious and far more interesting than we usually imagine it to be. Certainly anyone reading this may well wonder: Did Isaac Babel really have all these experiences in the summer of 1936? Or was he losing his mind? Could he really no longer distinguish his stories of childhood from his actual childhood? Or is this just Babel playing around, reinventing his past, giving himself adventures he always wished had been his. Perhaps the work is the product of boredom, a diversion during a dull period when he was undergoing medical treatments and needed to keep his mind occupied. Or is it a result of his overheated imagination during the period when the Old Bolsheviks were on trial. An attempt to connect himself to the great events of his day.

If any journalist or biographer ever tracks down the letters I have written to Zhenya and Natasha, and to Mera and Mother, or checks the archives of official agencies (if archives survive), they will be able to follow many of my movements this summer. Such documents will show that, yes, I took the train to Odessa in August and back to Moscow in early November. Yes, I did go to Yalta to work with Eisenstein on *Bezhin Meadow*. Yes, I did take extensive medical treatments at the Lermontov, including heat lamps, showers, mud baths, and massages. Yes, I did go to a synagogue once, and deliver an impromptu speech one night at the Sibiriyalovsky Theater, and give a public reading.

But no matter how much effort goes into the research, the real story always takes place in the space between the documents. Between the words, too. Any writer knows that. Which means you have to wonder about the romantic interlude. Nadja, looking so much like Galina Rubtsov. The lover who turns out to be a spy. Anyone who knows me well will know that, wherever I am, there is bound to be at least one lover. And anyone who knows the Soviet Union in 1936 knows that there is bound to be at least one spy, and probably more than one. As for the political tale, the story about making arrangements for Kamenev to escape, surely that has to contain a great deal of fantasy. Will history be able to imagine the Boss letting somebody escape? Not too likely. But as we all know, Russians are much better at giving orders than at carrying them out. And lots of people here give orders without our ever knowing the reasons for them.

Always it comes down to a matter of style, in life and in art. The style of this work is far too plain, too straightforward for Babel. He couldn't have written anything like this. He was too poetic, too sensitive, too Jewish. You know the type. A mama's boy who always remained fearful, evasive, sickly. The guy in this manuscript is something of a scoundrel. All those women. The Boss is right, how could he be such a lady's man? To tell the truth, this sounds very much like one of those doctored works that the Russian secret police have always specialized in turning out. Like the *Protocols of the Elders of Zion*. Russia is the last country in the modern world where you can still get people to believe such stuff. That's what I learned during the war with Poland. That's why I created the character of Gedali and had him call for a Fourth International, an international of Just Men. Even then I knew we wouldn't get anything resembling justice out of the regime we were beginning to build. But knowledge doesn't destroy hope. Only living can do that.

As for taking the ship to France, don't think it's not a strong temptation. Many is the afternoon I wander down to the harbor and look at the freighters with the names of foreign home ports and think about Paris and my daughter and wonder: What do I have to leave to her? What do I have to leave anybody other than words? It would be so easy. It would be so difficult. It would be so different.

One day in the park near the great steps a very old man leaning on a cane next to me starts to speak:

A glorious view, isn't it? The most glorious in the world. You know the old saying, don't you? Odessa's just like Paris only Odessa is better.

You think so?

I know what I'm talking about young man. Believe me. I've been to Paris. Lived there for more than ten years plying my trade. I was a tailor. I worked in a small shop in the Marais. The French need good tailors, and there were lots of us there from Eastern Europe. It was good, Paris, but only for a while. You get sick and tired of the French and their crusty bread. You want to hear Russian. You want to see the sea. Times may be hard here, but I've never been sorry I came back. It's home. Odessa is the best.

How about Moscow? Ever been there?

He turns to look at me as if I am crazy.

Moscow? Once. That was enough. Lousy weather and too many goyim. You have to be nuts to live there.

Finally I have time enough to read the stories written by the police chief of Nikolayev. Let's hope I never meet him again and be asked to give a commentary. They are badly written, poorly plotted, full of wooden characters nobody in his right mind would believe. And yet the stories have a certain energy, the energy of brutality. The best parts are the moments when the Jewish cops act like cops anywhere in the world. Planting evidence against crooks they don't like. Using stool pigeons. Twisting the law. Beating helpless prisoners with rubber clubs and pistol butts. Beating them senseless. Leaving them bloody and unconscious in their cells. In these moments, the prose of the police chief is full of an excitement that is almost sexual.

One thing bad writing does for you—it lets your mind wander. It also shows you that your own ideas are pretty good. As I read the chief's stories, the ending of Benya Krik becomes clear to me. So busy do I get with writing that for two days I neglect to go to the Lermontov and I don't even take a swim. When I finish the story, I head directly to the post office and send a telegram to Nina with a simple message: *I'm coming home next week. Let's get married.*

44

So you want to hear about the fall of Benya Krik. The end of the King. You want to hear that sad story, you with that nose that sticks out so far you should have a red flag hanging from it to warn people away. You must need public liability on a dangerous instrument like that. But what company would dare insure it? No doubt Lloyd's of London. They will insure anything, even your bubbe's wig against fire, theft, and earthquake damage, if you only pay them enough. Then these same people will turn around and point at people like you and me and say we're the ones who love money so much we'll do anything for it.

So you want to hear about the end. Okay. Take a load off. Grab a comfy seat on that tombstone and open your ears and close your mouth, difficult as that is for you to do. Listen, I understand. This is not an age when people like to listen. Everyone is too busy rushing about, getting ahead, making deals, moving here, moving there, trying to blot out this place where it all ends. I watch them get carried in and think, Nu, nu, Mr. Bigshot, you had to make one more killing in business? You never had time to come here and visit your parents or your old friends or to go to the synagogue and say a prayer for them, and now here you are. Now you're lying down with them and who, may I ask, is going to take time to remember you?

Endings are not something we like to think about, though they give us a good cry and lots of us enjoy that. Beginnings are better. That's what they teach us. Beginnings are a time for hope. The whole world lies before us. With each new soul the world is born anew. This is what passes for wisdom. But what it ignores is that life is, as we know, life. It goes around and around. Nobody gets away with it. Things happen to everyone, good things, bad things, things you can never make up your mind about. Along the way we all hope for pretty much the same thing. That maybe we get lucky and have some moments of happiness. Every morning we pray for some happiness. Where would any of us be without our morning prayers?

Okay. So you didn't come here to hear philosophy. You came for an ending and an ending you will get. Maybe more than one, for there are many tales about the end of the King. But, on the way to the end, you need to hear about the final act. How Benya the King of Odessa becomes Benya the Bolshevik. To be perfectly honest, this transition was not as difficult as you might imagine. Because between a king and a Bolshevik there is less difference than there is between a Jew and a goy, or a mouse and a rat. Benya played the role as if he were born to it. Played it in that tailor-made uniform that so impressed Froim Grach. Played it on the back of a magnificent black stallion with colored ribbons twisted into its mane. It seemed sometimes that for Benya the Revolution was about a horse. Every day for hours on end he trained that stallion in the courtyard of the regimental barracks, trained it to do all sorts of tricks. This was a horse with style. It could walk moving both its right legs at the same time, or both its left legs, it could take big steps or little ones, it could prance, it could dance, it could go backward as easily as forward. Anything you or I could do, Benya's horse could do better. Except for one thing: go to war. For Benya, this horse was strictly for parades, and since there was only one single solitary parade in Odessa during all of the King's time as a Bolshevik, the horse may be the only creature in Russia you cannot blame even in part for the victory of the Reds and everything that came after.

Now you need to know this: If war is good for business, revolution can be even better. Every day of our life, there's lots of stuff we need, and in a revolution there's no organization to provide it. Nobody to say who it belongs to or where it should go or how to use it. Wheat, corn, olive oil, men's jackets, women's shoes, guns, cars, trucks, and electrical equipment. And don't forget, in a revolution there are still banks and bank vaults, jewelry stores, insurance companies, freighters in the harbors. Someone has to decide what to do with everything. How to organize it. All the peasants and workers who were joining the Bolsheviks after October barely knew how to read and write, so how could they know anything about how to keep keeping a modern society moving? But Benya knows. He already has an organization, one that during the war years has learned a lot about moving things around the country. So if, while helping to distribute goods, from each according to his talents, to each according to his needs, his boys took a small percentage for themselves, well who's to say they didn't have talents and needs too, including the need to eat?

Benya's organization became the N/th Revolutionary Regiment and in-

*stalled itself in a barracks that had housed over the last two years, if you are in-
terested in history, the cadets of the czar with their shiny boots, German caval-
rymen with spiked helmets, French infantry with ballooning red pants, Ukrainians with fur hats, and last but not least, a White regiment made up almost
entirely of officers with stripes from a hundred different prewar units. Benya's
regiment did not, as you can imagine, devote its precious time to studying military tactics, or marching in close-order drill, or practicing with rifles on a shooting range. Led by Froim Grach and Kolka Pavlovsky and a guy named Abdullah,
who preferred to be called The Persian, the N/th Regiment had better things to
do. Day and night they played cards, shot dice, worked a small printing press to
copy the latest local currency, divided up the spoils of small jobs—boxes of
brand-new pocket watches, cartons of cigars, crates of oranges—and enter-
tained in their narrow bunks women with wide hips and lots of makeup on their
faces. But none of this should take away from the plain fact that when Benya's
men had a job to do, they did it and they did it well. Three times, no less, they ambushed the rear guard of the White Army. Three times wiped out all the officers,
captured food, guns, and ammunition, and turned maybe 70 percent of the loot
over to Bolshevik headquarters. This is not a bad percentage. Better in fact than
that of any other guerilla regiment in all of southern Russia.*

*Life is funny. One day you are on top, the next looking up from the bottom.
One day a hero, the next a bum. A menace to society. Who knows which one, or
maybe more, of the Bolshevik leaders, local or national, started to get nervous
about being on the same side as Benya. The thinking must have been something
like: what's good for the likes of Benya cannot be good for the Revolution. During those lost times before the war it was no different. A chief of police once
said of Benya: in a country ruled by a czar, you can't also have a king. Now the
words might be different but the sentiment was the same: in a country ruled by
people's commissars, you can't also have a king.*

*The event, the particular excuse for disbanding the regiment and getting rid
of Benya, could have been any one of a number of little jobs some of the boys
pulled off in their spare time, usually without the permission of the King, all of
whose time was taken up with training his horse and assuring delegations of local citizens from the Brody that he, the King, would never abandon Odessa to
the Whites. One afternoon, just for a lark, or maybe to keep in practice for the
time when life would get back to normal, a bunch of the boys looted the goods*

out of every last shop on Alexandrovski Avenue. Another day, some of them, without even bothering to cover their faces, marched into the Mutual Credit Society with pistols drawn and requested that the clerks put bales of money and valuables into a car waiting on the street.

The last public appearance of the N/th Revolutionary Regiment is recalled with pleasure to this day by the older folk in the Moldavanka. A parade right down the main street, Catherine Street, led by Benya on his magnificent steed, flanked by one-eyed Froim Grach on a Siberian pony and a commissar from the Red Army. Behind them marches a band consisting of a drum, two clarinets, and a tuba, alternately playing Mendelssohn's wedding march and the Internationale. And behind them a crew of former bandits wearing tin helmets and machine-gun belts, some carrying rifles, some with pistols, some with packs on their backs, some wearing breeches, some in long pants, some in boots, some barefoot, some in patent-leather dancing shoes. And behind them a mob of civilians, wives, mothers, sweethearts, babies in perambulators, all crying, shrieking, yelling farewells. At the corner of DeRibas, a beautiful young girl clad in nothing but a burlap sack, dodges into the street, pulls out of her bosom a rose wrapped in a newspaper, and hands it up to Benya. He signals with his arm to stop the parade, dismounts, lets the girl pin the rose on his chest and then, would you believe, he pulls a diamond-studded ring from his pocket, slips it onto her finger, and kisses the girl on her two blushing cheeks.

That, my young friend with the nose, is the last clear view anyone has of Benya Krik. What we know is that the parade starts up and marches off toward the port, and the N/th Revolutionary Regiment is never seen again, and never is the King. Weeks, months, years later people who claim to have been members of the regiment turn up in the Moldavanka with stories of a train ride, or of being disarmed by Red Army troops and sent off to labor camps and prisons. Nobody hears anything about Benya, or at least nobody witnessed anything, but the story begins to get around that he and Froim were isolated in a club car with some commissars, where for hours they drank and toasted the Revolution and liberty, and then the train stopped, and the commissars got themselves out in a hurry, and so did Grach, and Benya heard a roar of machine guns. He snapped open a blind, saw a field blazing with bonfires and, by the light of the bonfires, two companies of the Red Army, all their guns aimed at the train. He saluted, shut the blind, lit a cigarette, smiled, and awaited the end.

The only problem with this particular story is that other stories equally be-lievable began to circulate at the same time. One said the King was simply taken to the jailhouse and beaten to death with clubs by half a dozen commissars. An-other that he was shot from behind by Froim, who had struck a deal with the Bol-sheviks that allowed him to go to Tbilisi on a pension large enough to support a gorgeous woman who had once been a hooker. Another said the blow and the deal were struck by Mendel Krik, the King's own father, in revenge for the beat-ing Benya gave him many years before in the courtyard of his own house, before the heavy eyes of his neighbors and friends. All of these are good stories, but if you ask me, they are no more than Bolshevik propaganda, and I wouldn't for a moment believe a single one of them. Why? Because not one of them makes sense. Think about it. The King had been outsmarting the people in the Molda-vanka for years, and the Moldavanka is full of some of the smartest Jews in the world. So if you can outsmart the Jews of Moldavanka, does it make sense that a commissar from the Red Army can outsmart you? Not on your life. Not on Benya's.

So here and now, in this cemetery, sitting on this wall, I will reveal to you what really happened to Benya Krik. It's simple as spinning a dreidel. He got away. Through connections—and who had more connections than the King?— Benya stowed away on a boat that took him from Odessa across the Black Sea, through the Dardanelles, across the Mediterranean and the Atlantic and down the St. Lawrence River to Montreal, in Canada. That's where Benya ended up. Now Canada, you know, is a republic or a dominion, and even if nobody in the whole land can tell you the difference between the two, it is clear that in neither one can you also have a king. So Benya changed his title and his name and went into some familiar activities. Canada is a civilized country. So there was no need for guns, robberies, murders of colleagues. In Montreal, Benya went into num-bers and bookmaking. Like everyone else in the rackets, the legal rackets like making bombs or the illegal ones we know so well, Benya got rich during the Depression and even richer during the Second World War. He married again and had four kids, all boys and along with the Bronfmans, became one of the first Jews to move into the once sacred Protestant suburb of Westmount. Benya's kids went to college, and all but one entered legitimate rackets: one was a lawyer, one a doctor, one an academic. But the fourth child Benya trained in his old profession. Let's face it. He was a man with a sense of tradition and history. Smart enough to know that one day the Revolution would be over, and again it would be necessary for some Krik or other to come along and provide the kind of services that would make life in Odessa livable. Someday that kid of Benya's is going to return to Odessa. Just you wait and see.

You, with the nose and the glasses and the autumn sun telling you that a tale is coming to a close, are now waiting for the moral. A story must have a moral, right? Otherwise what good is it. Okay, I agree with you. To get the moral about Benya, you first have to ask exactly the same question you would ask about anyone else. Did his actions, all of them, taken together, help to leave the world a better place? Now I can't tell you how to answer such a question. An answer is not so easy. For how, in the final analysis, and how, in the scales of justice, do you weigh the good and the bad of a man's life and reach a satisfactory conclusion? And who, other than the Unnameable himself, is capable of doing the weighing? And He, let's face it, is pretty stingy about communicating his opinions on such things these days. So we down below are left to our own devices. One thing I know for certain is that I, personally, am not qualified to do the weighing. My job is to sit on this wall and watch the world and tell stories and leave the weighing to others. So far as I know, we all get one particular job to fill in a lifetime. This one seems to be mine. And what, may I ask, is yours?

Epilogue

Isaac Babel returned from Odessa to Moscow in late November 1936. His first letter to his mother contained the line: I am once again in Moscow's iron grip. Although he and Nina were never formally married, he was at her side when she gave birth to a daughter, Lida, early in 1937, and the couple lived together as husband and wife until the NKVD came to arrest Babel in his dacha at the Peredelkino writers' colony on the morning of May 15, 1939. Taken to cell 89 of the Lubyanka Prison, headquarters of the NKVD, he was interrogated relentlessly for more than two months. The questions focused on his connections with various groups and individuals said to be enemies of the state, such as Sergei Eisenstein and Yevgenia Yezhova, and also on his recruitment for espionage purposes by various foreign agents, including French writer André Malraux and Austrian engineer Bruno Shtainer. His formal trial before the military tribunal of the Supreme Court of the Soviet Union took place on January 26, 1940, and lasted twenty minutes. He was convicted of being a member of an anti-Soviet Trotskyist group, an agent of the French and Austrian intelligence services, and part of a conspiratorial terrorist organization that had been planning to kill, among others, Josif Stalin. He was shot at 1:30 A.M. on January 27, 1940, cremated the next day at the former Donskoi Monastery in central Moscow, and his ashes dropped into a common pit at the cemetery there.

Babel's first wife, Zhenya, along with their daughter, Natasha, spent the Second World War in a French provincial town and later immigrated to the United States. Yezhova, his lover in Berlin and subsequently his editor in Moscow, entered a sanitarium in 1938 and died within a month; there is some evidence that she was murdered by her husband, Nikolai Yezhov, head of the secret police. Yezhov himself was shot as a spy in February 1940, just one week after Babel's execution. Genrikh Yagoda had met the same fate two years before. Kashirina, the mother of Babel's son, Misha, survived him by more than five decades. So did Nina Pirozhkova. It was she who reported that, when he was being taken away by the NKVD, Babel's words, the last ones he would ever say in public, were: *I was not given time to finish.*

ISAAC BABEL'S
FRIENDS AND ASSOCIATES

ARYE LEIB
The rabbilike figure—actually a shammes, a man who helps out around the synagogue—who sits on the wall of the Jewish cemetery in Odessa and tells stories about Benya Krik.

BLOK, ALEXANDER
Russian symbolist poet (1880–1921), much beloved by Babel and his generation.

THE BOSS
The name that everyone used when speaking of Stalin.

BUDYENNY
Cossack cavalry general in whose division Babel worked as a correspondent during the Civil War. Denounced Babel's *Red Cavalry,* a collection of stories about his wartime experiences, as libelous toward the Cossacks and called Babel "womanish."

EISENSTEIN, SERGEI
The Soviet Union's most innovative and famous film director (1898–1948). Celebrated above all for his film *Potemkin,* and especially for the brilliant sequence shot on the steps of the Odessa waterfront.

GORKY, MAXIM
Novelist, memoirist, playwright (1868–1936). Russia's most internationally famous twentieth-century writer. Gorky maintained a love-hate relationship with the revolutionary regime from its outset until his death in the summer of 1936.

GRACH, FROIM
A character in Babel's Benya Krik stories, the most feared gangster in the Moldavanka until Benya Krik himself took over. He subsequently became Krik's chief lieutenant.

GRONFEIN, ZHENYA
Babel's first wife, whom he met in Kiev in 1916. They married in August 1919 and lived for a time near the Turkish border, in Batumi. She left him to immigrate to France in 1925. He fathered a daughter, Natasha, with her during a trip he made to Paris in 1927.

KAMENEV, LEV
One of the leading figures in the Central Committee of the Bolshevik Party during the October Revolution, in 1917. In the summer of 1936, Kamenev was in jail awaiting trial for supposed crimes against the state.

KASHIRINA
Well-known theater actress with whom Babel has an affair in the midtwenties. Together they have a son, Misha, who is later adopted by Kashirina's husband, Ivanov, when she eventually marries.

KATYA
The sister of Babel's mother and wife of Lyosha. A dentist who lives in Odessa.

KRIK, BENYA
Babel's most famous character; the most suave, dapper, and elegant criminal in the Moldavanka.

LYOSHA
Aunt Katya's husband, and petty criminal, with whom Babel has a somewhat strained relationship.

MALRAUX, ANDRÉ
Famous French adventurer, novelist, and political activist who led an air squadron for the Loyalists during the Spanish Civil War.

MANDELSTAM, OSIP
Celebrated Russian poet (1892–1940?) arrested in May 1934 for reciting a single poem against Stalin at a private party in Leningrad. He was first sent into internal exile and then, later, into the gulag, where he died.

MERA
Babel's younger sister. Married and living in Brussels, Belgium, with her husband, Boris, and with Fenya, her mother.

NIKITICH
A proofreader by profession, but also an athlete, who befriended the young Isaac Babel, taught him how to swim, and told him his early works had a spark of genius.

PASTERNAK, BORIS
Famed Russian poet and novelist (1890–1960).

PIROZHKOVA, NINA
A highly regarded engineer who in 1936 was working on the construction of the Moscow subway. She became Babel's lover in 1932. Later they lived together as husband and wife and had a daughter, Lida.

TROTSKY, LEON
Stalin's major rival for the position of general secretary of the Communist Party after Lenin's death, in 1924. Trotsky eventually lost the struggle with Stalin and was exiled in the late 1920s. He was thereafter used as a scapegoat, depicted as the great enemy of the Soviet Union, responsible for espionage and sabotage designed to overthrow the regime.

YAGODA, GENRIKH
Head of State Security (NKVD) for the USSR.

YEZHOV, NIKOLAI
Highly placed Party official who succeeded Genrikh Yagoda as head of the NKVD in the late summer of 1936 and oversaw the great purge, from 1936 to 1938. He was replaced in 1938 by Lavrenti Beria and subsequently arrested, following which he provided evidence that led to Babel's arrest.

YEZHOVA, YEVGENIA
Journal editor and wife of Nikolai Yezhov. She and Babel became lovers in Berlin in 1927 and remained friends and professional associates after the affair ended.

ZINOVIEV, GRIGORII
A leading figure in the Central Committee of the Bolshevik Party in October 1917 and later the head of the Comintern. In the summer of 1936, he was also in jail awaiting trial for alleged crimes against the state.

CHRONOLOGY
OF BABEL'S LIFE

1894 Born in Odessa, July 13.

1906 Enters Nicholas I Commercial School in Odessa.

1911 Enters the Institute of Finance and Business Studies in Kiev.

1913 Publishes his first short story, "Old Schloyme."

1916 Takes up residence in St. Petersburg to pursue career as a writer.
Meets Maxim Gorky, who begins to publish Babel's stories in his journal, *Letopis*.

1917 Serves in the Russian army in World War I on the Romanian front.
In December undertakes a risky journey to St. Petersburg (now Petrograd).

1918–19 During the Civil War, works in the People's Commissariat for Education.
Marries Zhenya Gronfein.

1920 Works as journalist with the First Cavalry Army of the Red Army in the Polish campaign.

1921 Publishes *The King*, the first of the Benya Krik gangster tales, set in Odessa. He and Zhenya move to Batumi.

1923 Father dies in July. Publishes *Odessa Stories*, a collection of Benya Krik tales, as well as the first stories from what will be *Red Cavalry*.

1924 Lenin dies in January and the power struggle between Trotsky and Stalin begins. General Budyenny mounts his first attack on *Red Cavalry*.

1925 Babel's wife, Zhenya, immigrates to Paris, and his sister immigrates to Brussels. Publishes *The Story of My Dovecote*, the first of his autobiographical stories.

1926 Babel's mother also immigrates to Brussels.
Publishes *Red Cavalry*, a collection of stories about his experiences during the war, and completes his play *Sunset*.
His son, Misha, is born in July to Kashirina.

1927 Leaves on his first trip abroad in July. Spends time in Berlin, visits his wife in Paris and his mother and sister in Brussels.

1928 In February *Sunset* opens and closes at Moscow Art Theater.
The critic Alexander Voronsky, an early supporter of Babel, criticizes him for his silence, and Budyenny's attack on *Red Cavalry* resumes.

1929	Trotsky is exiled in January.
	Babel's daughter, Natasha, is born in July in Paris.
1930	Tours countryside gathering material on agricultural collectivization and witnesses the famine in the Ukraine. Babel is accused of making anti-Soviet remarks in an interview he gave to a Polish journalist.
1932–33	Second trip abroad.
	Again visits his wife and daughter, and his mother and sister.
	Stays for some time with Maxim Gorky in Sorrento, Italy, and also becomes friendly with Ilya Ehrenburg, through whom he meets André Malraux.
1934	At the First Congress of Soviet Writers in Moscow, Babel speaks of himself as "master of silence."
	Develops friendship with André Malraux.
	In May, Osip Mandelstam is arrested, and Sergei Kirov is assassinated in December.
1935	Along with Boris Pasternak, travels in June to Paris to attend the anti-Fascist International Congress of Writers. Returns to the Soviet Union in August.
1936	Takes up residence in a dacha located in the artists' colony of Peredelkino, near Moscow. Visits Maxim Gorky in the Crimea, not long before Gorky's death, in June. Trial of Lev Kamenev and Grigorii Zinoviev takes place in August. In September Nikolai Yezhov replaces Genrikh Yagoda as the head of the NKVD.
1937	Nina gives birth to a daughter, Lida.
1938	Lavrenti Beria replaces Nikolai Yezhov as the head of the NKVD.
	Yezhov is subsequently arrested and offers testimony against Babel.
1939	Arrested in May by the NKVD and interrogated in prison.
1940	In January, tried and shot as agent of foreign governments.

ABOUT THE AUTHOR

Robert A. Rosenstone is the author of *Romantic Revolutionary: A Biography of John Reed,* the basis for the Academy Award–winning film *Reds.* He also has written *Crusade of the Left: The Lincoln Battalion in the Spanish Civil War; Mirror in the Shrine: American Encounters with Meiji Japan; Visions of the Past: The Challenge of Film to Our Idea of History;* and *The Man Who Swam into History,* a family memoir. Rosenstone is a professor of history at the California Institute of Technology. *King of Odessa* is his first novel.